MW01699670

Birthright

A NOVEL

LARRY L. BAILEY

DDP Literary Press

Birthright

Copyright © 1999 Larry L. Bailey

All rights reserved under International and Pan-American Copyright Conventions.
Published in the United States of America by DDP Literary Press, a division of Double Dragon Publishing, Markham, Ontario Canada.

No part of this book may be reproduced or transmitted in any form or by any means, graphic, electronic, or mechanical, including photocopying, recording, taping, or by any information storage or retrieval system, without the permission in writing from Double Dragon Publishing.

This book is a work of fiction. Names, characters, places and incidents are products of the author's imagination or are used fictitiously. Any resemblance to actual events or locales or persons, living or dead, is entirely coincidental.

A DDP Literary Press Book

Published by
Double Dragon Publishing
PO Box 54016
1-5762 Highway 7 East
Markham, Ontario L3P 7Y4 Canada
http://www.double-dragon-ebooks.com

ISBN: 1-55404-031-0
Library of Congress Catalog Number:
92-72078, 98-86296

A DDP First Edition March 2, 2003

Book Layout and
Cover Art by Deron Douglas

FOR MY ELDERS: My Grandmother, Jessie Hall Holdren, who gave me dreams. My Grandfather, Paul Holdren, who gave me strength.

CHAPTER I

The icy ground rang like iron beneath his frozen boots. Echoes sounded from the barn and machine shed, hard-edged, like winter shadows. The nearly new moon had long set. Only the cold glitter of stars refracted sparks through the dry snow.

Harry liked the cold. It sliced through the foggy membrane of the dream, forced back the dark eyes that mocked him, into the shadowed corners where he did not go. The bite of the wind brought tears and he blinked them away. In the dark corral, the steaming cattle stirred and jostled towards the feeder, certain there would be fragrant hay and some grain with a little molasses. Their warm, sweet smell rushed at him in waves, modulated the chill breeze.

He broke bales of alfalfa, rich with late-summer blue flowers. He used a two-pound Yuban can to sprinkle the soft hay with cracked corn from the steel barrel where they laced it with blackstrap. With his gloved hand he shattered the ice that skinned the round galvanized stock tank.

As the hungry cattle sorted themselves out along the pine- board feeder, Harry could see the results of his family's careful weaving of bloodlines. Patterns of skin markings ebbed and flowed through generations. As he watched them he scooped up a handful of the snow, let it melt on his tongue.

The hides were the visible witness of the subtle advantages sought by a good breeder. Tiny details of confirmation, feed usage, disease resistance and calving ability, were gently coaxed into dominant traits, as the animal adapted to its particular matrix of seasons and pastures and uses and markets.

None of that counted anymore. All that mattered was price. Corporate feedlots bought the calves cheap and fed them cheap, on by-products or industrial wastes. With the right mix of hormones and antibiotics, they could be kept alive the necessary few months while their sickened bodies bloated up to market weight. Well-marbled, the packers liked to call the flabby meat.

The Old Man, his grandfather, would not touch commercial beef. He had preferred to fatten and slaughter his own. A point of pride had been his freezer perpetually full of homegrown beef.

Now that the Old Man was gone, Dad didn't care how their food was grown. He would rather make the money to pay high grocery store prices for feedlot beef.

Harry was tempted to hold one of the yearling calves aside, hide it up at the old place and tell the banker they had counted wrong. If he split the meat with his parents, it would last them all a year. He would give his half to Judith. For the kids.

He gently pulled the ears of a couple of the new calves. They shook their heads in irritation. He whistled, and a ragged ball of fur he called Reject slid to a stop beside him. Harry had saved the brown and black and white Australian Shepherd from starvation and hand raised him. He was a good one.

The dog shivered with cold indignation that he had overslept, missed the start of the morning ritual. He cocked his head to the side and gave Harry that odd stare which came from his one brown eye and one blue eye, the badge of his mixed breed. Reject was always ready to chastise a runaway calf or bring the horses to be saddled. When it came to stock dogs, these half- breeds were the best.

Harry headed towards the far corral where they kept the last few horses. The dog danced around him, a patchwork tornado. The new snow squeaked low in protest beneath each step.

Wisps of the dream trailed across his vision. Eyes died in the flames, questions unanswered. The eyes became Long Joe's, accused, "You have killed our mother." The eyes were Judith's, crying, then Rebecca's, little Joe's, and he could not answer them.

He pulled up the collar on his faded field jacket, turned his back to the wind.

Harry's heavy beard and moustache stuck together with the icing of his breath. He passed the empty pig shed where the sweet scent of Old Manure drifted between the silver boards. The hogs were gone, sold in the early fall when prices were up, so they could save the cost of feed.

They had put the horses in what they still called "the Old Man's corral" five years after his death. Their death, Harry thought. His father's parents had died only a few months apart. Harry was sure that grandma had simply decided to follow the Old Man, as always.

Judith's mare, Shadow, stood in the far corner of the pole corral with the Old Man's last draft horse, an old, powerful mare. Shadow watched Harry calmly, eyes shining over the back of her yearling colt. Harry thought of Judith, saw her slim wraithlike figure cling to the racing mare, at dusk, as she made a wild and dangerous game of corralling the cows for the night.

He rubbed the soft nose that probed at him and automatically dug in his pocket for a sugar cube. Shadow's dark eyes calmed him like Judith's.

He thought again of that last time he had seen Judith's healing brown eyes. That foggy fall morning they had gone together to take little Joe to daycare for the first time and Rebecca to her new school. Then he had dropped Judith at a bus stop so she could go to work. The Seattle traffic was heavy and he hadn't really been able to say good-bye. She hurried from the pickup and he had lost sight of her in the crowd. Suddenly she had turned, and her eyes met his for an instant. She smiled, was gone, her small form indistinguishable among the hustling commuters. He shook off a feeling of vertigo and gave Reject a pat.

And now Shadow, too, would be gone. Auctioned!

Harry reached across the mare's back to give a cube to the spotted colt who begged from the safe far side of his mother. The yearling jerked the sugar away and dropped it on the ground. He nervously retrieved it and skitted to the other side of the pen to eat it. Shadow munched contentedly while Harry rubbed her strongly molded neck.

The Old Man had given Shadow to Judith. He always gave her things. If he had been younger it might have made Harry jealous. Not that the Old Man didn't give everyone things. But he had felt something special for Judith. They all saw it and wondered and were happy for her and for the Old Man.

Shadow was a fine horse as all the Old Man's things were fine. She was the well-crafted result of selection by a hundred generations of humans from a thousand generations of horses. She was an Appaloosa, descendant of the Palouse horses bred by the Nez Perce. Even as a two-year-old she had been fierce and independent, led the other horses in the wild upwind charges they loved.

When the Old Man had told Judith the horse was hers, he had said he was returning Shadow to her rightful owner. The family had all agreed as Judith began to train and ride the young mare that no one had ever looked more natural on a horse. Harry knew the Old Man was proud that Judith's grandmother, from Nespelem, on the Colville Reservation, was said to be descended from Thunder Rolling In The Mountains, Great Joseph himself, who had died there in exile.

Shadow tossed her head and probed for another sugar cube. "Stop it," he said gently and pushed her away. Her look quizzed him, one ear then the other aimed. He slapped her flank with a loud pop and she whirled, flashing into the dark.

5:27 his watch said. It sure didn't take long to feed the stock anymore. He had time to make coffee and still spend an hour at the old place before breakfast.

He'd have to eat breakfast with Mom and Dad, though. He was going to see the thing all the way through. He could have found an excuse, like his sister, Meg, although it was hard for a single, separated man to find real good excuses like parents of young children always have. Or he could take his brother, Jack's, route - promise to be there, then just not show up. He was sure Jack would not show up. Jack didn't have the guts. He would have an appointment, a showing or closing he just couldn't avoid, for the money - last minute thing. Unemployed people run short on excuses, too, so Harry would just have to see the thing through, and maybe feel better about it.

He whistled Reject to heel and circled the horse corral. He passed the barn with its ample, long empty stalls that had served the Old Man's Percheron teams. Those placid giants, too, were gone. The Old Man had found homes for them all, sold them for good money. He obviously had known that his time was short and that no one in the family had any real interest in draft horses. He'd put out the word through the Draft Horse Association Newsletter and soon a stream of prospective buyers appeared in various dilapidated trucks to chew straws and point at the horses and make their offers or suggestions. Soon all seven of the working horses were gone, scattered but secure. Only the ancient mare remained to carry the Old Man's spirit when it finally departed.

Harry could feel the temperature drop as always on winter mornings before dawn. The restless breeze steadied into a northerly ten knots and cut at his bare wrists with its icy blade. Skiffs of fresh powder licked his ankles. Stars reflected brightly from the dry snow, burst apart into colors against the hard crystals, and each step stirred stardust.

He walked behind the buildings, past his parents new house, past the deserted pad where Jack and Diane had lived in their mobile home, to the basalt studded acre up against the rocky bank of the canal where he had put his own trailer. The bank's trailer.

It hadn't seemed like a mobile home when Judith and the kids had been there with him, it was just home. Now he noticed the mill finish aluminum window-frames with their flecks of mildew, and the remnants of plastic woodgrain paneling, copied from the wood of some alien planet.

He heated water in an aluminum pan on the bright yellow electric stove, and got out his thermos, the coffee cone and a filter. He had a little Colombian left in a foil lined bag, roasted fresh daily some months before and hand-picked by Juan Valdez God knows when. It would still beat hell out of Folgers. One thing he disagreed with the Old Man about. Folgers was lousy coffee. He could hear the Old Man's chuckle of disagreement.

The dark rush of the coffee warmed his wind and star-chilled brain back to reality. He still had work to do and he was determined to walk around the old place once more. He'd already put the new canopy from the bank's three year old Ford onto the faithful 1972 International he had thought he would never need again. But it was paid off, they couldn't touch it, so he'd taken the canopy and the stereo and even the slick three-way side mirrors and switched them onto his old rig. The International didn't look too bad cleaned up, and it would carry his remaining possessions easily.

Almost everything was already gone, in Seattle with Judith and the kids. He had his own stuff... clothes, dishes, sleeping bag, a few books and pictures. He hadn't traveled so lightly in a long time, but old habits and the old truck were distantly familiar and he felt a little excited as he loaded up, almost as if he had somewhere to go.

He had loaded his guns earlier, as soon as he got up. He put the rifle and the shotgun behind the seat and the .357 in the side pocket. He hated this habit of always having a weapon in close reach, but he hated worse the dry-mouthed nakedness he felt when he was without one. "Guns," the Old Man said, "always lead to trouble."

Harry had no romantic firearms collection. To him, guns were tools. He made no pretense of hunting or target shooting or investing in the classics. He bought good, used, businesslike pieces. He shot them occasionally, without joy, cleaned them often, and waited.

He left Judith's loom to the last. He was almost afraid to touch it. She had broken it down the night she left, secured all the loose ends and wrapped it in the rug on which she always worked. He had loved to watch her at the loom, softly humming as her rhythmic hands ran through the ageless patterns. "The design is already there," she had told him, "I just have to put the threads in the right order. But the pattern is already there, if you can see it."

He couldn't, and when she had tried to teach him, his suddenly clumsy hands had found the movements difficult. He often had wished their fates could be in her sure, unhurried hands which always knew which thread came next. A family needed order and direction. Each day should not need to be created from nothing. An underlying pattern was required, a warp for the thread of your life.

It was almost ten years since they first had assembled her loom. She had wanted the legs left off. She always worked on the floor, Navajo style, in the center of a green Bolivian rug that crawled with embroidery of flowers and birds and furtive animals. At the loom, as she worked, she seemed to be in intense prayer and he had always kept a sacred distance.

Judith had saved for some really fine thread for a special project, for the family, just to remember. She had collected some brightly colored silk, red and blue and green, and some plain linen and proud Mexican cotton. She had carried in her mind for years, she said, an intricate pattern she longed to weave, and finally the time seemed right. She worked on it for several weeks, mostly when no one was around, and then last year had made it a family Christmas present. She had wrapped it and presented it to Harry to open while the kids watched. Rebecca and Joseph, too, knew it was something special.

It was just a length of fabric, a couple of yards, of linen and cotton mostly, but suffused with a rainbow glow of silk. He could see that a larger design floated like a shadow within the bright colors, but he did not want to tell her that he could not see what it was. He had looked at it and touched it and did not know what to say.

It was as if in that spectral tapestry, she had loomed their lives. It was not the fabric that mattered, or the design, but the motions of her hands in the air, again and again, as she inscribed the shadows and reflections of time. And the web of her loom had thralled them in the raveling of its pattern beneath her blessing hands.

Now, of her rainbow family, only he remained behind to pick up the pieces, a broken thread, tied off. He opened the top of the folded rug, to check the loom, and saw that Judith had wrapped her special weaving in a length of plain cotton, and left it there in the center for him to find.

Harry carefully loaded the loom on the back of the pickup. He wasn't sure what to do with it, but he had promised to care for it until Judith had room. He would not ask Meg or Jack to store it. And there was no room in the 36' 5th wheeler Dad had stashed at Uncle Paul's, the title in Paul's name to protect it from the bank. The whole family traveled pretty light, now.

He rolled Judith's weaving and buried it in the center of his old duffel bag, the closest thing he had to luggage.

Both the International's tanks were full and it seemed to run okay. He warmed it up for a few minutes and checked the oil. It was ready.

He went back inside to have another cup of coffee before he walked up to the old place. There would be some daylight by 6:00. He hadn't taken time to preheat the thermos and the coffee was half cold, steamed weakly with a taste like copper. He sipped it and unconsciously traced a number on the gold-flecked melamine table. He looked through his reflection in the window, stared into the vacant shadows along the canal bank.

When his finger began the number a second time, he became aware of the treachery and nearly spilled the coffee as he brushed the ghost number away.

He knew what the number had been. $585,000. In a way, that was better than the columns and reams of numbers there used to be. He struggled to put the offending numbers out of his mind. If he could concentrate on just this one number, $585,000, the others receded in their tributaries and backwaters. There was only one number that mattered now, the negative sum of all the family's knowledge and skill and effort, $585,000. That number had become a desperate goal. It tantalized him in bloody dreams, winked at him from scraps of yellow paper.

Usually, now, he saw the number in the young banker's handwriting, with a circle around it, written with a fine silver pen on a sheet of gold-embossed letterhead.

"Washington First National Savings Bank. $585,000." The final total of their lives. The young banker had looked at them with a faint smile as he drew the circle. "We'll work with you all we can," he'd said.

The four of them had filed out of his office, their shock hushed by the Whisper-Soft carpet Washington First had installed after the merger. They had walked stiffly out to the parking lot through a minefield of smiles and hellos from bank employees they had known for years.

That was in October, when they had hauled in the last of the corn crop at ruinous prices. They still had been left with a $47,000 operating deficit accumulated over two years, besides the land and machinery loans. Then there was the loan on the new house the young banker had encouraged Dad to build five years ago, to upgrade the place, he said, and to impress the investors he brought in from the coast to buy the loans he made to farmers. All together, there was no mistake about it, it added up to $585,000.

For a while it had seemed that the young banker always had more rabbits in his hat. He always found a way to borrow against something to pay off something else. The fee he had received each time seemed small enough, when you considered the service.

The Old Man had warned them before he died. "Don't mistake cleverness for intelligence," he'd said of the banker, "A dancin' dog is clever. This guy just has a routine."

Harry had seen the danger of the game. But, like most of their neighbors, they were too far in to extricate themselves. To go ahead, they knew, meant possible disaster, but to stop meant certain disaster.

The last couple of years had been sleepwalking, a dance of the already dead. No one would talk about it. They had smiled and worked and hoped that, as always before, perseverance and sweat would bring them through.

And faith, Harry thought. The farmers were truly the faithful. He had no mirror of faith to weave illusions of pattern and meaning.

"He said that they would work with us," Mom had said finally, in the car, halfway home.

"That isn't what he told Harry and me, the other day when he came out," Dad answered. "He said he would do what he could, but he thought the board would turn us down and foreclose." He turned, to show his face, make sure the women knew he was serious. "Since the bank merged with Washington First, they've changed a lot of the rules. The banker says he doesn't have a choice."

"How can they do that?" Judith asked, "Just change the rules?"

"They have no choice," Dad explained. "They had to merge, the government ordered it. Because of all the losses. They loaned a lot of money to speculators on land in the Black Sands and they never got water. Now they have to use new underwriting rules."

"That doesn't make sense," Mom said. "They don't know anything about farming."

"It isn't about farming," Dad said. "It's about money."

"Well, I know for sure," Mom said, "if it was still Farmer's Savings they wouldn't dare treat us this way."

They had spent frantic weeks going over the numbers on the farm's financial statement, over and over. Mom spent days on the telephone, patiently retelling the story to seemingly receptive lenders who invariably declined. When they did send out applications, there was always a series of questions beginning, "Have you ever been denied credit before?" And with each telling of the story, Mom had seemed a little older, a little grayer.

No matter how they stretched the values on equipment and land and livestock, there still was a huge gap, almost a hundred thousand dollars less than the young banker said they must have in equity to get an extension. That wasn't much if prices were good and you had the money to operate. With the loans called, and the new year's operating money refused, and no time, they could not make it work. If they could not refinance, they would have to sell.

Harry had gone over the numbers so many times himself that it seemed like he had written them on every piece of paper in the trailer. He was sure he could see the faint impression of the numbers in the tabletop.

For a while, he'd hoped that there would be a little money left after they sold out, enough to buy Mom and Dad the trailer they wanted, for retirement. There could even be enough to start over, small, maybe on the old place.

Farmland prices had plummeted, but still they could expect $1,000 an acre for the 200 acres of prime irrigated ground and half that for the same amount of more marginal farmland. 150 acres of rocky upland range was worth maybe $60,000. Machinery prices were good, beef was up and Jack had assured them he could sell the new house on five acres for nearly twice the $60,000 they still owed.

Maybe they could even save the old place, Jack had said. Harry could only think of how it always had been kept free and clear until they had put a mortgage against it for last year's operating loan. "Borrowed money," the Old Man said, "is worse than cancer.

Prices fell and buyers were scarce. Jack had finally rescinded the listing on the new house after four price drops.

"No market right now," he had said. "Maybe in the spring."

When Harry could no longer hope, he had raged. The numbers were leeches that clung to him, demanded blood. One night he had ransacked the trailer, burned every shred of paper that might have held one of the oppressive numbers. At that, the numbers had begun to run incessantly in his head, as if they had life of their own, and, deprived of the paper, had sought refuge in his mind.

Since then, it had been difficult to work with the household budget or even balance his checkbook. Any numbers awakened the shadow of those other, unthinkable numbers. Money felt greasy and repulsive, to be handled quickly and forgotten.

He hadn't liked having the children around. When they stopped their play and looked at him, he could see in their eyes only the shadow of coming disappointment, and he would send them to their rooms to play.

Rebecca always smiled at him, confident even when he was gruff with her. But little Joe would become upset and cry for his mother and Harry would feel helpless. It seemed just a short time ago that he had held up his infant son and turned slowly around so that he could see the whole farm and said, "Look good, Joe. Some day it will be yours."

Harry threw the last half-cup of the coffee on the floor. It splashed across the "Venetian" vinyl. Should be Venusian, he thought.

CHAPTER 2

Outside, the sky lightened. Harry was glad that it would be a clear day after three days of welcome February snow. It would be better for the auction.

The weather had been strange. There had been no snow until after Christmas. This year, it seemed, the solstice had not come. Great walls of stone gray clouds had blocked morning and evening, leaving desperately short days. No healing blanket of snow had marked the days, and no sun, just a faint lightening of the dark, a slight lessening of the depths of the shadows. When it finally had snowed, it was just an obligatory dusting. The Earth, withered and bare, had radiated into space her little store of heat, a green spark, tumbled in the sidereal wind.

His lips had split and bled in the frozen desert of those days. In the long northern nights, the ache of old wounds and other, deeper ills, had played their ghastly flickers across his darkened mind.

He crossed the shallow canal, slipped and caught himself on the thin ice. He liked to walk through the little strip of prairie on the upper side. It was only a short walk to the old place, across the canal from the sprinkler ponds, but it was also a different world. The canal marked the boundary between the "project" and the "dryland."

Below the canal was irrigated ground, heir to the bounty of the New Deal and Grand Coulee Dam. It possessed a right to an annual flood of cold, Canadian snow water, pumped and siphoned and ditched across the desert by the Bureau of Reclamation. Above the canal was rangeland and dryland wheat, dependent on the natural cycles, no different than it had been for a century. The good dryland places, like the Old Man's, had deep wells to irrigate gardens and orchards and hay fields.

When Harry's family had come there, in 1958, driven west by another of the droughts, which were part of the twenty-year cycles of the Great Plains, the Old Man had insisted on buying a place on the dry side. They could not deny him, because the sale of his place in Kansas had made the move possible.

There was plenty of land to choose from then, so they had found a place where they could buy the 200 acres of irrigated ground Dad wanted and his parents took the dryland quarter- section just across the canal. It had seemed a little crazy, to buy that close to the irrigation project, then have to drill a well. But the land was cheap and a dowser had found water for the Old Man, plenty, at 110 feet. Soon his homestead had begun to look very much like the place he and grandma had left behind, in Kansas.

Harry had been only ten when they moved and he had half- believed Mom when she said the Old Man was just clinging to the past. "He should throw away his old ways and be a modern farmer. Or, he could retire," Mom had said, "he's past sixty. He should stop working and just enjoy life. Dad can run the whole place perfectly well."

But the Old Man did not retire. Instead, he took his hundred and sixty acres of rocky ground on the wrong side of the canal and turned it into a smoothly running machine that soon provided the old couple with all they needed. And that included money.

Between his soft fruit orchard and the fresh vegetables he loved to grow, not to mention the various animals and fleeces and hides as well as the egg and milk business, the grandparents always had money coming in. Not a huge amount, but steady. And almost all of their own food came from the place. "If a man can't feed himself," the Old Man said, "his life belongs to whoever does."

Sixty or not, the Old Man had built his own house. The outbuildings came first, while the old couple had lived in a small trailer. Harry and Dad had helped him with the barn and chickenhouse and root cellar. The plans came from the Old Man's head. He said they were variations on plans he had helped his own grandfather build when he was a boy in Kansas and the Buffalo Grass still grew. They helped him plant trees where they were supposed to be. An orderly thicket of berry vines and grapes and other perennials began to swallow the house almost before it was finished.

Harry looked at the little house now, covered in snow, softened, as if it would melt back into the earth. It was difficult to determine where the house stopped and the earth began. There was no sharp boundary of board or brick to separate the human domain from nature.

The foundation was two giant coastal Cedar logs cut in half and laid on the sandy soil. The Old Man had bought them from a shake mill on the Skagit River and hauled them over the mountains in his old stock truck. The original surface underneath had been barely disturbed when the logs were laid on the volcanic sand, and the miniature life of mouse and insect and spider continued much as it always had.

Pungent red Tamarack timbers from the Kettle River Range lay across the Cedar logs, bearing the post and beam structure with ease. The siding was rough-sawn White Pine boards and battens, silvered by time. The floors and walls were tongue and groove Douglas Fir the Old Man had bought at a little sawmill high in the Cascades and finished himself. He'd laid a used brick chimney and a tile flue for the cookstove.

In summer, cottonwood trees shaded south side windows, which were open to the sun's heat and light in winter. The north wall held closets and utilities and the pantry. It blocked the winter cold and kept their stores of food cool in summer. The bedrooms, on the east, caught the earliest sun and the living room on the west was light late into the evenings.

Over the years the old place had lost any straight lines and hard edges in a constant interactive process of man and plants and Earth. As trees and vines had grown and lumber silvered, the place had taken on the contours of the land and wind and sun. The Old Man's magic was so easy that it almost seemed that the farmstead had grown by itself. He had known the art of arranging things so that the desired result was assured. It was like Judith's weaving. If you could string the loom correctly and lay the threads in the proper order, the pattern was inevitable and did not have to be thought about.

Harry stopped on the porch of the old house. The shadows of that world so recently gone lingered, enfolded him. Their scent was there, permeating the very boards of the old house. He wished that he had appreciated all of it more while they still lived.

One morning, about six months before he died, the Old Man had told Dad and Harry, "When I go, take my old body back to Kansas. That's where I belong." They had never talked about it after that.

Mom had tried to argue with Grandma, at first, pointed out how much less it would cost if they just buried him at the cemetery in town. She and Dad had several lots there, and they would sell one at a decent price. Besides, Kansas was a long way for Grandma to go just for a funeral.

But Grandma wouldn't hear it. "No," she said in her quiet, firm way, "Henry and I decided when we first came out that if we never went back any other way, we would be buried back home."

Mom hadn't felt up to the trip, so Harry had gone with Dad and Grandma. They went on the Amtrak train with the Old Man's coffin, and the trip had seemed endless. Harry supposed that the Old Man's spirit had fled on, impatiently, ahead of his body, and waited for them.

It felt strange to walk down the streets in the dusty little town he had not seen in more than twenty years and have people immediately recognize him. Or, if they did not know for sure who he was, there was no doubt he was an Isaacson. Relatives he didn't remember accosted him in the grocery store, waved him down to talk on Main Street.

The funeral in the Lutheran Church was packed and the potluck meal served afterwards was like the feast to welcome the prodigal son. There were routine condolences, but more than anything they had questions. Questions about Henry. What had he done since they left Kansas? Did he still have an answer for everything?

Harry and Dad and Grandma had accompanied the body to the cemetery, rode in one of the limousines. They still could not get grass to grow in the graveyard, except in little patches, and most of the area around the graves was covered with native weeds of all descriptions. Family members had cleared the Isaacson plot, and a fresh grave had been dug into the yellow adobe.

While Harry waited for them to maneuver the hearse into place for the pallbearers, he had looked at the headstones in the family plot. The oldest, a weathered sandstone marker, belonged to the Old Man's great uncle Benjamin who had been shot in 1877. There were several Henrys and Harrys and even another Joseph, who had died in 1922. Most of the wives were buried beside the men. There were three Margarets, an Elizabeth, a Pearl, but no Judith. There was a Rosa Elena, and Harry wondered if she was as dark as her name. He remembered the Memorial Day work parties when he was a child. The families would gather, hoe and rake and burn the weeds, set up any markers that had fallen over. And when it was all neat, they would assemble under the stunted elms for a Remembrance.

The last time he had been in the Pioneer Cemetery had been the Memorial Day before the move to Washington. One of the men had lit fire to a patch of dried weeds and burned a jackrabbit's nest. Scared little rabbits had run in all directions.

The Old Man caught one and gave it to Harry. Harry put it inside his jacket and it quieted, burrowed into his warmth. All during the service, while the old people spoke of the dead, he had felt the rabbit's heart beat rapidly against his chest. He wondered if his ancestors had eaten many of the rabbit's ancestors.

He had asked the Old Man why they held a service for those already gone, and the Old Man had said it was for continuity, so that people could feel that they belonged to something bigger than themselves. "But it isn't the dead that matter," he had said and put his arm around Harry. "It's always the living."

It had fallen to Harry to work the old place after the old man died. At first it had just been extra work. There were the berries and grapes, and plum and apricot and nectarine trees to care for, apples to prune, rhubarb and horseradish to weed, and a profusion of herbs, many of which Harry did not recognize, but tended out of duty. Judith was always eager to help with the herbs. There also had been flowerbeds, but he had let those go to weeds, mowed them once or twice.

Only as he worked the old place had he truly learned it. Everything there had to be touched, confronted directly, observed closely. Without the handwork it could not succeed, in this variety in this small space. There were so many interdependencies that he could not think about them all at once. But as he had followed the turns of the years, he had learned the patterns and micro-patterns and macro-patterns. In the near view, as he worked with each part of the fabric it was clear and even obvious. The work became easy.

There were moments, when he worked the old place, when he had looked down at his hands and had seen the Old Man's hands. There were the same bony ridges and hairy knuckles, the same strong-nailed fingers making the same motions. So many of the patterns seemed to be already there, in his hands.

Often, his hands seemed to make movements on their own and he had learned many things consciously by watching his hands work. Much of the knowledge, he knew, he had absorbed as a child, as he followed the Old Man around the place, casually at play, yet a part of him vitally alert to everything within range of his senses. While his mind had chased dragons, his hands had learned to prune and graft and plant.

His hands now taught him to transplant tomatoes as they sightlessly buried the roots deep in the mud. They already knew when the soil moisture was right for the steady growth that produced number one potatoes instead of knobby culls. And they showed him the early signs of scale on the undersides of bean leaves.

Despite the handwork, the old place was not that difficult. It was just more constant, required a different level of attention. You had to use every angle, maximize each harvest, but if you knew how, you could provide yourself with plenty.

Without the milk and egg business, or the chickens and rabbits, just with the vegetable garden and the fruits and berries and other perennials, he and Judith had made over $10,000 a year the last two years, part time, on the side. And that didn't include what they had eaten and given away. The Old Man's machine coasted on.

When his eyes grew accustomed to the dark inside the kitchen, Harry saw that the cookstove was still there. He would have to get it. It was a green enameled Monarch that had been with the old couple since their marriage in Kansas in 1921. He would store it with the loom, somewhere. He touched the cold, deserted top of the stove and thought of how many times the Old Man had made coffee on that same stove, in the same stainless Dripolator. "My one vice," he had said.

Anyone who had known the Old Man well, knew that much of his life followed patterns of habits so old that he could not remember their beginnings. The day was a pattern and the week, the month, the year. Tasks, large and small, followed familiar routines, varied only when he could see a clear improvement.

Parts of the patterns came from the Old Man's father and grandfather and who knows how many generations before. Though tools and crops changed, ancient programs remained. "The way my granddad did things," the Old Man said and slid into the ancestral Western drawl, "was mostly right. Nobody went hungry, and nobody ever belonged to the bank."

Sometimes it seemed to Harry that the Old Man must have lived several simultaneous lives. He had seen and done and thought more than all the rest of them. While his life had rhythmically proceeded, a part of his mind was free to watch and think and consider. "A man has to do his own thinkin'," he always said. "What's the use of havin' a brain if somebody else is doin' your thinkin'? Might as well have your head amputated."

The Old Man always had his hands into everything. He loved to reuse junk, and had always preferred to adapt something he had rather than to buy something new. If a new tool appeared, he would know instantly if it was truly useful or designed just to open his pocketbook. "You have to see what's in front of your face," he would say, "not what someone else tells you is in front of your face."

His long silences had been often misinterpreted, even by the family. He had not been unconscious or angry as some people supposed. Harry had seen it in the Old Man's last few years. He seemed to know everything about everything, from farming to politics to the weather that could be expected next winter, as if he learned by osmosis.

As the Earth moved, he had moved, so that it often seemed that the Earth moved with him. To the Old Man, it hadn't mattered. "You just do the best you can," he said, "and the world will take care of itself. It's a good thing, too, or it wouldn't have lasted until we got here to take care of it."

He scoffed at the idea that God had given man the Earth and all its creatures like the preacher said.

"God had more sense than that," he said. "If he was goin' to give somebody dominion over everything, it would have been horses or some other sensible creature."

Harry had often heard Mom bang dishes and slam cupboard doors after her religious arguments with the Old Man.

It still seemed impossible, sometimes, that he could be gone. His voice still whispered audibly in their ears. Harry roamed the old house for a few minutes. Dad had just closed it up after grandma died and Harry had only come in once since then, to collect the tools from the shop for the auction, and he had hardly looked around him then.

He saw now that the years of desertion had taken a toll. Spider webs supported peeling wallpaper. Rodents and birds had found their way in and nested here and there. The old folks wouldn't have minded that.

He had to absorb it all, now. It would be gone, TODAY. At least for him. He would not be back. "When a thing is done, it's done," the Old Man always said.

Harry carefully closed the door and went to walk the ghostly rounds of the empty homestead. It seemed that the old place, too, had become just another collection of winter shadows, disintegrating beneath the soft sameness of the snow.

The Old Man's spirit weighed heavily on him today. He remembered the last day, when grandma had come running along the canal bank to tell them she'd found the Old Man dead. Her eyes had been bright, grieving, but excited. Their time had come.

Harry knew how it had been. The Old Man had gotten up that day at 5:00 as usual. Each day, at 5:00, he was simply no longer asleep. He would have built a fire in the cookstove and made coffee for himself. He had filled both wood boxes the night before, as always. After the coffee, he had taken a little time to put his tools in careful order and cleaned his small shop, probably lectured himself a little for the condition he had found it all in.

The Old Man always tried to return things to their places, hated to waste time searching for a tool when he should be using it. It was the one area in which he was a tyrant. You could always use his tools, but God help you if you misplaced one. The loss of a chisel or pliers could provoke him into recounting the entire history of the tool, as though it was a vanished talisman whose spirit he must lay to rest.

When his shop satisfied him, the Old Man always put on his black wool coat and went out to take care of the animals. His dogs met him at the door, a young, feisty male Australian Shepherd and an older Border Collie female that had served him as a stock dog for years. He scratched their ears and promised them some food.

He threw a little scratch to the chickens and chuckled at their frantic competition. The ducks and geese, as usual, ignored him. They were only a step away from the wild, kept from flying south only by cracked corn and clipped wings.

The goats crowded the front of the pen, anxious not for food but for a touch, a look, a word that would renew and continue a pleasurable association. They were skittish and suspicious, nuzzled his hands fiercely for reassurance.

In contrast, the cattle drew back from his touch, flicked their ears and insistently nosed the bottom of the feeder. The Old Man fed them and turned back through the orchard and berry patches, checked it all as he passed.

His path made a large circle and ended as his morning ritual always did, with the horses. As always, they transported him. No longer able to ride, he had loved to walk with them, remembering. He could see in the leg strength of his old mare the power of the great-great-grandsire he had bought as a colt. The old farmer had told him the history of the entire bloodline. Dad's tall Appaloosa gelding carried in its blanket markings a lopsided star that had recurred every other generation in his family's saddle horses since his grandfather was a boy. And Shadow had the familiar carriage of head and arch of the neck he loved.

Once more they walked the Spring Earth together, that morning, the Old Man and the few remaining horses. Although they had become dependents instead of servants, he could not have imagined being without them. They went out to the corner of the pasture and back. The old Percheron mare nearly rested her huge head on his frail shoulder as they walked. Two yearling foals, just learning the routine, galloped back and forth as scouts for the procession.

When he had completed his rounds, the Old Man had left his muddy boots ready on the porch and returned to the radiant kitchen. He hung his coat on the hook beside the stove, warmed his gnarled hands. When they moved to his satisfaction, he had gotten out the leather bridle he had promised to repair for Judith. Grandma found him there when she got up, in the comfortable kitchen, slumped over the table, the bridle in one hand and an old wooden handled awl, a legacy from his own grandfather, cradled in the other.

CHAPTER 3

Harry completed his circle, waded snow through the stark orchard as the gray shades of daylight reddened to dawn. Near sunup, he thought, and was not surprised to hear the Old Man's voice. He was careful to connect his tracks at the front porch, finish the thing. He wasn't superstitious, but he felt like doing it.

He looked at his watch. Twenty minutes until breakfast. He would rearrange his load, make room for the cookstove. As the light quickened to yellow, he saw their equipment, drawn up in martial rows to await the day's ceremonies. It was ranked according to age and therefore presumed value, newer generally signifying better.

The remnants of the Old Man's equipment were relegated to the very back with the hand tools and household goods. The old horse-drawn stuff would have some curiosity and antique value. The thirty-year-old tractor and the plow and cultivator bars would probably go cheap.

The family didn't need any of it anymore, that was for sure. Besides it was all on the equipment schedules that went with the operating loan. The young banker was very thorough. "Maximize your collateral," he said.

His investors loved the long lists of tractors and discs and harrows. Made the place sound like a real farm. And the old equipment could always be valued at replacement cost on the loan applications. He even had listed the old mare at fifteen hundred dollars. The young banker definitely knew the angles.

Harry avoided the horse barn on the way back to his place. No point in stirring things up over there again. It would be hard enough, for them. It was light enough to see clearly, now, although the temperature continued to drop as any remaining heat was sucked into the vacuum of the coming day.

He repacked his small load. It would look better with the cookstove, almost full, like a family waited for it. He checked the guns and made sure the money belt was under the seat. It was only eighteen hundred dollars, but he felt lucky to have that. After they had rented Judith's apartment and moved her stuff, they split what was left.

Even with his head under the canopy Harry could hear Ron's turbocharged Mitsubishi as it worked its way up the lane from the county road. He turned and sat on the International's tailgate. Ron's sleek coupe rocked gently at his dismount. The red and green glow of the dashboard slid across the glass as he closed the door.

"Mornin' Harry."

"Mornin'."

"How's it goin'?" Ron asked automatically.

"Fine," Harry answered. "We're ready."

"How's your folks?"

"Fine. I guess. I haven't seen 'em this mornin'."

"Wanta go for breakfast? Into town? I'll buy. The Owl, anywhere you want."

"No. I better stay. I told Mom I'd be here all day."

"How's she doin'?"

"Okay. Prayin' a lot. That's what she calls it. Sounds to me like she's just runnin' down her bitch list. To the Lord. And remindin' him how hard this man of hers always tried."

"Well, maybe it does her some good."

"Yeah. Maybe. Drives Dad crazy. I know he's thinkin' about bein' in that thirty-six-foot trailer with her prayin' and watchin' Oral Roberts and Jimmy Swaggart all day." He laughed. "Hell of a retirement."

"Is Jack comin'?"

"Shit. You know Jack. Mr. Big Business. He'll find somethin' he has to do. He's tryin' his damnedest to stay away from this mess. His customers might lose confidence in his judgment."

"He's been tellin' people it's your fault, you know. How you put the place in hock tryin' to get the co-op goin'."

"Doesn't surprise me. I lost the Viet Nam War, too."

"Yeah, I heard him talkin' once about how tight him and Rod Thornton was. As I remember, Rod thought Jack was a punk."

"It don't matter anymore," Harry said. "If I spent all my time tryin' to straighten out Jack's lies I wouldn't have time for nothin' else."

"I gotta go," Ron said. "I'll be back, though. About lunch- time. I want to see how the big stuff goes. We'd like to sell ours and get the hell out of here. But we're not gonna get raped."

"Yeah. I know the feelin."

"You may do all right. I heard both Sunny Dale and United Farms was goin' to send buyers.

"Maybe they'll kill each other, biddin'."

They both laughed and Ron left with a thumb's up. Harry heard him punch the accelerator when he hit the pavement half a mile away. The whine of the turbo-charger faded fast, trailed off towards the State Highway.

Harry thought Ron had looked ridiculous, shivering in his black leather bomber jacket and running shoes, like he was already in Seattle. The Radfords had been right, though, about the money. They always were. Their crops never were worth a damn, but they got the money part of it right. Dad said they collected at least a dollar from every subsidy known to man. The Old Man had said the Radfords never met a chemical they didn't like.

They knew how to wheel and deal with the land. Jack said that they got almost half a million dollars, cash, for the mobile home park they'd built on a scrappy ten acre piece next to the high voltage lines. Jack had tried to sell it for them, but some Realtor from the coast, with a bunch of hungry tax investors, had come through buying anything that even looked like a mobile home park.

The Radfords also had been one of the first to sell to Farm Management Corporation when it was put together by a local broker five years before. The investors just wanted the tax breaks, they didn't care what happened to the land right now.

The Radfords had leased their land back for a nominal rent and were able to have a much higher profit margin than when they owned their own land. The broker had used the favorable numbers from the Radfords' low-rent operation to sell the next wave of investors. Meantime, Ron's dad had invested his money in a nursing home, which had a far better return, he said, than farming. So now Ron was a Vice President of Radford Retirement Environments.

As he walked towards the new house, Harry thought it still looked out of place, even though it had been there almost five years. It didn't look anything like a farmhouse. It was a split- entry, picked out of a catalog because Mom thought it looked like the nice suburban homes she saw in Lake Hills and West Seattle when they went on trips to the coast.

Harry had argued that no one built split entries anymore and that they were ugly and inefficient. He knew from his construction experience that it was a cheap design intended to give the illusion of space in a tiny house. But, it was Mom's decision Dad had said, and she made it.

They had trucked in over two hundred yards of fill from up on the rangeland to build a mound high enough so the entry would work. They had put some boulders around with the loader, and contoured the fill the best they could, but the way it poked up from the field the house was an alien thing.

At Harry's approach, Dad appeared on the deck the way they do in Sunset Magazine, with a wave and almost a smile, one hand on the railing.

"Breakfast's ready," he said. "Bacon and eggs. And biscuits."

Sure, biscuits, Harry thought, out of a can. And watery eggs with microwaved bacon. He wished he had gone with Ron.

"Okay," he said, "I'll be right there."

He walked around to the front of the house and went in. Mom was at the top of the half-flight of stairs. "Good morning, son," she said and forced a smile down at him, "God bless you."

"Not likely," Harry said. He took off the frozen boots on the landing and went upstairs in his socks. "Is there any coffee?"

Mom already had on her uniform of the day, a black polyester pants suit with a severe white blouse and high heeled shoes. She poured him a cup of weak coffee from a plastic percolator. "Well, we're ready," she said. "I guess. You're father had a bad night. It isn't easy for him, you know. He's worked hard all his life."

"He isn't complaining."

"He never does. You know that. They all learned that, in the war."

"War does that," Harry said. "Makes you not complain. That's why they should draft women."

Mom glared, ready to fight.

"Not today," Dad said from the table. "Let's eat." He started in, said no more.

"Is the banker coming?" Mom asked weakly, when it was apparent that Dad would not say another word until doomsday.

"I suppose," Dad said, did not acknowledge her.

"He wouldn't miss it," Harry said.

"That's not fair, Harry," Mom said. "He's been real helpful, handling the other creditors and everything."

"Yeah, morticians are helpful, too. Drive Mercedes, too, just like him. People get paid well to do things no one else wants to do. Except for soldiers."

"Well, I think he's been very nice to us, considering."

"Yeah, considering himself." "He's only done his job," Mom said. "And if he's done anything wrong, I'm sure the Lord will forgive him."

"Well, I won't."

"Don't say that, son," she said, tearing a little. "You can't ask for forgiveness yourself, if you don't forgive others?" "I haven't asked for forgiveness," Harry said, looking at Dad. "I take responsibility, myself, for what I do."

"Stop it," Dad said, paused for a quick look at them. "Both of you. There's nothin' we can do now," he said to his plate.

Harry had eaten all he could. He carried his plate to the sink and scraped and rinsed it. Mom started to say something as he walked towards the living room, but Harry looked her in the eye and she stopped. He turned on the television to the Morning Show and sat down on the big leather hassock to watch.

Polly James interviewed some stock-market expert. It was clear from the direction of the interview that she was primarily concerned about her own portfolio. Apparently she was into pharmaceuticals.

Harry's attention wandered out the window towards the distant highway. The early sun still cast long shadows. A couple of fat ravens called from one of the Poplars along the lane and flapped away to join their departing flock. He thought he saw a car start up the driveway and then stop. He wasn't sure if it backed again onto the highway or stayed there in the Poplar shadows. It was black, like the banker's Mercedes.

"The banker's coming," he said and saw Dad start slightly.

Mom just looked at Harry as if it was his fault.

After five minutes, the car hadn't appeared over the low rise near the house.

"I wonder what the hell he's doing, lurking around out there," Harry said. "I think I'll go get my rifle and have a look."

Mom glared. Dad took his plate into the kitchen. Harry stood up, tried to get a better angle to see whatever was under the Poplars.

"That bastard," he said, "He'll probably just sit out there, make sure we don't try to take anything away at the last minute."

The young banker had come to town about five years before. The first time Harry remembered him was when he got a job at Farmers Savings as a junior loan officer.

He would drive around the county in his old Plymouth, visit farmers and offer to do their financing. The day he had first pitched Harry and Dad he wore a cheap brown suit and a narrow tie and looked at them earnestly through his skinny gold-rimmed glasses.

The value of their property was soaring, he said, and generous credit was only a mortgage away. Dad's two-hundred-acre farm unit that had cost maybe $30,000 to buy and develop twenty years before could be sold easily for ten times as much. The tax benefits for those who invested in farmland were great.

Dad had taken a liking to the young banker. He knew every angle on qualifying for loans. If they wanted something, he would find a way to get it. He could show them, on paper, in black and white, that their net worth was far greater than they had ever imagined. They were in a new era, now, he liked to say, and the farmer would soon come into his own.

Dad and his friends broke ancient country taboos, began to talk openly about getting their just due. They would finally catch up with the city boys who'd been their rivals since World War II. They borrowed money to buy Cadillacs and motor-homes and to build split-level houses among the bean and potato fields.

The speed of the new equipment allowed them to use their newfound money to expand and still have Winnebago Winters in Arizona. They also had more time to socialize. The cocktail lounges in Moses Lake and Quincy and Othello flourished. Always, it seemed to Harry, the young banker was there, buying drinks, listening with fascination to the World War II stories.

Dad had talked Harry into going to the equipment show that winter in Spokane. The young banker put a thousand dollars for the trip in their operating loan that year, said they needed to get some new machinery. The show had opened with the National Anthem, a Pledge of Allegiance and a taped greeting from President Reagan. It was obvious that the two-sentence salutation had been added to some patriotic speech that didn't mention farming at all. But it worked. Before that first day was over, the show had become a drunken reminiscence of the Good War.

Led by salesmen from Ortho and Dow, John Deere and International Harvester, rowdy brigades of middle-aged farmers in baseball caps invaded all the bars within marching distance of the Ridpath Hotel. Arm in arm they staggered across plush-carpeted beachheads and took up top-grain forward positions in the best lounges.

Once more they cast monstrous shadows. For lack of Krauts or Japs, they intimidated all the women in their newly occupied Rhinelands. The young banker was there, sober as a judge, but encouraged them to enjoy themselves. And if any of them got too drunk, he would help them back to their rooms. They deserved a celebration.

No one was sure where the young banker had come from. Montana, some said, while others had heard it was Wyoming.

"Some decent, God-fearing place," Mom said.

Harry had noticed that the banker's accent seemed to change as he talked to different people.

He continued to wear the baggy synthetic suits but he traded the old Plymouth for a new Lee Iacocca Dodge and joined the local Young Republicans. Mom was one of many who said he reminded them of Rod Thornton.

Harry reminded her that the banker was younger than Rod would have been, and smaller, and wasn't actually in the war, or the military.

Mom said it didn't matter. It was something else.

The young banker became a loud supporter of the High School teams, especially football, and the next Spring married Lucy Bright, a newly graduated cheerleader. After an elegant Baptist wedding and a huge reception at the Elks', they moved into the fine split-level house he had built in a new subdivision Farmers' Savings had financed.

The Farmer's Savings Board of Directors, who were local businessmen and farmers and a doctor, really had no choice but to move the young banker quickly through the ranks to the presidency. Old Matt Johnson had gotten behind the times and clearly would never catch up. He had become an impediment to the young banker's obviously successful policies.

Harry remembered the party when the golden mantle settled on the young banker's narrow shoulders. He invited all his customers and friends and new in-laws to a great bash at the brand-new Desert Aire Motel-Restaurant on the edge of town alongside the Interstate. Farmers, business people, doctors, dentists attended. Even the local chiropractor was there, having financed his Volvo at Farmer's Savings. The young banker had asked Harry and Ron to leave, said they were obviously taking drugs. Ron said you didn't need drugs to think the whole thing was ridiculous.

CHAPTER 4

Harry still could not see into the Poplar shadows. He sat down again to watch the Morning Report from Spokane. Dad came in and sat in his recliner and became engrossed in the news. Mom stayed at the table, furiously smoked a cigarette and gulped the weak coffee.

A dog food commercial finished with a long fuzzy fade of a china plate heaped with little plastic-looking pork chops and T- bones and drumsticks.

"Farm Formula," the announcer announced. "The best to put that country golden glow in your dog's coat."

Debbie White's tan, blonde face replaced the Technicolor protein. She looked particularly good today. Her flawless hair coiled perfectly around bottomless blue eyes. Harry could feel the moistness of her professionally bowed lips. A plunging silk blouse with embroidered roses invited him down to contemplate barely discernible nipples. Her breasts swelled with each line she read.

Debbie introduced a story of her own, the last in a series on the homeless. Already she had talked to the experts; they had shown her the statistics. There were, indeed, a lot of homeless people in the country, in Washington State and even in Spokane. Of course the problem was much worse in Seattle where there was a large international district and many transients and foreigners to deal with, not to mention drug addicts. She had shown a lot of footage from the sister station in Seattle and from New York and Washington, D.C., but today she would interview some actually homeless people in Spokane.

As the videotape replaced her live image, she had changed into some tight acid-washed Levis and tied her ash-tinted hair back in a designer scarf so she would not intimidate her subjects.

First, she talked to a few winos, on Riverside. They mostly grunted and nodded, but none of them disputed the facts and figures she discussed with them. One of them generously offered her a swig of Tokay and leered at the camera.

Debbie had found a runaway, a skinny punker girl of about fourteen, at the bus station, and got her to talk about how her step-father raped her and how she had barely escaped from a vicious pimp in Portland. Then she cut to a strong finale at the Salvation Army Shelter. She talked to a black woman in baggy stretch pants and an old parka, with three little kids desperately hanging onto her as she talked. "I dunno, ma'am," the woman said finally and blinked back tears while she juggled the children. "I dunno what they ought to do about it. I just try to get by day to day with these kids. I just love 'em all I can."

After a decent silence, Debbie was back. The scarf rippled dramatically in the cold wind against a background of old brick. "As a mother myself," she said and paused for a brief smile, "I know how they must feel. How awful to have missed out on this great economic boom and not even be able to feed your children!" Again she held a sincere pause while the director dissolved from tape to studio.

"But, now for some better news," Debbie's carefully contrived male anchor-partner faultlessly responded, "and speaking of economic booms, Debbie." He turned to face her, live again, in the adjoining chair. "The stock market continues to rise. Most investors this year have seen record growth in the value of their portfolios." He warmed to his subject. "Dividends also have set records this year. Falling interest rates and the new, more generous Federal regulations, have allowed investors to multiply their profits. And, of course, we will all pay less taxes on those profits thanks to the Reagan tax reform. Some liberal economists point to plummeting productivity," his brow furrowed cautiously as he read, just a little, "as well as gigantic government and trade deficits," then the serene smile returned, "but administration experts assure us that old notions of economic laws need not concern us in this era of great expansion."

"And now, Debbie," he beamed at his female reflection, "we want to congratulate you for your excellent series on the homeless. Looks like Emmy material to us. Your deep personal concern and empathy for these people certainly made the series newsworthy. Once again, congratulations."

Their simultaneous smiles rotated to face the #1 camera, faded like Siamese Cheshire cats into an advertisement for AT&T computers.

Harry went into the dining room to get another cup of coffee. "Harry," his mother said, quietly, "I would like to talk to you later, alone."

"About what?"

"I just want to talk to you. I'm your mother, don't I at least deserve that?"

"When I have time," Harry said and returned to the hassock. "AT&T's new system," the announcer said in a throaty voice with just a hint of menace, "Don't be left behind."

"I wonder if that would have helped us," Mom said from the dining room. No one answered her. "A computer I mean. It seems like everyone who has one is doing fine."

Harry just looked at her and said nothing.

Now a fat used car tycoon honked his wares for thirty seconds. Harry looked at the row of worn cars with their bright placards reading "Buy me Now" and "Sharp!!" and thought that it was probably the used car man's last fifteen hundred dollars that had bought the thirty-second commercial. If this didn't bring the buyers in, it was down the toilet with his little dream. The fat man crammed the rest of his pitch into the remaining ten seconds and electronically slid from the screen, still gesticulating.

Then Debbie was back with her nipples. "And now for the Farm Spotlight," she breathed, roses rising. "Derry Marigold has a report for us on the current shake-out in the agricultural industry, or Agri-Business as they now call it." She made a smooth ninety-degree turn to face the more intimate #2 camera.

Her lips were huge now, and soft, with her face in super close-up. "Tell us, Derry, just what is going on out there with all these farm families going bankrupt?"

"Well. Debbie," the voice preceded the sudden flash of a well-groomed male face replacing hers, "there are differing opinions on that." It was impossible to determine if Derry was sitting next to her or on tape.

"Farmers feel that the current situation, with hundreds of farm failures in our area alone, is a disaster." The camera zoomed back, showing Derry in front of a farm auction. Neat rows of equipment awaited the bidders. Cuts of a corral full of cattle and a large porch lined with household goods succeeded the original shot. Harry could not determine if Derry had gone to the auction or had just mixed it in at the studio.

The scene returned to Derry, hovering now well above the ground in a long shot of the equipment. "Others, experts in the field, say this is just a normal operation of the agricultural cycle. Every twenty years or so, they say, there is a winnowing out, as it were, of the chaff. That is, the marginal operations too small to compete in the modern world. The Agri-Business tree is being pruned."

Derry abruptly returned to solid ground, stood in front of a huge steel building, a long row of identical roll-up doors all tightly closed. "Behind me," he assured them, "is all the equipment needed to operate an efficient modern farm." Now he floated near a strangely silent Bearcat tractor that plowed at full speed, black loam rolling over obediently in a swath eighteen feet wide.

Undaunted but breathing deeper, Derry continued, "No horse and buggy business here. This is serious farming." He made a quick transition to harvest. Against a perfect cloud-laced sky under the most flattering of suns, a golden cascade of corn thundered into the back of a shiny GMC truck. Harry thought he recognized the shot from an old truck ad. Derry reached out as though to touch the iridescent flow.

"As you can see," he said in close-up, after a moment for breath catching, "with modern methods, comes the modern harvest. Not a trickle, as in our grandfathers' day and not a stream, as in our fathers' time, but a flood, a veritable torrent of food, plenty to feed all the hungry of the world and more."

Again the camera drew back to show Derry now seated snugly next to Debbie. "It truly is a miracle," he said sagaciously. "The farm we visited, United Farms, Inc., is very efficient. Their labor costs are far lower than the small family farms they took over. The farms are now kept neat and clean and the equipment is new. As you could see from our auction footage, the equipment on the failing farms is almost always old. And United Farm's profits are wonderful.

"And by buying the land at current bargain basement prices, these corporations are assuring us of inexpensive food for a long time to come. The family farm may be of some sentimental value to some people, but we are very fortunate that our future food supply does not depend on such an antiquated system."

"Well, thank you very much, Derry, for another of your fine rural pieces as our farm editor. This world does move fast. I understand that there is also a human-interest side to this story concerning Matt Swenson, the Manager of United Farms. I met him once, a very nice man. I hear he is getting a promotion."

"Yes, Debbie, because of his good work here, Mr. Swenson is leaving to head up a new project for the company in South America where they are processing millions of tons of useless jungle plants into cattle feed."

"Well, thank you again, Derry," Debbie said. She moistened her lips with just a hint of tongue. "We'll be right back."

Harry felt himself being drawn helplessly into that alluring smile when a row of dancing raisins appeared where her perfect teeth had been.

"God damn it," Dad said and killed the picture with the remote control. "God damn it."

Dad stood up and looked out the window. "I think I'll go see who that is, down there," he said and his eyes followed Harry's gaze. Then he looked at Mom. "You stay here, Harry," he said. I'll check it out."

Trapped, Harry thought. "Okay," he said, "I'll be out in a few minutes."

"Harry," Mom said before Dad could get the door closed, "please come in here. I need to talk to you."

Harry got up, went to the dining table and sat down across from her. He said nothing; he was tired of making it easy for her.

She looked at him hopefully. Finally, "I'm worried about Dad."

"You're always worried about him."

"I mean seriously worried. He's been real strange. Doesn't say anything, but I know he's real hurt."

"He doesn't act hurt to me. I think he's just glad it's over. It's too much work for him. He's ready to retire. He's always been ready to retire."

"That isn't true. He's worked real hard. And he cares a lot. He's always loved farming."

"Well he was sure as hell in a hurry to make a bunch of money and escape from something."

"Harry, you know your profanity just upsets me. I need to talk to you. I don't know what we should do about him."

"Why do we need to do anything. Why do we always talk about what he wants or what he feels when he isn't here. He's an adult; he can speak for himself. If he wants my help he can ask for it."

"You know he can't talk about things. He feels real bad about losing the place. He knows you really wanted it."

"How do you know what he feels. You said yourself, he doesn't talk about things. You're guessing."

"I just know, Harry."

"I think you just like to talk for him. Then you don't have to talk for yourself. It's always he said... he thinks..."

Mom took Harry's arm and looked at him earnestly with her tearful eyes. "Harry, he's acting like he did after the war. So quiet. Like he isn't here."

"He's always been quiet. A lot of farmers are quiet. We're known for it."

"No, Harry," she said, "I mean with me. He won't talk even to me. The last time he was like this was right after the war. He was really hard to live with for a couple of years after we got married. He was a lot like you were when you first came back. Couldn't settle down. Drinking all the time, him and Chuck. He was really different."

War is different." Harry said.

"He thinks you blame him. For losing the place."

"I do. He screwed it up. His father found a way to get him started. Twice, once in Kansas and once out here. When Dad came back from the war, the Old Man gave you and him that eighty acres of bottomland and helped Dad build a house. You always talked like you deserved it. When I came back I was generously given the opportunity to work for Dad, on his place. Only if things were tight, I didn't get paid, and had to work out to make my trailer payment."

"He had to keep the place together, that was our only chance. You have to compete with the big farms now."

"The Old Man didn't. He did fine on a hundred and sixty acres. He built the old place after he was sixty, you know. He didn't retire and watch the world through the windshield of a Winnebago."

"That generation was different, Harry. They were satisfied with a lot less."

"They never settled for less than we'll have after today," Harry said.

Mom burst into tears. Harry stared at her hunched shoulders and felt only contempt. Somewhere deep inside was a faint memory of a young woman, cheerful and pretty, who had been nice to a little boy who loved her a lot. Lately he had found it hard to believe that she ever had been that young woman.

"Who gave you and Dad the right to gamble with everything this family had worked for over generations? You've sold your children into slavery. And your grandchildren. You always agreed when the Old Man said working for someone else was just slavery with a different name."

"That old stuff is all gone, Harry," she said and controlled her sobbing. "You can't bring it back." "I don't think your grandchildren will understand about you mortgaging their birthright so you could drive a Chrysler and watch soap operas in air conditioned comfort. I think they will wonder what was wrong with you."

"We... Dad did the best he could. He always tried real hard."

"You know what the Old Man said about trying," Harry said, and Mom started to cry again. "Tryin'," the Old Man had said, "is just another word for failin'."

"You could have done more, Harry, if you wanted to. You always left it all up to him, the business."

"Left it up to him! When did he ever listen to anyone's opinion? He just wanted our signatures on the papers, so he could play Big Business with our lives.

"The banker always told all of us, 'read everything closely, it's a legal document.'"

"That son of a bitch," Harry said, "he knew we didn't have a choice."

"I can't let you talk that way, Harry. Not about a fellow Christian." Mom made a little drama of getting up and going into the kitchen.

Harry just watched her and said nothing. The truth was, he had hated the business of it, the dealing with bankers who reeked of falseness and chemical salesmen with their oily, mechanical pitches.

Even if he had gotten the farm, Harry knew that it had a limited remaining useful life. Salts from fertilizers and pesticides were building up, fertility draining away year after year. He had seen the brown, dead slime along the drainage canals. Everyone had seen it, but they did not talk about it. Only the old place had been kept in a chemical free rotation.

For years it had been at the Old Man's insistence. After his death there was a kind of fear that if the Old Man's spirit were allowed to wither away completely, the family would die.

"If we come out of this with a deficiency judgment," Harry said, "I'll never be able to get started again, I won't be able to get any credit. And I'm not going to spend my life paying off Dad's bills."

"We won't have any deficiency judgment," Mom said, and straightened herself. "The banker and Dad both said we would come out with some money. Dad plans to give you half. He didn't want me to tell you."

"Well, you know about half of nothing."

"Even if we did lose everything," Mom said and drew herself more erect in a way that reminded Harry of a hen, "Sometimes, some people have to sacrifice so that the country as a whole can be better off. Just like in the war. This is a war, they say, an economic war, with Japan and Germany. Nobody ever wants it to be their turn to sacrifice."

"Us going bankrupt isn't going to help anyone. Some corporation will buy this place cheap from the bank and run it into the ground to make money for rich shareholders for a few years. Who is that going to help? It's a sacrifice, all right. Lambs to the slaughter."

"It will all work out for the good, Harry. God is watching."

"He seems to watch pretty quietly."

"The hand of the Lord works in mysterious ways," she misquoted.

Harry shook his head. "We had to make the same bargain the Indians made. Sell the future of your children for immediate survival. And if you don't understand what bargain you're making, so much the better."

"Oh, Harry, ever since you went to college you're so dramatic about everything. You sound like a professor." She looked at him hard and tried to control the quivering of her lips. "This isn't the end of the world."

"It's the end of my world. It's the end of your grandchildren's world. How much more of an end can there be?"

"Harry, what are you going to do? Why won't you tell us?"

"What the hell am I supposed to do. Maybe I should vacation in the South of France."

"How about Judith and the kids? Are you going to be near them? I would like to see my grandchildren sometime."

"I don't know. Judith lost her job a couple of weeks ago. She may have to go on welfare. I have eighteen hundred dollars. Period. And I'm unemployable."

"How are you unemployable? You're a young, healthy man with a college education.

It should be easy for you to get a job. Maybe not here, but somewhere. They say the economy is good."

"Where? I'm not trained for anything besides farming. They only hire Mexicans, now, to drive tractors for minimum wage. And they want Mexicans, they're afraid to complain."

"You have a college degree," she said and Harry was surprised at the note of pride when she said it.

"In Anthropology," he said. "To work in that field I'd need at least five more years of graduate school. If I could afford that I would be 43 when I was finished. No one wants a middle- aged instructor or assistant professor. It's too embarrassing. No one even wants a middle-aged laborer. Especially one with a psychiatric record."

"You don't have a psychiatric record."

"Of course I do. Why do you think I was in Harborview and down at Western State?"

"But that was temporary. And it was for depression from the war the doctors said. And they cured it. It isn't like you were mentally ill. And you're fine, now."

"Yeah," Harry said. "I'm fine, now." He stopped rinsing dishes and went into the living room and lay back in Dad's Lazy Boy.

Yeah, he thought, I'm okay, now. Compared to then. But the depression was back, a silent, shadow-like despair that could be seen only in retrospect. If he stopped at any time, any day, he could not identify the depression within him. But when he looked back over the months, the dark outlines could be plainly seen, slowly eclipsing the universe of his life.

He could not go to Judith and the kids. Unspoken even in his mind, was the knowledge that if it got really bad for them, his family would not qualify for any help as long as he was around. To the bureaucrats he was an employable male; to employers he was an aging casualty of a lost war.

At least there was a place for Judith, a niche. Single mother. It had become almost an honor. And there was help. Little enough, but something. But there was no equivalent place for him. Unemployed, separated males were not the targets for much sympathy. He had seen what they became in the cities, not only untouchables, but unmentionables, shadows sliding along unlit walls. With practice, he knew, it was possible to not see them at all. Just a shuffling, irritating interference drifted occasionally across the screen of the mind. But no face registered, no eyes pierced the onward flow of more pleasant and acceptable images.

"I'm going out and see what's keeping Dad," he said and stood up.

Mom looked in from the kitchen. "I would like to talk to you some more, Harry."

"We aren't talking," Harry said as he walked towards the door.

CHAPTER 5

The North wind still carried the chill of Cascade snow, but the sun was warm on Harry's face. In the near field, two pheasant cocks disputed ownership of a flock of hens. The intertwined flash of their bright feathers blazed up again and again among the cornstalks until their raucous calls drew an exuberant charge from Reject. The sudden throb of wings, as they sailed further into the stubble, startled Harry. The dog barked and danced in their wake.

Out by the rows of equipment Dad slowly walked along. Harry went the other way, into the cornfield. They should plow as soon as the weather broke. A few days of Chinook winds would strip away the snow and thaw the earth. Then it could all begin again. For someone.

He would miss the work more than anything. On the farm there was always something to do, something useful. After his sixty days in Western State Hospital, the farm had been the only place he could maintain his balance. He had been glad to get back on a tractor and he put in many twelve-hour days, healing as he worked the soil. Only on the farm did the shadows of the war substantially fade. It was better than all the medication and useless talk they had tried at the hospital.

The old, familiar movements, the certainty of what came next, soothed him, allowed him to think of better times, or at best, to not think at all, but just exist, there in the fields. That same immediate focus had caused his problems when he was first in Seattle. But here, instead of threat and confusion, the days were filled with a complex routine. And at night there was dreamless sleep.

He loved to plow the spring fields, watch the creamy gray volcanic loam stream behind into soft ridges. Dawn water changing, with the sharp splash of near ice, even choking in the golden dust of harvest, called up healing images from his Old World. Time, again, mattered only in an immediate sense: when was lunchtime or was it time to feed the stock. Time in the longer sense was irrelevant. It did not matter what year it was, or on what calendar it was counted.

Now, as he walked the fields, he felt loss and desperation and there was no refuge. To think of the future was impossible. If he was forced back to the city, he needed to be numb.

He turned back towards the house. Reject left off his chase and fell in at his heel. Mom came out on the deck, waited to talk some more. Harry did not acknowledge her, and turned instead towards his own place. He inverted a molasses bucket, and sat in the sun on the far side of the pickup, away from Mom and the north wind.

It had been a long time since he had not known where he would spend the night. He could go to Seattle. But, it would only deepen his depression to live again under the relentless waves of cold, humid darkness as the Pacific jet stream dumped one Gulf of Alaska storm after another on the coast. It had been that kind of winter when he went to Western State.

Five days after his discharge in Colorado Springs, the University of Washington Police had found him unconscious, drunk and drugged, lying in the mud in a little park dedicated to students who had died in wars. They turned him over to the Seattle Police who held him in the drunk tank. Early the next morning they took him into court, still soaked and shivering, which had seemed to the judge reason enough to put him in Harborview Hospital's Psychiatric Ward for three days of observation.

Harry had refused to claim his parents' address as home, he hadn't wanted to involve them. He didn't realize at first how much that would work against him.

"No address?" the judge had asked and looked at him suspiciously. "You must have an address. Why don't you want us to know where you live?"

Harry explained that he was just discharged and hadn't found a place. The judge told the bailiff to fill in the blank with NFA, No Fixed Address. It was clear that someone without an address was a criminal in his court. It didn't matter if you were just discharged from the Army or from prison.

That whole winter had been strange. There had been long lines at gas stations all across the high plains as Harry rode the Greyhound west and evil-tempered drivers fought for position. There had been a comet, too, called Kahoutek, hanging cyclopean over Seattle, its dirty yellow smudge obscuring the stars. Somehow, the physicists had calculated the orbit wrong and it drifted back into the outer solar system before they expected. Harry had sat all night in the Blue Moon tavern, listened to the arguments among physics majors and astrologers.

He couldn't remember how he got to the ceremonial grove on campus that night, or exactly what drugs he had taken after he left the Blue Moon as part of a spontaneous Comet Party. When the police took him from court to the Psychiatric Ward at Harborview he had laughed at their mock-parental concern. In his initial interview at the hospital, one young intern had said Harry could handle his drug and alcohol problems himself if he would just show some determination, act like a man.

Harry had dropped into a push-up brace and stayed there for twenty minutes, baited the pale, out of shape, intern to show his own determination. The resident returned, took one look, whispered with the intern and called security. When the orderlies threatened to put Harry in a straitjacket, he had stood up and punched the intern.

They did put him in the jacket after that, although it hadn't been easy and they called for more help. When the judge committed him to Western State, sixty day involuntary, Harry had a screaming headache from the injection they had given him. To calm him down, they said.

He had understood the game, then, and experienced an amazing recovery. He quickly learned to cheek the nasty little orange pills that plunged him into a hollow, acquiescent absence of feeling. He never again directly challenged their authority. The army had taught him that, too, how to hide and wait your chance. He played and lost endless games of solitaire and tried not to think too much.

Mom and Dad had driven to the hospital every weekend to visit and had taken him home when he was released. The diagnosis had been "Combat Related Stress" which, his file said, had been cured by Thorazine. A kindly, but confused, resident psychiatrist, Dr. Whelan, had taken a liking to Harry, and talked endlessly about his experiences as a medic in the Pacific thirty years before. Harry had amused himself by telling the doctor outlandish tales about his own service. He hadn't dared to tell him the things that truly bothered him. And he knew better than to mention the dream.

Dr. Whelan had not been able to understand Harry's guilt about the war. "War is different," he said, "it's a chance to do things you could never do at home, without guilt. And didn't you enjoy the excitement and the comradeship?"

Harry learned to give the right answers.

The spring and summer that followed his time at Western State, Harry had lived at home. Jack and Diane lived on the farm then, in their mobile home. Jack had talked his way into a partnership while Harry was in the army. The brothers got along all right, on the surface, but Harry knew that Jack was anxious for him to move along.

Jack's whole argument for a partnership had been based on Harry's lack of interest. After all, Harry had gone to the coast, to the University of Washington. The "intellectual" school, Jack often said in disgust. He should have gone to Washington State where you got useful degrees, in Agriculture or News Broadcasting. Jack had gone to WSU only two quarters himself, said it was a waste of time. Harry was sure Jack had flunked out.

The long hours Harry spent in the fields made Jack afraid Dad would split the farm three ways. But even then Harry had not been ready to farm. He wanted to finish his education. When he had been drafted, he had just begun to figure out what he wanted to learn.

That September, he had moved back to Seattle, into a boarding house in the University District, and went back to school as a twenty-six year old junior. The GI Bill was almost enough to live on, and he managed to find work-study jobs, first on the grounds crew, and later in the University's carpentry shop.

He went to his classes, and his job, and read and kept to himself. Only a few of his old friends were still around. Most of those who remained were now in graduate or professional schools, learning to think in ways that they insisted were not self-serving but just happened to be the convenient truth.

He met a few of them for a beer or an espresso, but there was almost no common ground. None of them had been in the service, and they had disagreed when he decided to go to Viet Nam instead of Canada. Now, either they avoided the subject entirely, with an occasional puzzled look to betray their tension, or they plied him with morbid questions about everything he'd done and seen. They always wanted to know if he had flashbacks. He was afraid to tell any of them about his time in Western State, and he never mentioned the dream.

He had returned to school for the challenge, the fearless pursuit of ideas he had craved as a freshman in 1968. He had been anxious to get back to it, to see what had been thought and written while he was gone. He longed for disagreements that did not turn into violence and for people who, whatever their side of an issue, discussed it intelligently and within a framework of shared values and definitions.

The first quarter he took classes with catalog descriptions that appealed to him. Political Anthropology 308 promised to "apply the techniques of objective anthropological fieldwork to the study of the institutions surrounding us." Geology 201 teased him with the statement that "the Grand Coulee may have been carved in a few days time by a gigantic prehistoric flood." Oceanography 101 seemed a logical choice. It would give him five credits in natural science and he had heard it was mostly movies and slides and multiple choice tests.

The new computer in the basement of the medieval Administration Building had assigned Dr. Diane Brown as his pre-major advisor. She was in the Comparative Literature Department, in a new brick office building hung from the steep escarpment on the east edge of the campus.

Inside, the building was firmly color-coordinated, in dark shades. An elevator hissed him to the third floor. A far cry from their old location in the dilapidated Victorian elegance of Parrington Hall, Harry thought. There were no classrooms in the new building, and the few students he saw hurried along the halls or sat patiently on hard, vinyl benches fixed to the walls outside each professor's door. He followed the numbers to the Northeast wing and knocked at a door marked "Dr. Brown."

"Have a seat, please," a sexy voice responded. "I'll be with you in a few minutes."

He sat on the dark blue bench, which matched the other dark blue benches and the dark blue wall stripe in that particular wing of the third floor. When she called him in, Dr. Brown sat in a dark blue swivel chair behind a walnut desk, which exactly matched the walnut bookshelves behind her.

The tangle of long reddish hair and the obvious coke spoon on a gold serpentine chain half-visible in the cleft of a batik blouse were not what he expected. Neither were the laughing blue eyes that caught his and stirred his responses as she offered him a chair.

There were flirtatious overtones as she approved his choices and insisted that he also take the one remaining of three required freshman English courses. He protested briefly, he had been able to duck that class for two years, but a look stopped him. She asked him how old he was and he was sure she was younger.

She looked at his records and asked where he had been for almost four years and when he told her the army, then working for his Dad, her eyes narrowed. "Viet Nam?" she asked. He nodded, and before he could elaborate, she handed his registration card back and said, "Thank you, Mr. Isaacson. Good luck." Her voice hadn't sounded friendly any longer.

CHAPTER 6

The only good thing that had come of his time at the University was Judith. He thought again about going to Seattle. He could just drop in on her. Or maybe hang around the Pike Place Market, see her again as he first had seen her, dark braids shining to her waist, while her laugh challenged the sun. Maybe he would have the nerve again to walk up to her and tell her she was beautiful as he had then, to his own surprise.

He had thought she was Asian at first, but she was at home, in her own country. She wore a long, liquid, yellow skirt, her eyes were deep in shadow. Her hand rested on a bin of oranges while she argued the price with the stall proprietor.

Harry had felt foreign, a stranger. It was as if he had suddenly awakened. She looked at him and her black eyes accused him.

She didn't speak, but he thought he heard her say, "Him, he did it. He killed them." He was afraid of her. Of all of them. They all wanted to kill him, now. The ground might give way at any moment, or one of the oranges, tossed at him, would explode and she would laugh at him as he died. There was blood in the shadow of the stall but he didn't know whose. A baby cried somewhere, and he wanted to scream at the mother to shut it up.

His vision cleared and the calls of the seabirds reminded him where he was. The fear passed. She was not Asian, at all, but Mexican or Italian or perhaps Lebanese.

He had wanted to tell her that the saffron yellow skirt, the red cotton blouse and green scarf, caught the essence of the market that fall morning, that her voice was the sound of the waves as they softly licked the pilings, the haunted cries of the gulls.

What he really had said was, "You're very beautiful," and then he had almost fled at the sound of it.

But she laughed and touched his arm and turned those eyes on him. "Thank you," she said, "But it's the day that is beautiful." And she had made him take her side, about the price of oranges, and when she bought them she asked him if he'd like to share one with her.

They walked up to the still empty stalls, on the north end of the market, where you could see all of Elliot Bay. They looked down on the tangle of watercraft, runabouts and fishermen and a brand-new five-hundred-passenger car ferry. Several rust bottomed freighters lay anchored near the docks.

Along the new southern piers, beneath the orange mantis container cranes, were crisp trading ships with Japanese characters and names that ended in Maru on their bows. Out towards Bainbridge Island, almost invisible in the lingering fog, a shadow-gray line of navy ships slipped out to sea.

"What a waste," she said, "this bay was once a beautiful place." She looked at him and offered him another orange. "My name is Judith."

"I'm Harry," he said. He couldn't think of much to add.

He ate orange after orange, tried to keep her there, until the oranges were almost all gone and she teased him. "I didn't know you were starving."

She was a student, too, she said, at the University, but in the Experimental College. He asked what courses and she said she studied medicinal plants and holistic healing, but that she also was in a workshop on spinning and weaving and a yoga class to stay in shape.

Harry knew that there was an Experimental College but few of the courses were for credit so he had never been interested. But she seemed so serious, not a hippie or a mystic.

She told him that the next quarter she would be in a Native American History course. The teacher was an anthropology instructor and Judith said that he would have elders from several tribes in to talk to the class. Harry could tell by the respect in her voice what the truth of her birth must be. He hoped that she was pressing him to take the class so that she could see more of him. He certainly wanted to see more of her.

The next quarter Harry got a copy of the Experimental College catalog as soon as it came out. He found the class Judith had talked about and signed up for it. It met Tuesday and Thursday evenings from seven until nine, and when he went to Denny Hall that first evening he was more anxious than he liked.

Judith was there, already sitting across the room when he came in. She was dressed in jeans and a sweater and there was a ski-jacket draped across the back of her chair. She wore her hair loose and it seemed a lighter color. She looked much less Native American than she had that first time. He wondered if he'd been mistaken, had projected some Asian image onto her when he had seen her at the market. But then she looked at him and he knew from her eyes that he had been right.

After the class they went for a cup of coffee and they talked for two hours in a quiet corner of the HUB. On Thursday they sat together in class and the coffee dates became a regular ritual. Her intensity and her quest for real, useful knowledge was genuine.

He felt proud, as he sat with her in class, obviously her friend, when the elders came. Each of them, when they looked into her eyes could see her mixed ancestry and treated her as a daughter. There were elders from several of the tribes around Puget Sound, the Puyallup and Lummi and Tulalip.

Judith told him about a Nez Perce elder from the Colville Reservation, a man they called Little Eagle, who would visit the class. He had been raised mostly in the old ways by elders from before white settlement. She said her family knew Little Eagle, he was a distant relation.

The class studied the Indian treaties and the battles. They read Cheyenne Autumn and Bury My Heart at Wounded Knee and Custer Died for Your Sins.

The class shrank; there were many arguments. None of the white students wanted to accept the truth of it. A couple of black students insisted that everything be used as a parallel for black history, although it was clear that most Native Americans had suffered more. They learned that in the heart of Dixie there had been laws to protect slaves at a time when there was a bounty on "savages" and the army gave them smallpox infected blankets to warm their frozen children. The bravery and tenacity of the tribes, as they fought their long delaying action against the end of their world, reminded him of the small, dark Asian enemy he had been trained to hate.

Then came the evening that Little Eagle was to visit the class. Harry could hear a drum, soft, almost subliminal, before he entered the building. As faint as the drumming was, the Earth seemed to pulse slightly with each beat. As he descended the stairs to the basement classroom, the fast four-beat rhythm seemed to grab him, pull him down. Something about the throb was insistent, partly inside his head. It made him think of Western State and Thorazine. And as he stepped into the cold concrete hallway it brought the dream. He could not wake himself and escape as he had learned to do.

They crossed the field slowly, all of them together. Four men bore four small bundles wrapped in old cloth. He knew the women cried, although he could not hear them. For the first time he noticed that they had a drum. The colors and outlines were so sharp that his eyes hurt. They passed closer to him than usual and as they passed they all turned their heads so that he could see their eyes.

It seemed forever before the graves were filled and the procession returned to Gook Town. His back was against the damp, plastered wall and he realized that tears streamed down his face. Several students and a professor had stopped to stare at him and he heard one say "Acid." He hurried into the men's room and wiped his eyes in one of the stalls. He wanted to run, forget the class, go back to his room and get drunk. But there was Judith. She would not understand if he missed this night.

He wondered how many had seen him cry like a fool in the hallway. For nothing. He forced himself to walk to the classroom. It was crowded and the drum was a loud annoyance. He stood in the back and looked for Judith, but he could not see her. There were a lot of people, mostly Native Americans, who had not been in the class before. A group of about a dozen, all in braids, sat in the front center.

A tall, pockmarked man with long leather-bound braids stood near the teacher's desk and beat a small drum with his fingertips. The famous Little Eagle, Harry thought.

He looked again for Judith, and she turned and smiled quickly, then again faced the drummer. She was in braids for the first time since he had first seen her at the Pike Place Market. The ends were wrapped with thongs and tipped with small pieces of fur. With her back to him, she was just two more braids in the group near the front. It made him uneasy to see her that way.

Several of the white students started to talk and were silenced by a glance from the drummer. The whole class was restive except for the group in front. Then Harry noticed that Judith and the others did not focus on the drummer at all. They watched a small man in blue jeans and a Navajo patterned shirt who sat cross-legged on the teacher's desk, faced away from the class. Harry wondered why it had taken him so long to notice the little man.

Suddenly the man on the desk began to shake a rattle and the drummer quickened his beat and left out the heavy accent on every fourth. They seemed to go faster and faster until the sounds blurred together and abruptly stopped.

The man on the desk slowly uncrossed his legs and turned to face them. "Hello," he said, "I am Little Eagle. I have just come back from another world."

Images collided in Harry's mind. He laughed silently. He knew "Little Eagle." At Western State the staff had called him Patient Joseph Longeaux. He had introduced himself to Harry as Long Joe.

He wondered if anyone else knew. Long Joe looked directly at him and he looked back, smiled. The dark eyes showed no recognition. Okay Long Joe, Harry thought, don't worry, I won't tell them. Harry remembered the soft, strong voice from the hospital dayroom.

"The world I've just been to, is a world anyone can visit. My people say that the drum is their horse or canoe that carries them to this magic world. The world I am talking about is in your mind. Most of you have never been there."

There were chuckles but Long Joe ignored them. "In all of our minds, the Great Mother put all of the knowledge we need, to live, to heal ourselves, to solve any problem we need to solve. The trick is to find that knowledge."

"Most of us," Long Joe said, and Harry knew he meant, "all of you." "Most of us never leave the shallow, easy waters along the shoreline of waking. We let others tell us what is in the deeper waters, because we are afraid to go there ourselves. We have been told that it is frightening or foolish or forbidden. So we let the priests and physicists and philosophers explain it all to us."

"But all they know is the knowledge the Great Mother gave to them. The knowledge given everyone else is ignored. We must have all the knowledge, all the dreams. Every dream is a question or an answer needed by us all to survive."

It seemed to Harry that the little man kept his eyes on him, bored into him, talked to him alone.

"Some of you have had strange thoughts while the drum beat, as if you dreamed while you were awake. I would say that is because this is a sacred drum that can transport you into that other world, the world you call dreams. Your scientists would say that it is because the rhythm is similar to that of theta waves which are associated with dreams. I don't think it matters. What matters is that we use the knowledge that all our minds already contain to help us all."

"This is a history class, so I will talk to you of history. But I will also tell you that I do not think the history really matters. It is just part of the shallow waters."

Long Joe sat on the desktop and talked of the old days, how the seamless web of the people had been torn into factional fragments, their power shattered.

"People have to eat," he said. "The game disappeared, the good hunters were dead, or in jail. White men lined the rivers and claimed the fish. Our gathering grounds for camas and berries were plowed up to grow hay for the army's horses."

"If the Methodists gave us food, we were Methodists for that time. When the Presbyterian missionaries brought in some wagon loads of corn, we all got baptized again, this time as Presbyterians."

He narrowed his face and raised his eyes heavenward, folded his hands in mock prayer.

"We did not understand about religion, because when a whole way of life is sacred, the people do not have to build churches and sing hymns on Sundays. And we did not understand about preachers because people have to be told what to believe only when they no longer believe it."

"Soon all the white churches and traders, even the military forts, had their little groups of dependent People who would then vote their way in the councils and treaty negotiations. Many fortunes in land were made at the cost of a few barrels of flour."

"They turned tribe against tribe, band against band, family against family, men against women, mothers against children, children against the elders. When you must have power to live and power depends on exploitation, then each person must exploit whoever they can."

"Many of the treaties required that we follow certain laws, punish with hanging and flogging. And the men who administered the laws, the Indian Agents, knew their business well. The first Governor of this state, Isaac Stevens, who was also the Indian Agent, had an assistant named Benjamin Shaw. The newspapers reported that Shaw bragged, 'I can get the Indians to sign their Death Warrants.'"

Little Eagle admitted that there had been factions and disagreements and fighting, before "the white problem," and he told several funny stories of absurd conflicts and unnecessary battles. "We have kept these stories, not to glorify fighting but because in each of them is a teaching. We must learn how foolish it is to fight."

"There were fights before the white man came. But," he said and looked at each of them in turn, a long pause, "There must have been some difference, because in all that time, my people prospered, and multiplied, and we were wealthy in our own eyes."

"One of your experts, then, described our lives as 'nasty, brutish and short.' Your scientists will tell you now that our way of life required only fifteen hours a week to provide the things that are necessary to be comfortable. All the other time was free, to play with our children, to love, to make beautiful things, to wonder about the universe. And our way could have gone on in harmony with the Great Mother forever."

There was a longer pause and a couple of the students decided he was finished and started to talk. Long Joe froze them with one of his looks and then continued deliberately. "Never before, at least here, on this continent, had one people set out to totally destroy another and steal everything, even the Earth. It was unthinkable, so we could not see it."

"When the whites first came, we sometimes welcomed them, sometimes quarreled with them, but always just as newcomers, the new kid on the block. We never questioned the whites' right to exist. There they were."

"They, too must be children of the Great Mother. And for sure, then, there was room for all of us, all colors. Much of the land was empty. We always knew that some day people would come to fill it with their songs. We had legends that told us these new people would be bearded and white. We did not begin to think of exterminating whites until it became clear that was happening to us."

"It was not that you needed our land, we could have lived side by side. You did not like how we lived, so you decided to force us to change. If that meant killing most of us, too bad. At least those who survived would be Christian."

"What you would not admit then is what your physicists tell you now-there are many simultaneous realities and the closer you look at something the harder it is to see it. If you want to get to your knowledge by building huge machines and going to the Moon and other things, which convince you that knowledge is outside, then you may do that. We would rather get directly to it."

"We were amazed that you would tell us how we should live. It should have been the other way around, because, like it or not, here we are your elders. By many thousands of years. You said your way was right, as if there could be only one right way, and everything else was wrong. But it is obvious that there must be as many rights as wrongs, or the Universe would be out of balance."

"You forced us to cut our hair." Long Joe ran his braid through his fingers then flipped it back over his shoulder. "To us, our hair is sacred, it contains power. It is to be cut only as an offering to the dead. Our beautiful braids were collected together in great piles and burned. Just as your priests, when they accused someone of witchcraft, first shaved all the hair from their bodies, to steal their power. Your priests and missionaries are soul vampires."

"The missionaries said that your God had told them to do all this, in talking papers written thousands of years ago. They said they were this God's holy men, yet they had no knowledge of the Great Mother. When we asked about their God, they described something very like themselves, jealous and angry and murderous. Then we knew the truth, the white man's God is just a mirror in the sky."

"I will tell you how we felt. Smohalla was a Dreamer. He founded the religion of Dreamers after a five-year spirit quest through California, Mexico and Arizona. He brought back many ceremonies, even some beautiful Mexican Catholic rituals. He taught that some day the Earth herself would rise up against the evil ways of the white man and cleanse herself. The newspapers wrote that he prophesied a great flood, or volcanic eruptions, as if he was writing a new Bible. What he meant, of course, is what goes on around us this very day."

"Smohalla also said that the spirits of our dead people would return and restore the land. The reporters said that the Dreamers thought they could resurrect all their dead through weird ceremonies and make war on the whites. What Smohalla meant was reincarnation. As I look into your eyes tonight I see, here and there, little flashes of recognition, and I know that for a moment I have looked into the eyes of one of my own ancestors.

"The soldiers told Smohalla that there was a new law, that his people must become farmers and miners or their children would be taken away to the white school. Here is his answer.

"'My young men shall never work. Men who work cannot dream and wisdom comes in dreams. You ask me to plow the ground? Shall I take a knife and tear my mother's breast? Then when I die she will not take me to her bosom to rest. You ask me to dig for stone. Shall I dig under Her skin for bones? Then when I die I cannot enter her body and be born again. You ask me to cut grass and make hay and sell it and be rich like the white man. But how can I cut off my mother's hair? It is a bad law and my people cannot obey it. I want my people to stay with me here. All the dead humans will come to life again. We must wait here in the house of our ancestors and be ready to meet in the body of our mother.'"

"Of course, the soldiers came and took away the children." Abruptly Long Joe got up and said, "Thank you for your time."

Judith walked over to him as he was surrounded by his own people and the class. She turned and led him to where Harry stood and said, "Little Eagle, I would like you to meet Harry."

The little man's eyes met Harry's, then looked at Judith then back at him and Harry could see that he had figured it all out. "Hello, Harry," he said softly. "It's good to see you again."

"Hello..." Harry began, then stopped.

"It doesn't matter what you call me," Long Joe said. "Between friends, names do not matter. Names are for strangers."

Judith did not seem surprised that they knew each other.

"What did you think? Of Little Eagle?" she asked him when they got to the HUB.

"I thought he was very interesting," Harry said and groped for something else. "I mean, I think what he said is true. Mostly."

"But his energy, his life," Judith said. "Isn't he an amazing person? He was raised the old way. Those people are always so different. They know so much more than anyone else. They can do anything. Have you ever been to the museums to see what they used to make? They could make their whole lives with their hands. Anything they needed."

It made Harry think of the Old Man and his always busy hands.

CHAPTER 7

Judith did not give Harry any of the signals he was used to. She deftly blocked anything, which could lead to him asking her out. Coffee after class was the only exception. He had seen her turn aside other men's flirtation with clear words and direct looks. She seemed to feel differently about him, more open and intimate, but he could not be sure.

He was afraid that the end of the quarter would mean the end of the friendship. Besides her classes, she worked at Sureco Insurance headquarters, which did not leave her much free time.

He asked her what Experimental College classes she would take in the spring term, and she said she would skip that quarter so that she could spend several weekends in Eastern Washington with her family. Easter, she said, was a special time for them.

He decided that on the last Thursday evening of the class he would somehow arrange to see her again. Before he could say anything Judith again blocked his plans. She would not be there on Thursday. She told him she was leaving that morning to spend four days at home. She wanted to do some early scouting for medicinal plants to gather later in the season.

He was glad that the class was not for credit, because he heard nothing of the remainder of the session. His mind raced, searched for a way not to lose her. He felt stifled and angry and he hoped the violent waves of emotion were not visible to the other class members, especially not to Judith. He could deal with rejection, if it came to that. But to be trapped within himself, unable to move, was unbearable.

He decided that he would just go home, skip the HUB and get the good-byes over with as fast as he could. But before he could flee, she touched his arm in that way that became so familiar, and said, "It's my turn to buy."

As always, with her, he was helpless. He spilled coffee on himself as they stood in line, and he barely suppressed an urge to throw the Styrofoam cup and its scalding contents at the student cashier who talked to a friend instead of working. As if she sensed his crisis, Judith leaned softly against him at that moment, and smiled, and the energy of his anger was diverted.

The Husky Den was crowded and noisy and they had to sit at a table already occupied by a disheveled guy in a Sigma Alpha Mu fraternity sweater. He had coffee, half-eaten doughnuts and books spread wide in pre-finals frenzy.

Harry looked at Judith, in braids again, and he wished he hadn't come, that he had made some lame excuse.

"Would you like to go?" she asked without transition. "Across the mountains with me?"

He was not sure he had heard what she said and turned towards her almost in anger. "What?" he asked dully.

She laughed and pulled her chair a little closer. "Do you want to go with me on Thursday? We can stay with my parents in Electric City. I already talked to my mom."

"But next week is finals," he heard himself say. "We would be back on Sunday. You could take some books, if you need to."

"I guess I could," he said and it sounded so lame that he laughed and the tension was broken.

Their table-mate looked as if he was sure Harry had lost his mind. Clearly, he would have been able to say yes.

"Good," Judith said, and leaned against him again, pressed her leg urgently against his.

They made arrangements for her to pick him up at 6:00 that Thursday morning. When they parted, outside the HUB, she drew him into the shadows and kissed him lightly and pressed her body against his. He walked home semi-conscious.

Harry watched out the window, peering through the dense fog, when he saw Judith's Mustang park in front of the boarding house a few minutes before 6:00 on Thursday morning. He put his backpack and sleeping bag in the trunk and shivered in the damp cold. He wondered if she wanted him to drive, but it was clear that she didn't and he sat on the passenger side.

"We'll go across Stevens Pass," she said as she headed the Mustang north on Lake City Way, "It's nicer than Snoqualmie. They haven't cut all the trees and the trucks don't go that way as much."

When they were out of the city, she drove fast, ignored the speed limit. She slowed down for the small towns on Highway 2, Monroe and Sultan and Skykomish, but in between they flew.

Several of the small, transient waterfalls that had given the mountains their name splashed onto the roadway and Judith dodged around them without slowing. Along the Sky River, the fog clung to the trees and rocks, slicked everything with dampness.

A few sloppy snowflakes fell with the hard rain as they climbed the last four-mile grade to the summit. On top a parking attendant tried to direct them into one of the jammed ski area parking lots with his flashlight.

Judith laughed and said, "This is where their world ends. They can't imagine why anyone would go on across."

Harry lay back in the seat and noticed how immediately and drastically the climate changed across the Cascades. The clouds from the Pacific were held on the West Side, then finally driven high up and over, leaving a rain-shadow a hundred miles wide.

The rain stopped before they were five miles down the eastern slope, and the air felt dryer. The dark groves of tall Douglas Firs were gone, replaced by an open forest of smaller firs and a few pines. The dense undergrowth of Oregon Grape and salal gave way to scattered buckbrush. Even the snow looked dryer, ablaze with translucent fire. The jagged clouds, now high above them, broke apart and were harried eastward by the jetstream.

They hardly talked during the precipitous descent, and it seemed like only a few minutes later when they entered the twisted stretch of Highway 2 along the Wenatchee River rapids through Tumwater Canyon. Judith drove the Mustang like someone used to mountain roads, accelerated into the curves, floated along the few straight-aways. She knew a German bakery in Leavenworth, and they stopped for a few minutes, drank espresso and Harry ate some pastry.

They flew on. She skirted Wenatchee, followed the truck route across the Columbia River and continued on Highway 2 through the dryland wheat and sagebrush to Coulee City. Here, the snow was all gone and the winter wheat shimmered green.

As she got closer to home, Judith started to talk about her family. She had a brother in high school, and two sisters still in junior high. Her mother didn't work any more, so she would be at home.

Her father, she told him, was a Bureau of Reclamation engineer who had come west from New England to help design the system of pumps and canals and tunnel siphons for the irrigation project. Judith's mother had worked for the Bureau, too, a secretary fresh out of high school, when she met and married him

Judith was anxious to get to the reservation on Saturday to see her mother's mother in Nespelem. "Hattie is Little Eagle's second cousin," she told him proudly. "She knows so much about medicine. She said she would go with me up the San Poil River and show me how to gather the strongest plants."

She told Harry that she often had stayed with her grandmother when she was a child. What she remembered most was the walks they used to take. They didn't just go for a stroll, or a hike, like other people. They often took the whole household, whoever was around, and sometimes they walked for two or three days, slept in blankets on the ground at night.

That was when she had first met Little Eagle, she said. The family had walked from Nespelem to the San Poil River, about twenty miles along Cache Creek. They stopped at several homesteads scattered through the highlands, which belonged to relatives of her grandmother. Her People lived in a very primitive way, she said, without electricity or running water, and their only heat was woodstoves.

"But, they knew so much about the Earth, about what plants you can eat or use for medicine. And their ceremonies were so beautiful. I've always wished I had paid more attention."

Electric City was a random collection of buildings grouped along a few crooked gravel streets, a town he had passed through often but never left the highway. There still were a few temporary military barracks left from the construction of Grand Coulee Dam as well as a small general store, a failing automotive shop and a few other dilapidated businesses beside the highway. Judith made a sharp left turn in a way so unconscious that Harry knew she had made that turn many times.

She stopped in front of a small white house. She sat quietly for a moment, just looked, then said, "This is it. I hope it never changes." They got out and she led Harry by the hand. She knocked softly and opened the door.

The house was comfortable, but small by Seattle standards, and old-fashioned with its formal dining room and wide front porch. Judith's mother was baking when they got there. Her hair was caught at the nape of her neck in a Navajo silver clasp and fell below her waist. She held her sticky hands behind her and Judith wiped a smudge of flour from her mother's dark face and kissed her.

She smiled at Harry with a smile very like Judith's, and he realized that their eyes were identical.

"Welcome, Harry," she said, "my name is Helen."

"Thank you." He sensed the same strength in her that he had seen in her daughter. "I hope it isn't too much trouble. If it is I could go down and stay with my family, in Ephrata," he said, let her know he was local, not from the coast.

"No trouble if you don't mind the accommodations." She smiled.

Judith took Harry to show him her room in the basement. The house was on a slope so the room had two large windows, which looked out to the north and east. Through them you could see the foothills of the Kettle River Range on the reservation side of the Columbia.

The room itself was large and the floor was layered with rugs, some with Navajo patterns, a couple were handmade rag ovals. The walls were hung with weavings of many kinds, mostly in bright, primary colors. Her bed was covered with a patchwork quilt, a large red Mandala on a yellow and green background. There was another door that opened into the garden back of the house. She took him outside to see the garden and the chickens her mother kept in a comfortable chickenhouse at the back of the property.

They went inside and talked in the living room while Helen finished her baking. Then she came in with coffee for them and Harry listened to the two women catch up on family gossip. Judith told her mother they'd seen Little Eagle.

"Ah, Joseph," the older woman said. "How is he doing? Was he drinking?"

"No," Judith said, "he was doing good. I don't think he was drinking at all. You would have been so proud of him, Mom. He told the class how it really was." Both women glanced at Harry and he had that feeling again, of foreignness and of not belonging.

Judith moved closer, touched his knee with hers.

After about an hour, Judith told her mother that she wanted to show Harry around. Her mother smiled and Judith flushed a little.

They drove up the highway, through the older town of Grand Coulee. They crossed the river on the bridge below the dam and drove through the newer town of Coulee Dam, on the north side of the river. They crossed back over the river and Judith stopped at the Wildlife Cafe. They ate some pie and drank some coffee and talked.

Several of the local people recognized Judith and came over to say hello. She introduced him as "my friend, Harry," and she seemed nervous. They finished the pie and coffee and got back in the car.

As she drove Southwest along Banks Lake, Harry was able to see the effects of the Great Spokane Flood he'd learned about in Geology. It was so obvious now. It seemed impossible that anyone, particularly generations of geologists, had ever thought that the great coulee was just a smaller Grand Canyon worn through the bedrock over millions of years. The sudden violence of its making was evident all around him.

The ragged canyons south of Grand Coulee Dam had been a favorite haunt for him and Ron Radford and Rod Thornton when they were in high school. It had been easy to disappear into the maze of deserted dirt roads to drink beer and maybe target shoot a little.

He had stopped several times at the Dry Falls Museum, on the northern rim of the Grand Coulee. The exhibits in the museum told of an ice jam at the present site of Grand Coulee Dam which must have caused the water of the Columbia to rise high enough to overflow and slowly carve these now dry canyons sometime during the last ice age. Dry Falls, they said, thundered with the roar of forty Niagras for thousands of years. There was a large, back- lighted artist's rendering of the mighty falls with a family of mammoths and a fierce saber-toothed tiger in place of the museum. Tourists were always impressed.

Now, that long accepted scheme had been overturned by a new theory full of violence and drama. There was an ice dam, but it was far off in Montana, in the valley of the Clark Fork River, where it held back a huge melt-water lake while the glaciers receded. The scientists now called it Lake Bonneville.

Suddenly, in the warmth of some post-glacial Spring, the enormous ice wall had weakened, then burst, and loosed a vast tidal wave of ice and water across Montana and Idaho to Washington State where it overwhelmed the Columbia and rolled south across the Basin. It temporarily straightened out the Big Bend of the river and gouged the tangled coulees.

The water from Lake Bonneville, they said, was all in the Pacific within two weeks, and most of it rushed through the Wallula Gap in three days with a crest hundreds of feet above the tops of the present-day cliffs.

As she drove down the coulee then back, they looked for more evidence of the great flood. Whole half-mile sections of sedimentary rock lay at random angles, their aeons-thick bands of red and yellow and lavender thrown against each other. Judith parked at the observation point on the cliffs and they walked to the edge and studied the formations. The great pool they saw at the base of Dry Falls lay not in a cavity slowly churned away by a constant river, but rather in a crater, blasted from the volcanic rock by an explosion of water. The irrigation water for the entire Columbia Basin Project now made a small trickle across the crater floor.

In steps above the canyons, whole plateaus had been scoured clean of their topsoil by the flood and become barren scablands, deserted but for marmots and jackrabbits and the rattlesnakes and badgers that eat them.

It was as if the inexorable advance of geologic time had been compressed into fast forward and left a jumble of epochs in its wake. Nothing was what you expected or where you expected it to be. In places, water now flowed along above older dry channels, at times in the opposite direction. There were several little dead-end drainages where surrounding watercourses collected into small lakes, each brackish and dead for lack of an outlet.

They picked up her sisters from school at 3:30. Both girls looked a lot like Judith and had their mother's powerful eyes. They were excited to see their sister, clearly idolized her. She'd brought gifts for them both, a book of Native American art for fourteen year old Sara and some silver earrings for Rachel, the younger. They sat in the back seat and both talked at once.

They all went back to the house and Harry read in the living room. Judith's brother came in after a while, in blue sweats with gold letters that said "Grand Coulee Track and Field." He introduced himself as Joseph. "Everyone else calls me Joe," he said, "but Mom insists that I use Joseph in her house." He was nearly as dark as his mother, tall and handsome, with those same eyes. He excused himself on the grounds of homework and Harry laughed and held up his own book.

Judith's father was Matthew Adams. He was a large, blond man with a Yankee twang in his voice. He was such a contrast with the others that it was disconcerting at first. But the family was close and affectionate and Harry wished his own was as good.

The dinner, steak and mashed potatoes with gravy, green beans and a salad might have come from his grandparents' table and he felt at home. There was good homemade chocolate cake for dessert.

They watched the news and then Harry went back to his book, although mostly he listened to the easy conversation around him. Helen was the center of the family, but Matt was not shy or silent, the way Harry's father so often was.

After a while, when the younger girls had done the dishes and Joseph disappeared again into his room, Harry and Judith and her parents talked for a while. By ten everyone in the family had gone to their own rooms, left Harry and Judith alone on the sofa. She kissed him on the neck and said, "Let's go to my room." and led him downstairs.

She closed the door and smiled wickedly at him. She unbuttoned her blouse and freed her breasts from her bra as she pulled him down on the bed. Again, he felt that he should be in control and he wasn't.

"What will your family say?" he asked her.

"They won't say anything," she replied. "They would prefer that I do what I choose to do in my mother's home. If they had objected, they would not have left us alone." She laughed and pressed her breasts against him. "You would still be listening to my father talk about flow rates and acre feet."

CHAPTER 8

They were greeted with smiles at breakfast, but several times Harry saw Judith's sisters giggle behind their hands. Before Matt left for work he asked Harry to play chess with him that evening.

After breakfast, Judith asked him if he would like to go for a drive, up the San Poil River, maybe as far as Republic if they felt like it. Harry agreed and Helen helped Judith to pack a lunch for them.

A few miles north of Coulee Dam Judith turned off the highway and drove east on the Manila Creek road. She said she wanted to check the lower part of the San Poil Valley for stands of mullein and yarrow and dryland Oregon grape that were not sprayed. She planned to collect medicinal herbs on her vacation the next August.

Two miles up the grade the paved county road changed abruptly to gravel. They soon climbed into scattered black and yellow pines. Here and there, in the clefts and notches of the hills, groves of white-trunked aspen quaked in pale green anticipation of spring. Along the dry watercourses the swollen buds on the red willows glowed scarlet as the sun drew up their sap. In the deepest shadows snow remnants gave up the last of their water.

When they reached the summit Judith pulled off the road onto a wide snowplow turnaround to show Harry the view. They sat on the hood of the Mustang and he pulled her close while she talked.

Below them they could see about twenty miles of Lake Roosevelt, from just above the buoy chain which guarded the great dam, far to the east. Along the river, directly down the slope from them, a riverside farm stretched its fields to the water's edge.

She pointed to the farm. "That's Bill Newlaw's place," she said. "He's about the best farmer the tribe has." Across the canyon, the shadow-darkened line of the southern cliffs hovered far above the mists of the morning river.

He kissed her. She responded warmly, eagerly, the reticence gone. In the startling stillness, a blackbird buzzed its melody. Up the ridge, a loud flock of ravens started up, strung out in a skirmish line and flew north.

They got back into the car and she drove on, through several tight switchbacks as the road picked a precarious path down the rocky east side of the ridge. There were two crude detours where the spring thaw had loosened the entire roadbed and large chunks of it had slid several yards down the slope.

In one of these spots a spring bubbled from the exposed hillside and washed a thick slurry of mud from the ruined road down the slope which forced Judith to drive almost through the yard of a faded ranch house. Two dark children in boots and jeans watched them maneuver the rutted bypass. Judith waved at them and they frantically waved back. Harry wondered if she knew them. She seemed to know everyone.

Further down, they went around a sudden corner and were at the intersection with the state highway that paralleled the San Poil. Judith turned north, a small sign said "Republic," and she sped along the narrow unmarked pavement.

Her eyes searched the riverbanks and small meadows for the plants she wanted to collect. She stopped several times, once with a screech of tires as she shifted into reverse and the Mustang shot backwards. They got out and she showed him the brown and withered remains of the previous summer's bumper crop of yarrow, which blanketed the mouth of a small valley.

He asked her if it was okay to gather the plants, and she told him that almost all the land on the reservation belonged to the tribe as a whole, 1.3 million acres, from the Columbia to the Okanogan Valley and north as far as Omak.

"It used to be twice as big," she said, "the reservation used to go north all the way to Canada, all of Ferry County and about half of Okanogan County. But they discovered gold, up by Republic, in about 1900, and they made the People sign a new treaty which gave the north half back. Talk about Indian Givers."

She slowed again, looked towards the river, then drove on.

"The best plants," she said, "used to grow right along the river, but they're all covered now, by the lake. They call it San Poil Bay, now, but the dam ruined a lot of things. I wish the river could run free again."

"We used to talk about that, me and my cousins, about blowing up the dams and letting the rivers loose again. We could just see that mountain of water crash through Wenatchee and the Tri-cities, ripping out all the bridges and smaller dams as it went. We used to argue about whether the flood would be big enough to wash Portland into the ocean." She laughed.

Up the valley, above the dam's elevation, the San Poil flowed without impediment. It was little more than a creek, which wound through small meadows and splashed over tiny rapids. Judith said the headwaters were up around Republic, among the old gold mines, where several creeks collected together then flowed south, straight as an arrow, to strike the Columbia.

As they drove through the narrow upper valley, the snow- covered cliffs were buttressed with step-like benches thick with Ponderosa Pines. She told him that the San Poil had been a favorite route for her mother's people in their north-south migrations, or when they had to run from the Pony Soldiers.

"They called it the Valley of the Cliffs, then," she said. "It was beautiful and peaceful and led them straight north to the Kettle River and into Canada, to hide in the Old Lady's Skirts. They would have liked going this fast, though."

She pushed the Mustang above a hundred miles an hour on a straightaway. Harry saw how she would have looked, in the old days, fiercely astride an Appaloosa, with a baby on her back and another child balanced in front of her, headed north for a cool summer in the high country.

She gave him the tour of the valley all the way to Republic, sixty miles from the Columbia. The little gold and cattle town was mostly deteriorated frontier leftovers.

Judith stopped in front of a two-story brown-painted wooden building. There were two storefront windows and a sign that said "Walt's Fountain." Inside were a couple of old wooden dining tables and an assortment of chairs. Beyond a half-wall divider, Harry saw a pool table and some pinball machines and video games. They sat on round red pedestal stools at the chipped green melamine counter and Judith recommended the homemade soup.

An older couple bustled about, served lunch and talked to everyone.

"Terrible day," the man said to them with a leprechaun grin, "If the sun keeps shining like this, summer will come." He shook his head mournfully.

He seemed to enjoy their love for each other and several times returned to make some silly joke.

The locals called him 'Corny.' Bert, Corny's wife, cleared their soup bowls and asked them if they wanted some pie for dessert. Judith said yes. Bert showed them several steaming pies, which cooled, on a shelf and she said "Apple, rhubarb, peach, banana cream and coconut cream."

"Rhubarb," Harry said.

Judith had apple and Bert refilled their coffee cups.

"Aren't you an Antoine?" she asked and scrutinized Judith's face.

"Yes," Judith answered, "my mother is. We're from Nespelem." "Ah, I thought so," Bert said and smiled at her, "I just wasn't sure if I should know you."

Corny yelled a goodbye at them when they left and Harry could hear him amuse his customers by saying "And don't do anything I wouldn't do." There was a ripple of good-natured laughter as Harry closed the door.

They headed back to the south. The sun was high and warm. The cold air on the valley floor stirred into brief gusts, whirled eddies of leaves and dust. Judith didn't stop until they came to a road marked Cache Creek. "We'll go back that way," she said, pointed up the road, "when we go."

She crossed over a wooden bridge hidden by the riverside brush and turned onto a rough two-wheel track that paralleled the river. The Mustang's tires lost traction, spun, slipped sideways in the spring mud, and Harry was afraid that she would get them stuck. But as soon as they were out of sight of the highway, she stopped and said, "Come on, I want to show you something."

She took a blanket out of the back seat and led him along an overgrown path that twisted along the riverbank. She spread the blanket out on a little grass-covered ledge and pulled him down to her.

"Isn't it beautiful?" she asked, and he could only agree.

"Let's go into the water," she said after he had kissed her.

They stripped and she led him into the icy stream. The shock of cold water took his breath and he shuddered, but she pulled him on. Even in the center of the stream the water was only hip deep and not too fast.

She made him kneel with her on the sandy bottom and he had never felt colder. His ears rang, a sharp pain lanced at his temple. She held him down and in a moment the ringing and the pain cleared. The water no longer felt cold, but caressed him, and he guessed that he was numb. She let her hair loose and it floated, mingled with the stream. She pulled his face to hers and kissed him with icy lips and laughed as she quickly dunked his whole head under.

He came up, sputtered, angry at first, in his surprise. He looked at her there, as she smiled up at him from the water like the spirit of the river, and he knelt again and caressed her dark body. Then he carried her out of the river and made love to her on the blanket.

They lay for a while, in the sun. He entirely forgot that he had been cold, and instead, felt more alive than he could remember. He asked her, then, to marry him, but she smiled in a way he thought was aloof, and she said, "No, Harry. Not now, anyway." And she kissed away his disappointment.

Harry awakened with a start, recoiled from the icy splash of water. He heard Judith laugh and another handful of the San Poil stung his naked body. She knelt again in the river, which split around her, as though she were some ancient, familiar rock. "Come on, Harry," she said and threw more water at him, "this will wake you up."

He smiled at her, then lay back down and stared into the intense blue sky. He was happier than he had been since he was drafted. He couldn't think of anything he wanted more than to marry her, have children with her, build a family like hers. But she had refused him.

"No," he said to her, "too cold for me." He started to put on his jeans, shivered and the day felt cold again. She looked at him and got out of the water herself and dressed quietly. They did not talk as she backed the Mustang out of the muddy little track and crossed back to the highway. She took the Cache Creek road to the west. The sign said "Nespelem."

After a few miles, they broke out of the trees into a large, clear upland plateau. Patches of snow lay still in the darkest shade. They passed a deserted homestead, its silvered buildings already half-melted back into the earth. In the distance, within a line of trees, he could just see another house that looked as old, but wood smoke came from it's two brick chimneys.

"Little Eagle and Hattie both grew up here," Judith said, "about five miles over that ridge," and she pointed past the deserted house.

The wind flowed free at this elevation, stirred waves in the dry grass.

"There should be horses, somewhere," she said. She searched the grassland, nearly drove off the road, then pointed into the distance. "There."

She stopped the Mustang while he strained his eyes to see what she saw. Finally, he could discern movement, far away to the southeast across the plain. He would not have known it was horses.

"They're coming this way," she said. There was great excitement in her voice.

Soon Harry could make out the individual horses in silhouette as they traversed a bare ridge. They were a mixture of colors and patterns. Many showed Appaloosa markings. They trotted, not fast, but steadily, and followed each other in single file. They dropped out of sight in a draw, then after several minutes, suddenly reappeared over the rise only fifty yards away from the car. The lead mare stopped the line and looked at them and flared her nostrils. Harry heard Judith catch her breath. She reached for his hand and squeezed it hard.

In a moment the mare decided they were no threat, and she led on, trotted again for a hundred yards or so, then broke into a gallop. As they passed, several of the horses turned dark eyes to look at them, manes flying, tails streaming behind. The pulse of their hoofbeats was almost below the range of his hearing, like the sound of faraway drums carried on the wind. He didn't count, but there must have been fifty of them, more horses than he had ever seen in one herd, running free. He felt Judith's hand tremble in his.

"They like to run into the wind," she said, "it's an instinct. If they move into the wind, they are safe. A predator has to be behind them, downwind, to catch the scent. Once the horses have the lead, they can never be caught and they can smell whatever danger is ahead."

"Whose horses are they," he asked her.

"They could belong to many people," she said. "Some belong to Little Eagle's family, probably the most. But several families turn their horses loose here. It's tribal grazing land. Some people go to the auctions and buy horses they like, just so they can let them run free up here."

"Don't they get lost?" The old fences across the grassland were down in places and the gates lay open. "Or eaten by cougars or coyotes?"

She laughed and squeezed his hand. "How can they be lost? This is their home. A few get killed, weak foals mostly, and sick older ones. But even a cougar usually stays away from full grown horses, especially a herd this large."

"But what good are they? No one can ride them. They're too wild. How would you catch them?"

"Oh, we can catch them when we want to. And ride them for a while. We're much better at that than cowboys are." She laughed playfully. "But then we turn them loose again, after a few weeks or months. No spirit should be forced to always serve another."

When the horses disappeared over a ridge to the west, she started the car again and drove on. The road soon left the high plateau and followed another small creek down towards Nespelem.

"Chief Joseph's grave is here," she told him. "This is where they brought him after the long fight and his time in prison camp. The army wanted to punish him, so they would not let him go back to the Wallowas."

Nespelem looked like many other small western towns, but almost every face Harry saw was Native. Some were light skinned, obviously mixed. Kids played along the streets, looked up at their approach and most of them waved at Judith. She waved back. He knew from the way she looked at the houses and up the side streets that she knew everyone in town.

The street they followed turned to the left and Judith drove very slowly. Ahead Harry could see a random collection of cars and pickups in front of a concrete block building. There was a sign that said "War Bonnet Tavern," emblazoned with a neon picture of a feather headdress. A group of men stood around. Some leaned on a shiny new black Trans Am. Several of them were obviously drunk, waved bottles and talked loudly. Harry looked away, but when the Mustang was abreast of the group, one of them shouted "Judith," and staggered towards the car.

Judith stopped. A couple of other men started towards them. One of them also called her name and held out a beer bottle towards them. The one who had first shouted stuck his head in the window and tried to kiss her. She pushed him back and laughed and Harry smelled the fetid alcohol on his breath.

"Stop it, Nathan," she said, "you're drunk."

"Yeah, you want some?" He held out a half-full quart of Rainier.

"No," she said, "How are you doing? How's your mom."

"Not too good," he leaned down again to look at Harry. "She has cancer. In her liver. Who's this?"

"This is Harry. Harry, this is Nathan. He lives up on Cache Creek."

Nathan reached across Judith to shake hands with Harry. He squeezed hard, caught Harry by surprise and made him wince.

"Hello, Nathan," Harry said.

Nathan just looked at him then back at Judith. Harry noticed that several of his teeth were missing, and his face was pocked, but still he was handsome, almost beautiful. His straight black hair was tied at the back and fell thickly to his waist. He had those same strong eyes.

"How long you here for?" Nathan asked Judith. Then he grinned lasciviously. "Are you going to come see us." He looked over again at Harry.

"Maybe," she said.

Nathan tried to kiss her again, laughing, but as Judith pushed him away, Harry saw the fury in his eyes.

The other men laughed, too, and as she drove away from them, there were tears in Judith's eyes. They drove the few miles back to Electric City in silence.

When they got back to the house, Harry said, "I think I'll go visit my family tomorrow. I can call my brother and he'll come and get me. You could pick me up on Sunday." He did not want to be in the way.

Harry was quiet at dinner. Judith and her family didn't seem to notice and chattered as they had the night before. After dinner he played two games of chess with Matt, but he couldn't concentrate and lost badly both times. He hoped Matt didn't think he was stupid. Joseph left to study with someone.

"A girl," Sara said and giggled.

Harry fell asleep on the couch in the living room and pretended not to awaken when Judith kissed him and asked him if he wanted to go downstairs with her.

Joseph came home about midnight and woke him and said, "Hey, man, it's bedtime. Judith's downstairs." Harry mumbled at him and went back to sleep.

It was not yet daylight when Judith switched on a lamp and kissed him again and asked, "Are you sure you don't want to go with me? I think you would like Hattie. She's like Little Eagle."

Harry shook himself awake and looked at her. "No," he said, "I better go see my folks."

"Okay," Judith said. "I'll see you tomorrow morning. Early. I'll call you."

He wrote down the number and she kissed him again.

Harry sat on the couch and read until Helen got up and started breakfast. She brought him coffee and smiled Judith's smile at him. "Good morning, Harry. Did you sleep well?"

"Yes," he said. "Good enough." He knew he flushed.

"Bacon and eggs for breakfast. And biscuits. Do you like biscuits?"

"Yes," Harry said.

Helen returned to the kitchen and he returned to his book. Matt came out of the back, said hello to Harry and went into the dining room for his coffee. Soon Harry could hear Judith's sisters talking and giggling. The bacon smelled wonderful and so did the biscuits. By the time Helen called them, Harry was so hungry he could hardly read.

The two girls came out of the hallway dressed in house-robes and Helen said, "We're not too formal on Saturdays."

Sara sat beside her father and Rachel took the next chair. "Say 'good-morning,' girls," Matt said.

"Good-morning, Harry," Sara said in a very adult way.

Rachel could not speak but looked at him with a wide, intense smile.

Helen brought bacon and eggs and a warming dish piled high with homemade biscuits.

"Start it off," Matt said.

Harry took two eggs and a strip of bacon.

"Don't save the bacon, or the eggs," Helen said with that smile. "The eggs are from the backyard and my brother raises the bacon."

Harry took another piece of bacon and passed the plate to Rachel. He took a biscuit, looked up at Helen's mock-frown, then took another. The food tasted better than it had smelled and he took another egg, some bacon and more biscuits with only a little prodding. And he had to try Helen's huckleberry jam.

After he had eaten, Harry excused himself and took a fresh cup of coffee with him and went back to his book.

The girls dawdled over breakfast and talked. From the couch, Harry could not understand the conversation. When he looked up they smiled, then looked away. They did not seem hostile, just interested. They did not seem to know that he had not slept with Judith last night.

They reminded him of Gook Town, of the girls he had seen there and wished he could get to know them. That was in the good days, before that Fourth of July. Some even seemed friendly, then. But Rod's outfit had come in for resupply and decided to teach them a little respect.

He had often wondered what it was the girls talked about behind their hands and why they rolled their eyes in an indecipherable way when he walked by. Sometimes he was sure it was him they talked about and not in a totally uninterested way. But the army discouraged unnecessary knowledge of the language and, besides, he would probably never have gotten close enough to them to talk.

There were always the whores, they talked broken English but they never had anything of interest to say. The whores' kids knew English well enough, they could ask for anything. He remembered when he first saw mixed kids in Gook Town. They were a brother and sister, the girl about seven years old and her little brother about four. Their half-American faces with sharp noses, round eyes and freckles on their cheeks jarred him. At first he wondered what was wrong with them. The girl held her brother's hand firmly and smiled at Harry, blocked his way. She didn't beg as he'd expected, but just said "Hi, GI" in a high- pitched, melodic voice, "You Daddy." She smiled and waited for him to respond.

Harry was with Jeff Lasker, as usual, and was embarrassed. Besides, they were there to pick up Sergeant Hicks.

"Move it, kid," Jeff said. "You ain't got no Daddy."

They had brushed on past, but after that Harry had seen the two children many times. They would follow him whenever they saw him and the little girl would whisper behind her hand to her brother. He began to dream of their dark, round eyes and he hated to be sent to the village.

"Daddy," Rachel said and Harry saw that they all were coming into the living room. "Are we going to the party at Grandma Hattie's tonight?"

"Yes," Matt said, "we planned to." He sat down on the far end of the couch from Harry.

"All right," Harry heard Sara say as the girls went back to their bedrooms, "Everybody's going to be there. Joseph said he would pick up Nathan."

"Would you like to play another game of chess?" Matt asked him.

"No," Harry said. "You're too good for me."

CHAPTER 9

Jack came for him a little after noon. When they were out of town, Jack turned to Harry with a grin. "So, a little squaw," he said. "Is she as good-looking as her mother and sisters? That Sara looked like a sweet little piece."

Harry's jaws went tight and he curled his fist and almost hit Jack before he checked himself. Instead, he glared at his brother and the grin disappeared.

"Okay," Jack said, "Jesus, you're touchy. Ever since you came back. You have no sense of humor anymore. That's what everyone says."

"Like who?"

"Like Mom."

"War doesn't help your sense of humor."

"I suppose not, especially if you lose it."

Harry's anger rose again. "I didn't lose it," he said and Jack recoiled as if burned by his look. "But at least I did fight."

"That's not what everyone says," Jack said and Harry could see that his brother watched him closely, afraid he would be hit. "Everyone says our guys didn't have any guts, not like in World War II. They just sat on their butts and did dope, and didn't fight. Got the shit kicked out of them by a bunch of little gooks in black pajamas."

"Who's everyone?"

"Oh, Chuck and Jim, a lot of the guys who were in World War II."

"I didn't see any of them in Viet Nam. Or you." "I wish I had been old enough," Jack said. "I would have been happy to go."

"Yeah, that's easy as hell to say. I don't hear anyone who was there say that we didn't fight."

"Some do. And, of course the guys who were the bravest and did fight are dead. Like Rod. They're collectin' money to build him a memorial in town, you know. A statue or somethin'. At least we had one guy from here who wasn't chickenshit."

"You don't know everything about that." Harry was tempted to tell him about the last time he had seen Rod, but it wouldn't do any good. Jack wouldn't believe him anyway.

"Are you sayin' Rod didn't fight? How'd he get a Silver Star for gallantry under fire?"

"Oh, he fought all right," Harry said. "Like everyone. You just don't know everything there is to know about it."

"Well, you better not go around here sayin' Rod wasn't a hero. Everyone here is proud of Rod. Even Mom says she wishes you had got a medal or somethin', not just come back and wound up in the nut house."

Harry reclined his seat and looked out the window, made it clear he wouldn't talk any more. Jack drove on in silence. It would be a surprise to Rod, Harry thought, that he was a hero. Everyone was sure he had died trying to win the war. Rod wouldn't have done drugs. Rod wouldn't have become one of these half-cripples with the wild eyes they had seen come back.

But Rod's eyes had been wild enough when Harry had last seen him. His teeth chattered in withdrawal, his emaciated body quaked with cold in the steaming jungle compound. He had been brave all right. Braver than they knew. He had made his decision and carried it through and sometimes Harry wished he had done the same.

Jack tried to talk to him several times on the drive home, but Harry refused even to answer him. His eyes roamed the great coulee. Torn clouds in many shades of gray milled about a dull azure sky. Spring flocks of ducks and geese settled in the smooth shallows and onto the green nesting grounds. He had read that in the ice age the flocks of waterfowl were huge and plentiful. It must have looked much the same then. There had been a melt-water lake where the reservoir now was and the weather near the receding glaciers was supposed to have been damp and unsettled.

Harry could feel the humidity of the lake on his face and bare arms as he watched small gusts press their tracks through the choppy waves. The gulls that swirled around the canal head- gates on Dry Falls Dam seemed to call to him from another time. Jack turned the corner past the Dry Falls Cafe, and Harry half expected to see a mammoth family stalked by a saber-tooth where the museum was supposed to be.

He started to tell Jack about the flood but Jack interrupted him. "What the hell is the point. How are you ever going to make any money thinking about that sort of shit?"

When they got to the farm, Harry took his duffel bag out of the trunk and carried it into the trailer where Mom and Dad lived. Dad had the TV on, college basketball, and invited Harry to join him. Harry sat at the breakfast bar where he could see the game, but not too close. Mom offered him coffee and he accepted and she came in to sit across from him.

"Jack said you were visiting a girl." She looked at him and he knew she wanted the whole story.

"Yes," he said. "I met her at the University. She's from Electric City."

"Is she a Christian girl?"

"I don't know," Harry said. "I never asked her."

"You know what I mean."

"I don't think she goes to church much," Harry said.

"But what kind of girl is she?"

"You mean have I gone to bed with her?"

"No, that's not what I meant," she said and the lie was in her eyes.

"She's a very nice girl and her father is an engineer for the Bureau," Harry said. He couldn't think of anything else safe to say.

"Well, your father and I always hoped you would marry a nice Christian girl."

Harry watched the game and ignored her. At half-time Dad got up and came into the kitchen for a beer.

"How's the job? On the, what do you call it crew?"

"The grounds crew, "Harry said. "It's fine. It's like miniature farming. We have lawn tractors and little wagons. It's kind of funny."

"So, when are you going back?"

"Tomorrow," Harry said, then. "You got somethin' I could drive this afternoon? I want to go see Uncle Paul."

Mom frowned and Dad looked at her, then back at Harry. "Yeah," he said, "the two-ton is behind the hayshed. It's got the stock-racks on so take it easy."

"Sure," Harry said. "I'm just goin' over to Uncle Paul's."

"When will you be back?" Mom asked him.

"Later," Harry said and frowned back at her.

Uncle Paul lived out in the rocks. He had irrigation water, from the Project, because his eighty acres lay below the canal. But it was one of those areas where the surveyors had been forced to route the canal around some scrappy land so that the elevations would work further along.

They hadn't even bothered to put turnouts in the canal, at first, because no one thought that the land would ever be farmed. But now it was, by a collection of unlikely and unlucky farmers. They weren't all poor. A couple of them had quite a bit of money, and most of them were sharp traders and managed their resources well. But they were definitely unconventional.

Mom wouldn't even go there except on rare occasions. She didn't want to be associated with that bunch, she said. Why did they have to be so trashy, with all those rock piles and old junk around? The junk was mostly machinery, still serviceable but not modern, and usually unpainted. They did have a reluctance to throw anything away, but that was because most of it would be used again, somehow, someday. So they put things in rows and piles and stuffed them in makeshift shelters.

The rocks didn't help appearances. There were piles and rows and ridges of rocks, from pebble size to those it took two men to lift. They were the remnants of some ancient glacier melt scattered across the volcanic plain in drifts and deltas like so much windblown sand.

In most of the Basin the rocks were covered by a fine, thick layer of topsoil blown in by huge dust storms during relentless Pleistocene droughts. But here, in these scablands, the Great Spokane Flood had stolen the topsoil.

The rocks had to be picked up by hand and thrown or wrestled onto trucks and wagons and dumped around the edges of the fields and along the roadways. One farmer had made a corral of rocks and another had built his house of them. On every farm they were used for something, but still the hills of unused rocks grew.

And every spring it had to be done all over again, because plowing and winter heaving of the soil brought up more of the rocks that rested beneath the surface. The geologists said that in twenty years there might be a consistent rock-free foot of topsoil.

The trade-off for all this apparent misery was price. Uncle Paul had bought his eighty acres for just five thousand dollars and his was one of the better places. If you had enough money, or time, or children to remove the rocks, the soil was fertile enough and the Project water was cheap. The good farmers in the rocks, like Paul, had broad fields of alfalfa and grain irrigated by wheel-line sprinklers. Except for the inevitable mounds of rocks, you couldn't tell that their farms had been bought by sweat, not money.

Others in the area had been buried by their rock-piles. Some had seen the dollar price, but not the work. Some had seen the work, but overestimated themselves. A few were just lazy and shiftless anyway and it was as good a place as any to be lazy and shiftless.

It was easy to remember the turn to Uncle Paul's. His neighbor on the corner liked windmills. There was a double windmill that made the wheels of a bicycle turn and a little wooden man pump furiously in the warm Chinook. A propeller drove a loose-jointed logger to chop frantically at a tin can log that was never cut. There were vertical windmills, Dutch windmills, airplane windmills. An old-fashioned Great Plains windmill pumped water for the stock. There was a wind generator connected to the house. When the wind was brisk it was easy to get dizzy there. Mom hated the place. She said she didn't need any reminders that the wind never stopped blowing.

Harry had been told all his life that he looked more like Paul's son than Dad's. Paul was shorter, and stocky compared to Dad's rangy cowboy frame. Like Harry, he had darker hair and skin. More like the Old Man.

But Paul couldn't have been his father, because when Harry was conceived, Paul was still in the hospital, in Los Angeles, where they sent him just before Japan surrendered. He had almost made it, four years in the Pacific with no serious wounds. That was a miracle, for a marine.

Then just before the end, as they held fast to the rugged islands, waited for the rumored secret weapon that would bring Japan to her knees, a Jap sapper, bent on immortality, had tossed a grenade into an outdoor latrine full of marines. One of them was Paul.

He had lost a lung, two fingers and three years of his life. And he had never been the same, they said. He had a lot of scars, including one across his face that made him seem to wink when he didn't. And he didn't talk much. When Harry was younger some of his friends were afraid of Paul, or feigned to be, and used to tease Harry about the living dead.

They showed Harry a tabloid story about the "Kill Crazy" marine divisions sent to their deaths in the Pacific. The story said that military psychologists had told the command that two veteran marine divisions had been so altered by their continuous exposure to incredible combat conditions, including grisly atrocities on both sides, that they would pose a threat to the social order if they were returned to civilian life. So they were thrown time after time into suicide missions where they won many medals and eventually only a few survived. His friends were sure that Paul was one of the survivors.

Harry had finally gotten up the courage to ask Paul about it when he was fourteen. Paul had hired him to drive his old truck while he and a crew of Mexicans picked up the first bumper crop of rocks from his eighty acres. Paul had said the whole story was nonsense, but would say no more. Harry had hoped then that Paul would tell him his war stories. Paul was the only veteran Harry knew who didn't love to talk about World War II.

As Harry pulled into the rock-lined driveway, he could see Paul out beside the unpainted clapboard shop working on his offset disc. It was still hitched to the tractor so it must have broken down in the middle of a job. Harry parked the truck near the county road and walked down the muddy, rutted lane. Paul continued with his work until Harry was a few feet away, then he looked up.

"Oh, Hi, Harry," he said. "I thought it was your dad."

"Hi, Paul," Harry said. "Need some help?"

"Nah. Just finishin' up. Broke another damned disc. On the rocks. This place eats discs. And everything else. People, too, I guess. Ain't ate me yet, though."

"Not likely," Harry said. "You'd be a tough piece of meat."

Paul smiled and his eye winked inadvertently. The scar was an angry red from his exertion. "Too ugly to eat," he said.

"How's it goin'?" Harry asked.

"Not too bad. I'm gettin' ready to plant some barley over on that bad twenty. Don't dare plow in all them rocks so I'm tryin' to scratch it up with this old disc."

"Barley, huh? Hog food?"

"Yep. I got me four sows out there gonna' pop any minute.

I'll have forty, fifty pigs runnin' everywhere one of these days."

"How's prices?"

"Not that bad. I sold ten last year to a butcher over by Moses Lake that sells what they call 'natural' meat. I guess they sell it to health food stores or somethin' like that. Anyway he give me ten cents a pound more since I don't use no chemicals. Don't need no chemicals anyway."

Paul finished tightening the nut on the end of the axle, then banged his wrench on the new disc, rang it like a gong. "What you up to Harry?"

"Not much. Just visitin' till tomorrow."

"You still goin' to school?"

"Yep, still goin'. Got the GI Bill and I'm still mowin' lawns and plantin' shrubs." Harry laughed.

"Learnin' anything interestin'?"

"Sure," Harry said. He told Paul a short version of the flood story.

"Damn," Paul said, "I wonder how deep that water was when it went right over here." He looked up as if he could see the ghostly crest of the cataclysm high above them. "So that's why we all slave our butts off out in these rocks. Some flood millions of years ago. Now that's interestin'"

"So, you got a cup of coffee?" Harry asked him.

"Sure do," Paul said, "and I could use one too.

Paul lived in an old trailer, just eight feet wide and fifty long. He had added a full-length wooden addition to the back and a wide covered porch in the front. It was plenty, he said, for a permanent bachelor. He put some Yuban in a percolator and set it on the gas stove. The faint smell of propane mixed with the brewing coffee made Harry feel at home and he relaxed more than he had in a while. He didn't have to prove anything to Paul.

"Not gettin' along with your folks?" Paul asked when he poured their coffee.

"No, it's not that. Mom just gets on my nerves after a while."

"Yeah, mine too," Paul said. "She thinks you're wastin' your time goin' to school. You know how she thinks. If it don't make a buck, don't do it."

"She wants me to be like Jack," Harry said. "Farm in the day time, study real estate at night."

"Farmin's okay," Paul said, "for us dummies."

"Dummy hell," Harry said, "you know more than most of the people I go to school with."

"Nothin' that counts," Paul said. "At least in money. So what's on your mind? If it ain't your folks, it must be a woman."

"Yeah," Harry said. "I guess. Her name is Judith."

"So what's the problem? Won't go to bed with you?"

"No," Harry said, "It's not that. But I love her and I thought she loved me, but she won't marry me."

"When did you ask her?"

"This weekend."

"And already you gave up? Maybe you just need to hang in there, prove yourself."

"I don't think so," Harry said. "She's different. She's Indian, well, half, and she's different."

"Maybe she just doesn't want to get married yet. Marriage isn't the only thing. Sometimes it just makes things worse."

"But I really love her," Harry said. "I want to be sure of the future."

"You can never be sure of the future, Harry. Marriage don't do that."

"It would help."

"No, I don't think so. Your Aunt Judy and me never got married, you know. So when she got restless and she started gettin' on my nerves, we talked and she decided to leave. We split things up the way we wanted and nobody could say shit about it. She still spends a week or two here, when she can. We get along better than anyone I know who got a divorce. Marriage isn't that big a deal."

"It is to me," Harry said.

"Well, give her some time," Paul said. "You never know."

Harry was sure Judith had spent the rest of the weekend with Nathan, or someone. That was why she had said no. She was amusing herself with him, probably wanted to tease Nathan. He would ride with her, back to Seattle. Then he would get on with his life, quit mooning after the impossible.

She called about seven-thirty and asked for directions. She would be there by ten.

It was just past nine-thirty when he saw her Mustang come up the long poplar-lined lane from the highway. Despite his resolve, Harry's heart raced. He would ask her nothing. What she had done was her business.

He met her in the yard and led her into his parents' mobile home to meet them. Dad briefly looked away from the Sunday morning TV news, said "hello." Mom forced herself to be pleasant and offered them coffee. They both said yes, but Harry noticed that Judith didn't drink hers, either.

He was anxious to introduce her to his grandparents and took the first opportunity to escape. They walked along the canal, through the edge of the spring prairie. A Killdeer called from somewhere under the sage. Her hair, unplaited, rippled in the strong breeze. A dust devil cut a fleeting path through the young wheat below the canal. She took his hand, and he found that he had no power to resist her.

Grandma met them at the door, and greeted Judith warmly, smiled at Harry. The Old Man, she said, was out with the horses as usual. Judith wanted to see the horses so Harry took her out to the horse barn.

The Old Man was in one of the stalls. He knelt to examine the huge front hoof of one of the white Percheron geldings. Harry said nothing, and they watched while the Old Man talked softly to the horse and pried something out of the shoe with a sharp metal pick. The Old Man looked up at them and smiled in surprise.

"Harry. Now, I didn't hear you come in. My ears must be goin'."

"This is Judith," Harry said and Judith held out her hand with a smile.

The Old Man pulled his right glove off and took her hand, looked into her eyes. "Hello, Judith," he said, "I'm glad to meet you." Then he patted Harry on the shoulder. Harry realized that his love for her was completely apparent to his grandfather.

"Okay, Ned," the Old Man said and rubbed the big horse's nose. "That'll do it for now."

"That's a beautiful horse," Judith said. "What breed is he?" "Percheron," the Old Man answered. "His brother Ed is in the next stall. Now, they're my best team. They'd pull this old barn over for me."

"We never had draft horses," she said, rubbed the giant's forehead. "But we always had lots of saddle horses."

The Old Man looked at her with approval. "Appaloosies, I'll bet" he said. "Now, I like Appaloosies. Even the big noses." Judith smiled and touched her own nose.

They went back inside and Grandma had the coffee ready. They talked for an hour or so, about horses, mostly, then Grandma took Judith out to show her the chickens. When Harry and the Old Man went outside half an hour later, the two women were in the garden. They talked furiously as they dug up some kind of plant.

When they saw the men, the two women stood up. "Oh, no, Judith," Grandma said. "It's time for you to go."

Judith smiled at Harry. "Not yet," she said, "Let's finish our digging. Harry would you mind bringing my car over so I can load these?" She tossed him the keys. As Harry walked away they talked again, but he could not hear what they said.

Harry returned in a few minutes with Judith's car. Grandma said Judith and the Old Man were back out at the horse barn. Harry found them leaning on the fence as they watched a tall sorrel mare and a small black foal. "Half Appaloosie," he heard the Old Man say, "from a stud that belongs to the neighbors. A show horse, they say."

Harry watched with them. The tiny foal stood in the shadow of her mother. The few white spots on her rump and the white forehead star shone brightly. Any way the mare turned, the foal stayed in her shadow and watched them.

"A little filly," the Old Man said. "Sure is a pretty little thing. I need a name for her."

"Shadow," Judith said, "you should call her Shadow."

"Shadow, it is," the Old Man said. "Good name."

They said their good-byes. Harry went to tell his parents they were leaving and get his pack. When he opened the trunk to load his stuff, there were several pots of the plants Judith and Grandma had dug. He asked Judith about them and she said, "It's mint - peppermint, spearmint and catnip. And some Greek oregano. I'm going to grow them in my kitchen window, for tea and seasoning. And the catnip is for my cat."

She told him that she wanted to take the Stevens Pass route again, even though it was an extra fifty miles, so they could avoid the tourists on I-90.

She was talkative and he mostly listened. She told him her plan to learn all the natural healing arts and return to her mother's people and help them.

"The doctors don't do them any good," she said. They just want the money. And they're thinking, 'this is just another drunk Indian. Nothing could help anyway,' and they take the money and write some prescription that just makes them sicker."

Once she had learned the natural ways, she would find an M.D. who wasn't completely brainwashed, to go with her and help the People. A woman was more likely to understand that there are many ways and that different ways can work together.

"Medicine is so messed up," she said. "Did you know that the infant mortality rate in the Bronx is higher than it is in Honduras?"

Harry shook his head.

"And I read a study," she said, "of how M.D.s work. When they talk to patients for the first time, to find out what's wrong, they listen to them an average of eighteen seconds. How can they help anyone that way? The tribe wastes a lot of money on medical care."

Hattie had agreed to train Judith to heal with natural power, what the whites called shamanism. But just to begin she would have to go live with Hattie all of a summer and eat only wild foods and abstain from drugs and alcohol.

"I hate alcohol," she said, "for what it does to the people. But the doctors don't help much with that. They don't even tell them that they are being poisoned. They just treat the superficial symptoms and take the money."

"Like, Nathan," she said. Her voice made Harry wonder if there were tears in her eyes again. "He used to be so nice, so smart. And he played basketball like Doctor J. Nespelem was in the state tournament when he was a junior. When he was a senior, he got kicked off the team for drinking too much. The coach didn't care. To him it was just a discipline problem. He wouldn't see how sick Nathan was. And look at him now. Whenever he gets his check, he buys a car and drinks up the rest. And usually wrecks the car."

"What kind of check?" Harry asked. "From the government?"

Judith looked at him for a moment, then said gravely, "No, Harry, not your government. From the tribe. Every member gets a share of the tribe's business every year. It's like a big family."

"What is Nathan? To you."

"A friend. And kind of a distant cousin."

"But, what else. I mean, he was trying to kiss you. Kissing cousins?"

"We used to go out," Judith said. "In high school. Then he started to drink. I couldn't take it."

"He still thinks he owns you."

"He's lonely, Harry. And sick. I go out with him sometimes when he's really down. Just to talk."

Much of the trip was silent. When she dropped him in front of the boarding house she leaned over to kiss him good-bye, but he pretended not to see. He got his stuff from the trunk, said, "See you later," and walked away. She sat there for a while; he didn't wait to see how long.

CHAPTER 10

Judith knocked on his door Sunday morning after finals week.

"Hello," Harry said.

"Hi," she said and came inside. "How about breakfast?" She studied his eyes. "I'll buy."

He looked away. "Sure. I guess."

"Well, if you're busy or something, just say so."

"No, it's okay."

She drove to a Greek cafe on University way for Feta cheese omelets. Fresh sun streamed through a wall of windows, fell through the leaves of a bank of plants and scattered across the checkerboard floor. Harry took a table in the corner, faced the door.

Judith sat with her back to the light. Her face, in shadow, made an oval frame for her eyes. "How'd finals go?" she asked.

"Okay. I'll keep my grade point for graduate school."

"You're for sure going to graduate school?"

"For a while at least. My GI Bill runs another year and a half after I graduate."

"Which department?"

"Anthro."

"You mean like archaeology?"

"Maybe. But I really like Political Anthropology."

"What's that about?"

"How power really works in different groups. Not what the rules or the laws are, but what really goes on."

"You mean studying Natives," she said. "The kind of stuff they use to manipulate them."

"No. Anthropologists just study. Just for knowledge."

"Sure," she said. "Then the CIA gets the information because the government gave some grant to the university. I don't think people should study people that way. They deceive the people."

"No," he said. "That's not how it works. There is a whole protocol on informing your informants."

"So, you only use informants who understand scientific protocols?"

"I don't want to argue," he said.

"Me either."

The omelets came and they did not talk. Harry took the check, insisted on paying. Judith wanted to walk the Avenue and he agreed.

The freaks were out. Incense and music poured from open shop doors, joints circulated openly. Harry was uneasy with the press of people, maneuvered into the gaps in the flow.

"Let's get some espresso," he said.

The Raven was nearly empty. They sat in a dark corner behind barricades of books. The coffee was thick and sharp and warmed him more than the sun.

"What are you doing this summer, Harry?"

"Working. In the carpenter shop. And a programmed French lab to get my second foreign language. For grad school."

"Is that all you do? Work?" She laughed, leaned against him. "You gotta have a little fun."

"Sure," he said. "I do. Sometimes. I go out. Not much."

She hesitated, watched his face. "Would you like to go to a retreat with me? The middle of July. It's out on the peninsula at Kalaloch. A lot of elders will be there. Maybe Little Eagle."

"I can't miss work."

"It's just Friday and a weekend."

"No. I can't. I'm up to my ears in books."

"I can see that," she said.

"And how's that girl," Mom asked. "Judith."

"I don't know. I haven't seen her for a couple of weeks."

"Well don't worry, Harry. There are lots of nice Christian girls out there."

"I'm not interested in girls right now. I called to see if you could send some of my stuff. The footlocker and the duffel bag. And my rifle. It's in Dad's gun cabinet. He knows which one."

"How am I supposed to send all this. The mailman won't take it."

"UPS or something. Greyhound."

"Well, I'll see if I can get Jack to drop it off at the bus station. I don't get to town much. Just to church. My life isn't easy."

"You can send it collect," Harry said. "I'll pay for it."

"Okay," Mom said. "I'll try."

"What's in that box?" the cab driver asked, handed it to Harry. "Looks like a gun."

"No. Just some tools." Harry wasn't sure why he lied.

"Funny lookin' box. Tools!"

Harry paid him, took the rifle and the duffel bag in first, came back for the footlocker. It was already wet from the rain.

He hoped his four days of beard hadn't made the damned nosy cab driver suspicious. He wasn't in the mood to answer any questions.

He unwrapped the sleek 30.06 and attached the scope, sighted on the door. It was cool and reassuring. He set it aside and opened the duffel bag. Mostly he wanted his old fatigues to wear when he was painting in the carpenter shop. He cut off the name tags with a razor blade, then the US Army patches and sergeants stripes.

He opened the footlocker. Two good pairs of combat boots still held a gloss under the dust. They might be useful for hikes. There were some pictures and folded-up Vietnamese newspapers, but he did not look at them. His old field jacket was on the bottom. He shook the jacket out. There was a familiar smell of jungle rain and alien mud. He put it on and it still fit him well, wrapped him like a green cocoon. He watched the rain drizzle down the window and was glad for the jacket's warmth.

The Century Tavern was packed. The only refuge was the last stool at the bar against the far wall. Harry pulled the field jacket close around him and shivered in the gust each time the door opened.

He had intended to read all night, until he fell asleep. But eyes floated before the page, looked back at him and scrambled the sense of what he read. He had learned that the only answer was alcohol.

Three pitchers should do it. He drank deliberately, watched each face as it came in the door. Even those who had known him a few weeks before didn't recognize him with his thick beard and field-jacket. He glanced at his own face among the bottles. Dark eyes stared back. He poured another glass. The bartender glanced at the half-empty pitcher, said nothing.

Smoke swirled from the back room. Waves of talk and laughter beat against the windows, came at him in distorted reflection. The inaudible television showed pictures of a hospital, men in uniform with arms and legs blown away, faces scarred. Then a blonde woman with large breasts pointed to a satellite picture. The clouds moved, a procession of cold fronts marched across the North Pacific all the way from Asia.

The bartender brought another pitcher, hesitated as if to say something, but did not. Harry drank quickly, just to get it down. He waved off the third pitcher, decided to get a six-pack on the way home.

"Harry," Her voice called from the Mustang before he was fifty feet from the door. "Harry, is that you."

He looked through the window as she rolled it down. A clump of wet yellow leaves fell, splattered against the windshield.

"Come on. I'll give you a ride."

"No," Harry said. "I like to walk. The rain feels good."

"I wanted to talk to you. How are you doing?"

"Okay. I've been working mostly."

"Why don't you get in? You'll get soaked standing there."

"No. I'm okay."

"I was on the San Poil last week-end. It's still warm over there. We had a big celebration at Hattie's. I saw Little Eagle. He asked about you.

"Oh," Harry said. "Was Nathan there."

She looked at him for a moment. "He's doing so good. He stopped drinking. Little Eagle agreed to teach him if he would stop."

"Teach him what?"

"Everything. The old ways."

"Oh. So what does he do with his check now?"

"You've been drinking."

"A little. You gotta have some fun you know."

"Is it fun?"

"The best I can do right now."

"I'm going back over in two weeks. Why don't you come with me?"

"No," Harry said. "No thanks. I'm too busy." "Give me a call, Harry," she said and touched his arm. "Soon."

"Sure," He said.

CHAPTER II

Harry got a printed invitation to an open house for Arts and Sciences seniors interested in graduate school. He decided he should go. If he was lucky there would be no one there that he knew. Strangers were easier to talk to. He'd gotten used to being part of the woodwork and he didn't want to change it yet.

The open house was scheduled for a late November Tuesday. He decided not to wear the field jacket, put on the tweed sports- coat from last year. He didn't like the way it felt and he avoided his reflection as he left.

There was almost no traffic on the side streets although he could hear the distant white-noise echo of the freeway as he crossed Cowen Ravine. The sound faltered and died in the foggy shadows of the iron bridge.

He had not been out at night for almost a month and he walked in an alien world that was the other side of his days. His eyes didn't want to adjust to the darkness and saw movement where there was none. The orange sodium lights flickered alive along Ravenna Boulevard. Bright reflections flamed in windows and settled to a dense glare that reminded him of Kahoutek.

In the little market the Italian proprietor waved to him and smiled from behind his vegetable bins. Harry's eyes fastened on the neat rows of oranges and delicious apples and purple-leather pomegranates. The incandescent light in the market was warm, sun- like, and the green of lettuce and moon-round cabbages drew him in. He ran his hand over the potatoes and briefly held a cantaloupe although he knew he didn't want it.

He bought some white grapes the proprietor recommended. The little man, whose head seemed too large for his body, weighed the grapes and put them in a paper bag. He reached again into the bin, held up a bunch of the grapes. He split off a side-branch handed it to Harry.

"A celebration?" he asked, and ate a grape, spit the seeds into the trash container.

"No," Harry said, "A meeting. At the U." He put a grape in his mouth. Penetrating sweetness then a wave of bitter as he bit into a seed.

"Ah," the proprietor said. He followed Harry to the door. "Beautiful full moon tonight." He smiled and held the door open. "Hunters' Moon, I believe."

Harry looked out, saw no moon. He studied the round face. "Ah," The proprietor said, smiled even more, "I see the reflection. In the glass, across the street." He pointed to a wavy moon on a glassed-in front porch.

"I should have seen it," Harry said, laughed. But all he had seen was the overhead glare of the sodiums. He felt a strong, steady hand close gently on his arm and guide him outside.

"Well," the proprietor said, "To the Moon, then." And he softly closed the door behind Harry.

When he looked into the distance the fog materialized before his eyes. The harsh sodium light could only partially penetrate the swirling shadows. Greek Row was quiet, damped by the fog, and the lights shone faintly against the night. Harry stayed in under the trees near the street. At 45th, there was a wide break and he saw the moon again. Not white and serene, in close proximity to the earth its face was ruddy, like smudged copper or Aztec gold and wisps of the fog drifted across it.

He crossed onto the campus. A few people walked to night classes or talked inaudibly in the doorways. The open house was in the HUB, the Ballroom, and his footsteps echoed in the side stairwell as he went up.

There was a circle of folding tables, each with an Instructor or Assistant Professor presiding. Small half circles of folding chairs enclosed each of the tables. Posters proclaimed each department.

A few people milled about inside this stockade, too few for him to remain anonymous. The overhead lights were painfully bright, glared off the hardwood floor. He knew that he was watched.

He took control of all his movements, made sure the watcher did not know that he knew. He moved smoothly from table to table. When he could do it naturally, he scanned the room for the eyes that watched him.

He sat down and listened to a pitch in which he had no interest. As he stood up he was caught and held by deep blue eyes in a tangle of copper hair. It was Diane Brown, his former advisor. Unmistakably it was she who watched him.

He avoided her area and did not again acknowledge her eyes. Wherever he went around the circle, she found a reason to face towards him. He thought of leaving, before coffee hour, but was held by curiosity.

Two student employees wheeled in a cafeteria cart with two urns of coffee and some leftover doughnuts and pastry. The department representatives turned all the chairs to face the center. Harry stepped towards the line that formed and felt her at his elbow.

"Hello, Mr. Isaacson," she said and smiled up at him. "Remember me?" She looked very sexy in the professional blue suit and ruffled blouse.

"Yes," Harry said, "Comparative Lit."

"Diane," she said, "Diane Brown."

"Right," he said, "Doctor Brown."

She stood behind him in the line. "Have you decided on a graduate school?" she asked him. Her eyes probed his as he turned.

"No," he said. "But I like Anthro a lot. Political Anthropology"

"Doctor Houck," she said. "He's supposed to be tough. You like him?"

"I like the way he looks at the world. Logically."

"Logic isn't everything," she said. She took his arm and he felt the shock of the contact. "Let's go have a drink," she said. "The Blue Moon."

"I don't like The Blue Moon," he said. "I had a bad experience there."

"Okay." she said, "How about the Robin?"

"Too far," he said, "I don't have a car."

"I do," she said, "But anyway there's the Century."

He started to say no. But he could use a drink and anyone who knew him would be surprised to see him there with her.

"Sure," he said.

She gathered her stuff from the table and put it in a blue leather attach? case. She started to fold up the chairs then waved her hand.

"They must have someone to do this," she said. She led Harry down the central stairs and out to a new, red RX7 in the closest parking lot. The kick of the little rotary engine surprised him and so did her ability to handle the car.

She took the back way that twisted up Ravenna Boulevard and scared him a little with the way she drove the fog-slick street.

The Century was half full as usual for a weeknight. Nearly everyone stopped to stare at them as they entered. Some of the regulars along the bar recognized him and they talked in surprised low tones.

She led him to a booth in the back corner, said, "I suppose you want your back to the wall." She sat down across from him.

When the bartender came over Harry ordered a beer and she asked for some kind of sweet wine drink.

"So you think logic is the answer?" She smiled, teased him, had other interests than philosophy.

"Yes," he said, irritated, "I think logic is the answer."

"What is the question?" Her eyes still beckoned him, did not care for the result of the argument.

Everything," he said. "Decisions should all be made logically. It's simple."

"All decisions?"

"Sure," he said. "Why not?"

"Like war," she said. "A logical way to handle a dispute."

"No it isn't," he said, "If you could see." He looked away.

"Ah," she said, "But logic is blind. And has no feelings. Logic is just a tool. A man shouldn't be slave to one tool. There are so many others."

He watched her, watched the room. The drinks came and she paid, silenced his protest with a look.

The bartender winked at Harry and left. Diane smiled at him and touched her lips with her tongue.

They talked about the University and Seattle and other things which interested neither of them. They drank several drinks. She continued to tease him with her eyes and her tongue. She came back from the restroom with the top two buttons of her blouse undone and he could see the swell of her breasts whenever she leaned towards him. She still had the coke spoon on the fine chain.

"Did you ever kill anyone," she asked him and he started, could not speak. "I mean in the war. You told me you were in Viet Nam, remember?"

"Yes," he said, "I remember."

"I'm sorry," she said.

"No," he said, "It's okay. Yes, I did. I've just never talked about it."

"You don't have to."

"It's okay."

"Was it many?"

"No," he said. "Not many. Not that I am sure of. Usually you never know. You just shoot at a movement, or help fire an artillery round." In the shadow her eyes could have been other eyes, dark eyes that mocked him as they died. He steadied himself on the table edge and started to get up.

Her hand was cool on his. "You know what else isn't logical?" she asked him.

"What?" he asked, too loud.

"When you want to make love to someone. That isn't logical."

"It could be," he said. "Why not?"

"Because I want to make love to you and that isn't logical."

He was supposed to make the approach long before, but it angered him that she had. "No," he said, "That isn't logical." "But I want to," she said. She got up, but he didn't follow.

"Come on," she said. "At least come up to my place and listen to some music. The smoke is getting to me." She pried his fingers from the edge of the table. "Come on, make a sacrifice."

Diane's house overlooked Cowen Park. She shared it with another instructor. Her roommate was out and the house was dark. She turned on a lamp and led him to the stereo. "How about Bob Marley?" she asked, "he isn't logical either."

"Sure," he said. He wasn't really sure who Bob Marley was.

"Catch a Fire," she said. The music came on and he remembered. Black music, Jamaican. Mom would call it nigger music. About the Concrete Jungle. The beat caught on to something in his mind and made him feel more alert, yet calm.

She opened a blind and let in the moon. "Isn't it beautiful?" she asked. "That isn't logical, either, to think that the music or the moon is beautiful".

"It is beautiful," he said. "But there's probably a logical explanation. We just don't know what it is."

"No," she said, "Beauty isn't logical, although logic can be beautiful." She slid a wood-backed mirror from under a shelf. It was etched with a full moon beneath which strode a naked woman followed by a wolf. Rays from the moon were incised little grooves, which refracted the moonlight from the window. Diane showed him the reflection of the real moon overlaid on the moon etched in the glass.

She dumped a little cocaine from a bronze glass vial onto the mirror and slowly chopped it with a razor blade. "This is beautiful, too," she said. "Pure spirit."

She took a golden engraved straw, drew a little of the powder into her nose, handed Harry the mirror and straw. He took a small hit, then another. He felt the fog of alcohol clear from his mind as he returned the mirror.

She took a little more then passed it back. "Finish it," she said. "That's enough for me."

He found himself greedy for the energy it gave him and he finished the two large lines that remained in the moon-ray grooves. The drug stung his sinuses and numbed his throat. The rush of energy was intense, not the dull rapture of the heroin Rod had given him in Viet Nam.

He put the mirror on the carpet and she leaned over to kiss him. When their lips touched, he found himself wild with lust for her. She encouraged him, stroked him through his pants while she struggled out of her suit with the other hand. He took off his shirt and jeans and she pulled down his shorts and stroked him harder. He fought with her bra, then slid down her panties. He wondered if that pale white body had ever seen sunlight. She pulled him to his knees and put her mouth on him and his whole body tensed with pleasure.

They made love on the floor and again in her bedroom. When he finally was exhausted they sat in the bed and she lit a joint. She smoked and passed it to him and he smoked a little.

She smoked again and handed the joint back to him, shuddered a little. "I've never made love to a killer, before," she said. "It's exciting."

"I'd better go," he said. "I have an eight-thirty class." "Okay," she said, "I'll drive you." She stood, stretched her body towards him.

"No," he said, "that's okay. I'll walk. It isn't far." "Okay," she said. She didn't kiss him at the door as he'd expected.

Harry walked through the trees along the north rim of the ravine, well off the street. His heart still raced from the sex and the coke and he felt himself dart from tree to tree. He tried to control it. The deep shadow of each tree comforted and held him, yet he knew he had to go on. To the next shadow and the next.

He was okay until he started to cross the broad clearing of 15th Northeast. He controlled his pace, at first, just a rapid walk. But a car came fast, over the crest of the ridge south of 52nd, and he ran for it. Even then he would have been okay, but he tripped on the curb and by reaction rolled into the brush.

The car stopped quickly, with no screech, and a light shone through the trees above him. An amplified voice followed. "Who's there? Come out, this is the police."

Relief shook him. His tongue stuck and he struggled to rise. The light immediately dropped to his face.

"Answer me," the voice said.

He could not, so he stood. He tried not to sway.

"Get your hands up, buddy. This isn't a game."

Unbelieving, he raised them. Finally, he could speak. "I'm just walking home," he said. He could not see into the light and adrenaline made his voice quaver.

"Sure. Well we want to talk to you a minute. Come over here. Slowly." He heard the amplifier switch off.

As he approached the car, he heard someone get out. The light moved and a hand closed on his arm. "In here." The other hand roughly guided his head through the door. Another light was in his face.

"Walking home, eh? Do you have some ID?"

"Where do you live?" the other asked.

Harry took out his wallet, showed them his driver's license. "Over on 17th," he said, "just two blocks up."

"Okay," the driver said. "We want to make one little call, here, then we'll give you a ride home." He picked up the microphone and asked for the dispatcher.

"Where you been? It's kinda late," the other policeman said. "I've... to see someone," Harry said. "A friend."

"And who would that friend be?"

"I'd rather not say," Harry said.

"Why not?"

"It was a... lady," Harry said and expected the kind of camaraderie common among men.

"Right," the other said.

The radio was talking. "Psychiatric commitments to Harborview and Western, 1973. For assault. Let's talk to him, he might be our boy."

"You heard the man," the driver said and rolled through a slow U-turn.

"I was just walking home," Harry said.

"Keep it quiet," the other said, "there'll be someone to talk to."

"Do you have an attorney?" the detective asked him.

"No," Harry said.

"Do you want to wait until you have one appointed by the court?"

"No," Harry said, "Why should I?"

"I don't know," the detective said. "I have to ask." He checked a small cassette recorder and switched it back on. "This is being recorded. Anything you say can and will be used against you in a court of law."

"For what?" Harry asked. "I was just walking home."

"And where is that?"

"It's right there, on the file."

"I'd rather have you tell me." Harry have him the address.

"And where had you been?"

"To a friend's house."

"Yes, the mysterious friend. A lady, you said?" "Yes."

"And her name was?"

"I'd rather not say."

"All this will go much faster if you tell me. Why don't you want me to know?"

"It's private," Harry said.

"Why private? Is she married?"

"No, she lives with a roommate."

"And what would her roommate's name be?"

"I don't know," Harry said, "She just said a roommate."

"How well do you know this person?"

"I met her at school, just once before."

"So we have a mysterious lady friend who you met just once, whose house you are leaving at 4 am and her roommate still isn't home? Is this making sense to you?"

Harry was silent, controlled his anger.

"Well, answer the question?"

"Yes," Harry said, "because it's the truth."

"But I don't know that. You have to convince me."

Harry didn't answer.

"Let me go at this another way. Have you had sex tonight?"

Harry started. "No," he said.

"An examination can determine that quick. Shall I call the Doc to have a look?"

"No," Harry said. "I had sex tonight."

"Why did you lie to me?"

"It's private."

"I'm getting tired of this private stuff. Who did you have sex with?"

"I can't say," Harry said. "It would embarrass her."

"Because it would embarrass her, or because it would send you to jail?"

"For what?" Harry asked.

"I'll ask the questions," the detective said.

"Have you taken any drugs tonight? Other than alcohol?"

"No," Harry said. "Yes, I did."

"What drugs."

"Cocaine."

Is that all?"

"Yes."

"If you'll just give us a urine sample we can check that out."

"No," Harry said. He remembered the joint. "I mean, I had another drug. Marijuana."

"And where did you get these drugs?"

"I can't say."

"I know, it's private. Well, selling drugs is not private. So this lady, your mysterious friend. She sells you drugs. And then has sex with you. Does that cost extra?"

"No," Harry said. "She gave them to me." The detective smiled. "The sex, too?" Harry glared.

"Yes."

"You better tell me who this mysterious lady is, Mr. Isaacson, or I'm going out in the other room and ask them to book you on a charge of first degree rape."

"Rape," Harry said. "I didn't rape her. If she told you that, she's lying."

"Let's ask her," the detective said. "I have a name here. Of a lady who was raped tonight, a few minutes before you were picked up. You give me another name and an address, and if I go out there and this friend of yours says she gave you drugs and had sex with you tonight, then you'll be out of here this morning. Otherwise I think the prosecutor will want you for trial. And I think we better get those samples. You can refuse, but I wouldn't if I were you."

"Okay," Harry said. "Her name is Diane Brown. I don't know the address."

"We have to have an address."

"I don't know," Harry said. "She drove me."

After another hour of repeating it all, the detective agreed to drive to the neighborhood and let Harry show him the house. He got another detective and they took Harry downstairs to the garage in handcuffs and put him in the back seat. By the time he showed them the house, it was eight-thirty and the sun was cutting the fog away.

They parked in front and the first detective went to the door. He was inside for a while, then Diane came out on the porch in a rose kimono. She shielded her eyes and squinted towards the car. She said something to the detective with her and he signaled to the one in the car.

"Get out," he said, and opened the door.

Harry got out and stood with his hands behind him and his head down.

"Get it up," the detective said, and pushed Harry's chin.

Harry raised his face and looked up at them. Diane looked at him and he thought he saw a faint smile. She nodded slightly and said something else to the detective. He came down the steps and got into the car.

"Pretty nice piece, for a slob like you," he said and laughed. The other joined him.

Harry didn't get out until evening and they made him stand in a couple of line-ups. Just to fill them out, Detective Johnson said, and he became almost friendly, tried to joke with Harry about that nice little piece.

Harry didn't feel like joking.

CHAPTER 12

The February sun was stronger than he expected. He stepped into the shade beside a cedar tree, let his eyes adjust. A squirrel chattered annoyance until he moved on. His head was clear. He hadn't had a drink or a hangover in more than two months, not since his night and day at the police station.

The field-jacket was too warm and he took it off, carried it over his shoulder. Sparse Saturday morning traffic sped by, stirred the static air. He wanted to talk to Judith. She would care that he had stopped drinking. They could at least be friends.

The Sureco building filled a block just off University Way. He was early, waited by the little fountain, out of the sun. She did not come out with the first lunch wave, so he moved closer to the door.

At quarter after she still had not appeared and he decided to go up to her floor, see if she was there. The sign above the double doors said "Underwriting." One door was open and he saw her at her desk, eating a sandwich, leafing through a magazine. She did not see him for a while as he watched her. Then she looked up, slowly smiled.

"Harry. Hi. What are you doing?"

"Looking for you," he said.

"Let's go outside. Just a minute." She put the sandwich away, came to the door. "I don't need a coat."

They walked three blocks to the campus, sat in the grass under the oaks behind Parrington Hall.

"How is your family?" she asked

"Okay. I haven't seen them in a while. I skipped Christmas. I wasn't too merry."

"I went home," she said. "It was beautiful, lots of snow on the reservation. There were eagles right down on the San Poil."

"How was Nathan?"

"I didn't see him. He was with Little Eagle at a solstice celebration in Canada. I don't see him that much. We're just friends, now."

They were silent while a couple passed near them.

"I applied to graduate school. Archaeology. More of a chance to get outside. I've had enough Political Anthro."

She smiled. "When will you know?"

"In the spring. But I'll get in. My grades are good and I got good recommendations."

"Great," she said. "It sounds exciting. I love the old places. Where people were in the old days."

"I quit drinking."

She seemed a little startled. "Okay!" she said. "I'm proud of you. I don't like alcohol."

"I know," he said.

"How long?"

"Two and a half months. Almost. Since November."

"Why did you stop? What happened?" Her eyes pressed him.

"Nothing," he said, watched a loud bus leave a stop on 15th. "I just needed to quit. For grad school. Grow up a little, I guess."

It was time for her to go.

"I wanted to see if you would be interested in going to a party, for the Anthro Department," he said as they crossed University Way. "Next Saturday."

"Yes," she said, "I would. What time."

The party was at eight in the auditorium downstairs in Lewis and Clark Hall. Judith wore a flowing batik skirt and a silk blouse painted with wildflowers. Her hair was clasped at the back with a silver and turquoise raven.

There was a tension in the room. Conversations were a little too loud, greetings a little too hearty. Everyone clearly wanted something. Dr. Houck was rumored to be in line as next department chairman and drew the most suitors. Other knots of power collected here and there. Harry would have been alone but for the succession of men who talked to him while they looked at Judith.

The party had no real format, supposedly a get-acquainted affair. After about an hour, Harry could stand it no longer, prepared to leave. Dr. Houck noticed, came over.

"Hello, Harry," he said. "And this is?"

"Judith," Harry said. "Judith, Dr. Houck." They shook hands, smiled.

"Harry," Dr. Houck said, put his heavy arm on Harry's shoulder, "I've been wanting to talk to you."

Harry waited.

"I need a teaching assistant next year. For the freshman survey. A total of three. I need one more."

"Sure," Harry said. "But I haven't been accepted."

"Don't worry," Dr. Houck said, leaned closer. "You will be. It's a deal then?"

"Sure," Harry said.

They stopped for coffee in the HUB when they left the party.

"For old times sake," Judith said. "So, that's a good job Dr. Houck offered you."

"Yes," Harry said. "A lot more money than I have now with the GI Bill and the carpenter shop."

They stayed only a few minutes. Outside, Judith took his hand. When they were out of the light he pulled her to him and kissed her.

She held it a long time, then said, "Let's go."

"Where?"

"To my place. I want to make love to you."

Their lovemaking was beyond anything Harry had known, beyond his imagination. But in the depths of their passion, he could not make eye contact with her. His eyes would tic and pull away, afraid of some great female beast of unbearable grace and beauty asleep there.

CHAPTER 13

The week after the solstice was the hottest of the summer. Judith's basement apartment was cooler than his room so they spent most of the nights there. They didn't make a pretense any more of going separate ways in the evening.

"We should move in together," he said. "We're always either at your place or mine. Running back and forth.

She pressed the cold ice tea glass against her cheek. "I like having my own place," she said. "I like privacy."

"But you're never here alone," he said. "When was the last time you slept here by yourself."

"I know," she said, laid her head against his arm. "But if I ever wanted to, I know I can."

"Why would you want to?"

"I don't know," she said. "It's just theoretical."

"We could get a big place he said. "You can have your own room. If we put our rent money together we could get a house. With a yard. You could grow herbs. I want a garden. I miss having a garden."

"I don't want to give this place up. Not yet. Maybe after my gathering trip the end of September."

"How long will you be gone?"

"A week, and two week-ends. You can go with me."

"Not the end of September. I'll be working for Dr. Houck. And classes start that week. Can't you go earlier?"

"No," she said. "The herbs won't be ready. And Hattie already made plans."

Nine days. He could no longer imagine her gone that long. "You can get a lot of reading done," she said, touched him with the warmth of her body. "I'll be back before you know it."

He worked hard, wandered the campus, drank desperate cups of coffee in the HUB. He read as many texts ahead of time as he could, but it seemed that whenever he started to study he would think of Nathan.

The students in his Quiz Section were dull and disinterested. He went through the drill, hoped he had it right. His graduate survey course paralleled the one he was teaching. Dr. Houck said something about it being on the next turn in the great spiral of knowledge, but Harry felt like there was no progress; it all looked too familiar.

On Sunday night he almost went in the Century when he walked by, but decided against it. Alcohol was not the answer. Besides, Judith would be home tomorrow.

She was dark from the desert sun. The Mustang was loaded with bags and boxes of dried plants. She even had a borrowed top carrier and the dusty car sounded like it would throw a rod when she parked in front of the boarding house. She hadn't even been to her place yet, because she wanted to show Harry her harvest. She was sure she had over a thousand dollars worth to sell to local shops.

Harry kissed her with relief and while she showed him her treasures, asked her if she had made a decision.

"Maybe," she said and kissed him again, and he knew that the answer was *yes*.

They found a house for rent on Ravenna Boulevard with two extra bedrooms and a large backyard that overlooked Cowen Ravine. Judith took one extra room for her loom and Harry used the other as a study. Before summer the backyard became a dense garden. Harry planted as many kinds of fruit and vegetables as he could make room for. The flowerbeds bloomed with Judith's herbs.

Judith followed her interest in healing wherever she could, took classes and seminars and read voraciously. She got any new book that was available and haunted the used bookstores for works on herbs and natural medicine that she said had been mainstream material before World War II. One of her prizes was a physician's reference called Materia Medica published in 1927. It was a trove of information on natural substances and their uses.

Harry had been a skeptic, but he saw her successes with friends and family members and he began to turn to her whenever he had some problem. He found great relief in the teas she made for him when he had a cold or sinus infection, from chickweed and wild cherry bark and plantain.

She routinely treated everything from bladder infections to migraine headaches among her friends and her reputation as a healer grew. She never took money for her work, because, she said, that interfered with the healing process.

Harry wanted to get married, but Judith wanted to wait. She would not give him a reason at first, but said it didn't seem necessary.

When he persisted, she finally said, "Something happens to most men when they get married. No matter how long and wonderful the courtship is, as soon as they are married, men think they own women. They're taught that. I love *you*, Harry. I don't want to see that ugly thing happen to *you*."

"It wouldn't," Harry said, "not ever. I love *you* too much."

"I know," she said and kissed him. "I love *you* too. But, let's just be equal. Like my people were in the old days.

CHAPTER 14

That first summer in the house on Ravenna was so busy that they had made only two quick overnight trips across the mountains. Finally, after fall quarter started, they managed a three-day weekend. Judith heard that Little Eagle needed a ride to Nespelem, so they drove to Fremont to get him. He met them at a bus stop, sat silent in the back seat.

It was one of those clear days interspersed between dark Pacific storms. Most of the broadleaf trees were bare. Here and there a bright straggler resisted. The lately fallen leaves, not yet beaten into the mud by the rain, made colored drifts against stark trunks.

The evergreens had taken on deeper winter shades and in the distance they cast black shadows upon the mountains. The mountains were deep gray shadows against the washed out sky. Wet pavement glistened, and below them the Sky River churned with the mud of yesterday's storm.

They did not talk as they climbed the pass. Several times Harry thought one or the other of them spoke, and he would turn to look where they looked. When he had asked Judith about the long silences her family sometimes fell into, she said, "We don't talk unless we have something to say." He wasn't sure if she mocked him.

When they reached the summit, Long Joe said, "Stop, please, Judith. I want to smoke." Judith pulled the Mustang near the trees at the back of the almost empty ski-area lot and they got out. A couple of motor homes and some campers on pickups clustered around the public bathroom.

Long Joe unwrapped a long pipe bound in leather. The bowl was a hawk or eagle, carved coast-Indian style, brooding eyes and a fierce beak. A single eagle feather fluttered at the end of a thong. Long Joe took a pinch of something from a beaded bag and tamped it into the bowl, lit it with a kitchen match. Suddenly he raised his arms high and presented the pipe to the four directions. The tourists stared.

After Long Joe smoked to the four directions, he handed the pipe to Judith. She also blew smoke in the four directions, ended with the west. She handed the pipe to Harry.

"What is it?" he asked.

"Tobacco and kinnickinnic," she said. "It won't hurt you. Start with the North."

He took a tentative puff. Sharp and sweet taste. He drew again and blew a little to the north, turned east, then south. He was out of smoke, had to draw again. He turned to the west and saw the tourists. He heard one say "drugs." He quickly blew out the smoke and handed the pipe to Long Joe. Long Joe sat cross-legged on the ground, smoked and stared back at the tourists until their gathering broke up in confusion.

East of the mountains it was a warm, late-harvest day. Apple pickers, mostly Mexican, were everywhere. They finished the year's northward wandering here, before the long return trip to winter in Mexico or California or Texas. Many of the old cars and vans that had brought them north were traded here for something a little better, a little newer and the used car lots thrived.

The bright Mexican cotton and dark faces added color to the streets in Yakima and Wenatchee and Omak, for a while each season, and each year more of them stayed, more of them found permanent work. The complexion of the valley slowly changed, closer to that of its original inhabitants.

Judith had packed a lunch and Harry said he was hungry. They found a place below Leavenworth where they could pull off the highway into an orchard. There was an upside-down apple bin near the driveway and they used it for a table. They ate smoked salmon sandwiches with onions and garlic. Judith had made some deviled eggs and vegetable sticks. Harry thought that anyone would mistake them for pickers.

A family walked by, Harry counted six children, and they all smiled and spoke in Spanish. The parents and two of the older children had picking bags on neck straps and two of the little ones carried a water bottle and what looked like lunch in a coarse red and green woven shoulder bag.

Joe and Judith both answered them in Spanish. Harry said nothing. The family continued on, out of sight. Their soft voices were murmured echoes among the trees, spirits of the orchard. Harry envied them. They still did farm work as a family, not as a solitary rite performed in an air-conditioned tractor cab.

"This is a nice place," he said.

"You can smell the chemicals," Long Joe said.

"It is bad," Judith said.

"They don't really have a choice," Harry said. "The orchardist, I mean. He has to use chemicals to get the appearance the packing sheds want. Otherwise he can't sell his fruit and feed his family."

"He eats his own grandchildren, this orchardist," Long Joe said. "And kills his mother."

Harry looked at him, but Long Joe continued to eat his Sandwich and looked into the distance.

He looked at Judith.

"To my mother's people the Earth is the mother of us all," she said. "to be treated with respect. The Earth is also the future of all our children and their children. What this orchardist does is a great sin.

"But it isn't this guy's fault. I mean if he wants to stay in business."

"Maybe he should find another business," Long Joe said.

"Then someone else would come along and do the same thing."

"That makes it all right for him? So because there are murderers and rapists out there, then it's okay for me to murder and rape. Someone else would just come along and do it anyway." Long Joe grinned. "So, really, there isn't anything I could do that's wrong. Now I understand. Since some of us are criminals, we may as well all be criminals. God will forgive us."

Harry was angry but he had walked into it. Still he felt a kinship for the orchardist, had sympathy for his dilemma.

"Okay," he said, "I see," and pretended to give in to get Long Joe off his back.

But Long Joe seemed to know his thoughts. "Harry," he said, "It's the same kind of argument they use to excuse the rich. There was an economics professor in one of the seminars that invited me to speak. So I asked him, after the session, why such an advanced society had very rich people and very poor people. In the old days we didn't have that. Everyone shared.

"He said we must have the rich because it is the only way to accumulate enough capital for business to do business. For the good of society.

"I asked him why, if their money was so important to us, we allowed them to spend so much of it on wine and yachts and endangered animal furs. He said because they were individuals, society had no right to control how they spent their money, so they could waste it if they wanted to.

"I said that in the old days, if someone accumulated more than he needed, he would have a Potlatch and give most of it away to prove his worth. The more he gave away, the more influence he had. This economist said that was a strange, backwards system to reward giving away.

"I asked him why it wouldn't be better if we rewarded the rich when they gave money to the poor. Then we wouldn't need welfare or food banks or Medicaid. And it wouldn't cost the taxpayer anything, only the rich. He said that didn't make sense because all the rich cared about was money, so there would be no way to reward them.

Judith drove on, passed Wenatchee and crossed the Columbia. They followed Highway 2 to the east, climbed away from the river. A sign marked a turnoff, "Badger Mountain Ski Area."

"Poor badgers," Long Joe said as they passed. "I hope they never name anything for me, 'Long Joe Gulch.' Uhhh." He shuddered.

"Why, Long Joe?" Harry asked.

"Because the white man names places for what he killed there. You see any wolves on Wolf Creek? Or Cheyennes in Cheyenne, Wyoming, except at the rodeo? How about Manhattan? No, it's very bad medicine when the white man names something for you."

Long Joe sat cross-legged in the middle of the back seat. He wore jeans and a black shirt and a ragged leather vest. His single long braid came over his shoulder and nearly reached his waist. As Harry watched him his face seemed to shift and change shape. It was hard to guess his age. Bright silver strands scattered through his hair but it was easy to believe they'd been there when he was twenty.

Alternate blocks of close-cropped yellow wheat stubble stretched across the Big

Bend country as far as they could see. The other half of the fields had lain fallow a year, were furred green with new winter wheat. A wide gang of rod-weeders behind a D-8 was parked in a field corner, the farmer gone to lunch. Harry wished he could climb on the cat and make a round or two, just for the feel of it.

"At least we'll have a farmer for president," he said.

"Carter?" asked Long Joe. "You like Carter? He's boring, grows peanuts."

"Better him than the Republicans. I'm sure you don't like the Republicans?"

"Reagan," Long Joe said. "He would have won. They should have let Reagan run."

"He's bad news," Harry said. "He wants to start a war."

"They all want to start a war," Long Joe said. "Carter came from the submarines. Reagan would have won."

"But he's full of wild ideas," Harry said

"White people love wild ideas. That's why he would have won. The idea that this whole continent can be run by one government is a wild idea."

"You have to have a national government," Harry said. "Some kind of national government."

"Why? What is it good for?" Long Joe asked. "There is only one thing national governments are good at. War. Everything else is better to do local. For war you have to have big governments."

"They do other things, too."

"Maybe," Long Joe said, "but they just do other things for an excuse. Welfare is better local, police is better local, health care is better local. Education is better local."

"But how about highways. And trade."

"So we must have a national government to build highways. Seems like a lot of overhead." Joe's face showed mock- puzzlement. "Trade. They don't help you and me trade. They help the corporations steal from everyone. You and I don't need them, Harry."

"So what do we do, Long Joe? What's your solution?"

"We won't do anything. It isn't ours to do. It will do itself."

Harry laid back in the seat, absorbed the yellow and green pulses of the planted and fallow fields. He watched with longing the triangular clouds of dust that followed the farm machinery wherever it worked.

They descended from the grain-covered highlands and passed by the Dry Falls Cafe. Across the dam, the road turned north and Judith sped along. Harry watched the color grow in her face and the light come to her eyes as she got near her family. He had begun to think of them as his family.

They took Long Joe to Nespelem and he got out of the car behind the War Bonnet, promised to meet them right there on Sunday morning. They spent what was left of Friday afternoon with Judith's mother and saw the whole family that evening.

Nathan came over in a loud Dodge pickup and talked to Judith for a few minutes while he waited for Joseph. He said hello to Harry but pretended not to see his offered hand.

On Saturday, they traveled the San Poil again. Whenever they were there they would see eagles or a bear or watch a kingfisher dive. This morning, they sat for two hours on the riverbank where they had made love the first spring.

"This place belonged to Nathan's Grandfather," Judith told him. He was a white man. Bill McTavish. He was accepted into the tribe. He made this pool. See the rocks? It's a dam he built to water his fields down in that big meadow below."

Harry had not noticed that the ridge of rocks, which created the pool, was man-made. "Let's walk down to the meadow," he said.

Judith showed him where an old sluiceway made of hand-hewn Tamarack ran along the riverbank. It was just a little higher than the present level of the pool. If you added just a few rocks, it could be made to run again. The bank had slid over the sluice in places and washed away from under it in others. The bottom was mostly rotten, but much of the upper structure could be salvaged. It would be better to reroute it a little where the contour of the bank had changed. His eyes surveyed the new route, told him the elevations would work.

The sluice had emptied into a long, shallow depression that had been a little canal along the higher side of the meadow. He could see how a system of laterals would irrigate the whole thing. The abandoned ditches seemed to open into the earth as he saw their faint impressions, like shadows, left by the old farmer, McTavish.

He could see also the shadow of the fields with their crops in neat rows and blocks, bounded by the contours of the laterals. A Stellar's Jay squawked from the brush on the edge of the meadow.

Judith pulled up some Oregon Grape and showed Harry the bright yellow inner bark that was the medicine. Mostly it was used for kidney and bladder problems, she said. She collected as much as she would need for the winter in a few minutes. She stripped away the leaves and broke the rhizomes into two-foot lengths and tied the lengths in a bundle. She waded across below the dam to cut branches from some willows, which grew almost in the water.

"Black Willow," she said, and at first Harry thought she said Black Widow. She laughed so hard as she waded back that she almost dropped the branches in the river. "Black Willow," she repeated. "What you call Pussy Willow in the spring. It's like aspirin. The bark has Salicylic acid. Look on your aspirin bottle, it will say active ingredient Salicylic acid. She bundled the branches as she had the Oregon Grape.

Then she led him up a deer path to a clear bench a few yards above the river where a patch of dark olive plants sprawled thickly. The leaves were glossy and oval and the branches were covered with small red berries.

"Kinnickinnic," Judith said and he tried to repeat it. She laughed and showed him how to strip the leaves in handfuls. They filled a white plastic bag.

Harry carried the bag and they started back to the car. On the edge of the meadow, in the shade of some brush, Judith saw something else. She bent down and uncurled a withered leaf for inspection.

"Echinacea," Judith said, almost in awe. "Hattie said there was still Echinacea around here. I've never found it before."

"Isn't it dead?" Harry asked.

"Dormant," she said. "Oh, the top is dead. What I want is the root. Above ground is just what it chooses to show us, but the important part is underground. Would you get my little shovel out of the trunk?"

Harry carried the bag of Kinnickinnic to the car and got Judith's camp shovel and returned. She nearly had dug up the plant with her fingers and had found three more. "I must leave one," she said, "So that it can continue. If I only found one, I couldn't take it."

She carefully extricated the long, dark roots and wrapped them in a neckscarf she had woven.

"Echinacea is strong medicine," she said. "They use it for all kinds of infections, and they say it sometimes cures cancer. It stimulates the body's immune system. The wild is the best."

She packed all her medicines in the trunk and they drove on to Republic and back, just for the drive and a piece of Bert's pie.

When they got back to Electric City, it was already dark and the family had eaten. Helen fixed plates for the two of them and sat and talked with them while they ate.

Long Joe waited for them as promised. He had a beautiful beaded ornament on a thong around his neck and had tied a feather to his braid. His eyes were clear and sharp and he only nodded at them as he got in. He took up his cross-legged position in the back seat and was silent. They drove down through the Grand Coulee to visit Harry's family on the way back.

Judith drove fast and they were there in just over an hour. The morning was warm, but the wind blew from the north and chilled them as they went into his parents' trailer. Dad watched the Sunday morning news and Mom sat at the kitchen bar, drank coffee and smoked a cigarette. She started slightly at the sight of Long Joe but forced a smile for Judith.

Dad came in and towered above Long Joe as he shook his hand.

"Nice to meet you," Long Joe said. Harry realized that it was the first time he had heard his voice that day. It was as though he could remember a conversation in the car.

Everyone but Long Joe seemed ill at ease. Harry got them out of the situation, said that he wanted Long Joe to meet the Old Man. But they would come back, he promised. On the porch, they met Jack and Diane who had walked over from their own trailer. Harry was even more glad to be going.

They crossed the canal and walked along the little strip of prairie. Long Joe pinched a sage tip, smelled it then threw it into the air. The cheat grass and brome was dormant for the year, old tops brown and broken. The barbed cheat grass seed clung to Harry's socks and stung him like a hundred needles. He looked down at the worthless street shoes. He should have worn boots.

"You should see the horses, Little Eagle," Judith said. "Draft horses and some Appaloosas. They have the prettiest little Appaloosa filly. I named her Shadow."

"Good name," Long Joe said.

"Judith," grandma said at the door. "It's so nice to see you. Come in, come in. I've just been digging my fall herbs. Come here, let me show you."

The Old Man came through the door from his shop and smiled at them.

"Judith," he said, "I have a new horse to show you. I bought another Appaloosie mare. They sold her so cheap at the auction I couldn't pass her up."

"This is Long Joe," Harry said. "Joseph Longeaux."

"Pleased to meet you," the Old Man said. "Henry Isaacson." Grandma smiled and put out her hand. "Rose," she said. Long Joe smiled at them but said nothing. That didn't seem to bother either of them.

Grandma took Judith into the kitchen and they talked while they looked at grandma's herbs.

Harry and Long Joe followed the Old Man into his shop and he showed them the horseshoes he was making from lengths of iron bar.

That interested Long Joe. "I haven't seen anyone make their own for a long time," he said. "Why don't you just buy them?"

"You can't find decent shoes anymore," the Old Man said. "Not for work horses. All they do with big horses now is show them. The shoes break if the horses do any real work."

He pumped the bellows with his foot and the coal in his small hooded forge glowed translucent red. He stuck an iron bar among the coals with some long-handled tongs. As he pumped, they watched the bar turn red and then white. Tiny storms of fire raged through the coals.

The Old Man turned the iron, pumped some more, then used the tongs to hold the edge of the bar against the rounded point of his huge anvil.

As he pounded the hot iron, golden sparks flew and the bar cooled to dull red under the hammer. He put the half-made shoe back in the forge and heated it again. When he had the curve he wanted, he turned up the ends and pounded them smooth.

"There," he said, "All I have to do is drill it and Ed has new shoes." The shoe hissed steam as he dunked it into a tub of water.

Long Joe took the tongs and held the shoe to look at it.

"Beautiful," he said.

They went back into the house. When there was a lull in the women's conversation, the Old Man called, "You ready to see that mare, now, Judith?"

She came in from the kitchen. "Sure," she said.

Everyone but grandma went out to the corral by the horse barn. The new mare was a red roan and they admired her for a while, but Judith wanted to show Long Joe the big horses.

They went into the barn and Long Joe whistled softly when he saw the Percherons. Judith laughed and said, "I told you. Aren't they wonderful?"

"Beautiful," Long Joe said. He looked at the Old Man with approval.

They went back into the house for coffee and Long Joe and the Old Man were old friends. Long Joe asked what crops they grew and the Old Man started what seemed like an endless list.

"I used to know an old gentleman," Long Joe said, "up on the San Poil when I was a boy. He married my aunt. He used to grow everything. We bought potatoes from him. They always had lots of food."

"Good food," the Old Man said. "The best food is what you grow yourself."

"That's what he always said." Long Joe laughed. "He loved those big horses, too."

They had talked for more than an hour when there was a knock on the door. It was Jack. "Mom wants you all to come over for lunch," he said.

"I've got too much to do," the Old Man said. "I gotta make Ned some new shoes now. You folks go ahead."

"Tell your mother, I'll be over later," grandma said to Harry. "I have to stay with these herbs until they're ready to dry."

"Okay," Harry said.

They followed Jack who immediately crossed the canal and led them along the bare dirt road on the bank. Their feet stirred small puffs of dust, which blew into the canal.

"When you movin' back?" Jack asked Harry.

"When I'm through with school," Harry said. "Maybe."

"It's a good time. We're sure makin' the money. Gonna have to expand soon."

"Expand?" Harry said. "Where?"

"Radfords are sellin' that hundred and sixty just north of us. They're buyin' a section out in the Black Sands. Four circles when they're done."

"How'd they get water to the Black Sands? I thought it was too high for the canal."

"Wells," Jack said, "Deep goddamned wells. Eighteen hundred feet. Costs twenty grand for the hole. And twenty-five for the circle. But the land is dirt cheap."

"What can they grow? It's just sand. The water will sink away as fast as you put it on."

"Not with circles. They've got circles, now, that make a round in eight hours, move fast as you can walk. They grow beans and potatoes. By the time the water gets to them they're dry and wilted. But it works. If your circle breaks down, then you got problems."

"Sounds crazy to me."

Mom had put the leaves in the dining table and set enough places for everyone.

"Where's your grandparents?" she asked Harry.

"They couldn't come," he said. "Stuff to do."

Mom made a sound of disbelief and noisily removed the two place settings.

Dad came in from the living room. "Is it ready?" he asked.

"Almost. Almost." Mom said. "Just a few last minute surprises."

Diane helped her carry in the lunch. It was clear that she and Mom were best friends. They brought cold cut sandwiches on white bread and some runny potato salad. There were three quarts of cheap soda to drink.

Mom sat down. "Dig in," she said. "I bought a cake at Safeway we can have for dessert." She passed Harry the plate of sandwiches. "Did you know Jack was going to school, too?"

Jack's flush was pleased and embarrassed. "Just night school," he said. "At Big Bend. Real Estate. I can get my license next year. Lot's of money in real estate."

"Lots of money," Mom said. "Diane is going to school, too. In at the Beauty College. She already has a job offer from the Wak 'n Yak. That's where I go." Diane smiled prettily.

Long Joe took a small sandwich and passed on the potato salad. Harry took a little of it. It was worse than he expected.

"Oh, dear, I forgot my medicine," Mom said.

"I'll get it," Diane stood up. Which one is it?"

"Oh, thank you, dear," Mom said and smiled at her. "It's the blue one."

Diane went into the kitchen and came back with the bottle.

"What's that for," Harry asked.

"Just my diabetes," Mom said. "I'm on a special diet, so I have to have supplements."

"I didn't know you had diabetes."

"Well, you haven't been around much, dear. I've been so upset. Dr. Grissom prescribed tranquilizers, too. Just to help me bear my burdens."

"How advanced is the diabetes," Judith asked.

"Oh, I don't know," Mom answered. "They didn't tell me much, just take this and this..."

"I have something that could help you," Judith said. "I'll get it after lunch."

"Oh, I would never take someone else's medicine," Mom said.

"It's not that kind of medicine," Judith said.

"It's an herb," Harry said. "We picked it yesterday."

"I'm not sure," Mom said. "I would have to ask Dr. Grissom."

When they had eaten, Judith went out to her car and came back in with a small paper bag half full of the Kinnickinnic leaves. She handed them to Mom and said, "When your blood sugar gets too high, make a tea of these leaves, one teaspoon in a cup of boiling water, steep for half an hour."

Mom took the bag carefully between her thumb and forefinger and set it gingerly on the counter. She looked at Diane and Diane giggled and turned her head.

Harry said it was time to go, and he noticed that Long Joe had gone to the car.

CHAPTER 15

Midway through his second year of graduate school Harry's GI Bill ran out. He was bored supervising quiz sections and grading papers. He knew for sure by then that he was not intended for the academic world. The petty squabbles and jealousies he saw among the junior professors and graduate students reminded him too much of the military.

He was tired of the lack of physical activity and hungered for something to do that was real, productive. He interviewed with several corporate recruiters on campus, but he couldn't get very excited about stock options and incentive bonuses.

"Find out what you don't do well," the Old Man had told him, "then don't do it."

He found a job with a homebuilder named Arne Olson. Arne did the work with his own people instead of sub-contracting to the lowest bidder like the big companies. Harry's experience with heavy equipment on the farm and his two years in the University carpenter shop made him valuable to Arne. The money was as good as corporate trainees got and Harry enjoyed the process. There were real problems to solve, not just paper puzzles. And he could see and touch and take pride in the product.

Harry thought he had found a career. Construction was not that different from farming. Success came from your own ability and motivation. And he enjoyed the people. Arne treated his customers with care and concern.

"They're our business," he told Harry. "Without them, there is no business."

Harry spent a lot of his time at "pickup work," finishing the fine details of a job that many contractors avoided. But if one of Arne's floors squeaked or a door didn't fit just right, they fixed it, even if the house had been finished for a couple of years.

"I think we should have a baby," Judith said. "What do you think, Harry?"

"I don't know. We could. We have the money, now."

"It's not the money. Our relationship. Kids have to have a stable home."

"We would need to get married."

"Why? I think we're doing fine this way."

"A baby needs to know who his parents are."

She laughed. "It would know its parents. I know lots of good parents who aren't really married."

"You mean on the reservation? I don't want to do that. I won't handicap a kid that way."

"Most reservation kids are happy. What handicaps people is a family that doesn't love them. Marriage doesn't change that."

"What if something happened to you? They might not let me have the baby."

"Yes they would. I could do a will."

"No," Harry said, "I can't do it. It isn't right."

It was two months before she agreed with him. And she made him promise that if anything bad happened between them they would part as friends, neither would contest a divorce. And he had to understand that her loom and her car and her other things would always be hers.

He couldn't see a problem with it.

She spent much of her free time for two months weaving a fine piece of linen for her wedding dress. Then she took three vacation days and a weekend to visit her mother and do the sewing. Harry kept busy and tried not to think about Nathan.

The wedding was in Judith's parents' backyard in Electric City on a bright June day with only an occasional cloud. Many of Judith's relatives from the reservation attended. Harry's parents and grandparents came and Jack and Diane. His sister, Meg, made a rare visit from Spokane where she worked as a nurse.

Judith was excited when she heard that Long Joe would be there. Harry hoped Long Joe wouldn't say or do anything outrageous during the ceremony.

Judith's brother, Joseph, came home from Stanford to be an usher. Harry thought that Judith's relatives were more excited to see Joseph than they were to bless the marriage.

Harry had asked Ron Radford to be best man. "Too bad Rod couldn't be here," Ron said as they dressed in Joseph's room. "In high school we always said we would be in each other's weddings. I always expected Rod to be first, the way the girls liked him."

"Yeah," Harry said, "me too."

They had borrowed folding chairs from the church and set them up on the back lawn. As the crowd gathered, the chickens clucked and cackled at the disturbance. Harry heard his mother say to Diane, "I suppose they gave the hens invitations, too." Diane giggled.

Mom had wanted Reverend Hale from her Baptist church to marry them, but Harry had refused. He had never liked the fat preacher who invariably had dirty cuffs with cheap cufflinks protruding from his cheap suit. He would press your hand obscenely with his thick, sweaty palm and quote some bible verse or make some unctuous pronouncement.

Instead, Judith and Harry had chosen the assistant pastor from the Presbyterian Church in Electric City. They wrote their own ceremony. They were to be married until they gave their bodies back to their Great Mother, the Earth. Mom wouldn't like that.

It was time to begin and Harry, Ron and Joseph waited in the chill shadow of a passing cloud for Judith and her father to enter from Judith's old room in the basement. The traditional march was played by one of Judith's cousins on an electric organ they had rented. The maid of honor and bridesmaid were also Judith's cousins and so were the ring-bearer and flower girl.

Jack and Diane had wanted their middle daughter, Tiffany, in the party, but Harry was afraid the half-wild five-year-old would ruin the ceremony.

Mom said it was because Judith didn't want to be shown up by a beautiful blonde.

Finally Judith and her father entered and Matt briefly touched Harry on the shoulder when the preacher asked who gave this woman to be married.

"Her mother and I," Matt responded.

The reception was in the church basement and Judith's relatives provided the food. Harry thought it was as fine as any of the catered affairs they had attended in Seattle.

Everyone agreed that Judith's dress was the most beautiful they had seen and rivaled anything in the magazines. It had alternating panels of Judith's linen and some Chinese silk she had bought. She had worked tiny, bright-colored feathers into the veil. Her bouquet was of spring wildflowers that she and Harry gathered in the San Poil Valley the day before, many of them from medicinal plants.

Harry was tense as he saw Nathan approach them in the reception line. He looked like some dark prince in a stark white shirt with nugget cuff links and an expensive deep gray suit.

He shook Harry's hand with mock-gravity, squeezed hard, as usual.

"Well," he said, "It's finally happened." Then he slapped Harry roughly on the back. "You know, we expect people to treat our women right."

Harry did not like the smile on his face. He had to look away as Nathan kissed Judith. The kiss seemed longer than the formality of kissing the bride required.

Mom let Diane know that she was not pleased with the beautiful homemade wedding cake with alternate white and chocolate layers under the traditional white frosting.

"Wedding cakes should be all white." She tasted it daintily. "I guess black is appropriate when you've lived together in sin as long as they have."

She and Diane sat and talked together, apart from the others, and refused to eat any of the other food. Dad did talk to some of Judith's relatives, but he glanced often in Mom's direction. Finally, Judith's father sought him out and talked to him for a while and he seemed to relax.

Grandma spent much of her time with Helen, helped her bring in more food and cleared away empty dishes. They seemed to get along well and Harry was glad to see grandma ignore several looks of disapproval from his mother.

The Old Man talked about horses with one of Judith's uncles. The two of them became so engrossed in their subject and so animated that they drew smiles and occasional participation from the others. Harry was sure that before it was over the two old men would trade a horse or two.

While Judith talked with her grandmother, Harry moved over to listen to the Old Man. Long Joe had told the others that the Old Man was a horse farmer. Most of those over forty had seen horse farming in their youth and were interested in what he had to say.

"Complexification," the Old Man said, "That's the problem. They complexify everything and tell you that you can't understand it. Then they sell you a way they say is easier. It ain't easier.

"It does take a few minutes to harness a horse. With a tractor you just hit the starter button and away you go. Right? No, because you need to warm it up for ten or fifteen minutes, burn up some diesel. I can harness a team in that time. Then, with the tractor, one mornin' you hit that old starter button and... nothin'. So, now you have to spend a few days and a few hundred dollars before you can work again. Now, that don't happen with a team. You can keep a spare horse cheap, a little hay and grain, a few shoes. And if one gets a sore foot it heals. You seen any iron heal lately? And in the end you don't have some old piece of junk the dealer tells you is now obsolete. Instead, you've got a herd of horses. There ain't no increase in iron."

"Iron is bad medicine," Long Joe said. He sat backwards on one of the folding chairs, leaned it forward to talk to the Old Man. "That's what Crazy Horse said. He sure was right. Iron and white men." There was an amused murmur around them.

The Old Man laughed. "Not all white men worship iron," he said.

"The great gods, Iron and Aluminum," Long Joe said.

"And plastic," the Old Man said. "I am deathly sick of plastic."

"We all are," Long Joe said."

"And aluminum pipe," the Old Man said. "I hate them aluminum sprinkler pipes. Have to wear gloves to touch 'em. They ruin your hands. And I hate listenin' to sprinklers run, them rainbirds? You get thirty or forty of them goin' and it sounds like a troop of monkeys chatterin'.

"Now, I like ditches. I would much rather listen to water trickle in ditches. Sprinklers ain't easier, they just make money for someone. Ditches is the way to go."

"Water flowing in ditches is very hypnotic," Long Joe said, "Strong medicine. It led to all the great civilizations. Don't forget who first irrigated the American deserts. It wasn't a white man."

"The Pueblos," the Old Man said. "I saw an article on that. They had canal and ditch systems long ago, good ones. In the driest part of the desert."

Long Joe nodded. "The Pueblos, the Hopi and the Zuni believe that it is very important to live in the harshest environment. When the great cycles change, they still can survive, because they have done it where it is the hardest. And the most stable."

Harry realized that the Old Man was listening to Mom and Diane. He also focused on them. He heard Mom say in a loud whisper to Diane, "It's a good thing Ron was best man. He was the only other white face in the whole wedding party."

The Old Man winked at Harry.

Judith came to get him and introduced him to a bunch of cousins. The Old Man remained, talked to Long Joe and the others. It went on so long that finally Dad worked his way through the crowd, touched his father on the shoulder and indicated Mom who waited impatiently on her folding chair by the door. Reluctantly the Old Man broke it off but promised to continue at some future time. Several of Judith's family made a point of saying goodbye to him as he slowly moved towards the door.

CHAPTER 16

They stopped birth control and within two months Judith was pregnant. They used most of their savings to buy a "horse acre" lot on the east side of Lake Washington. Harry got a VA loan, and Arne helped them design and build a house. They financed the house without disclosing that Judith was pregnant. If the bank had known, the loan would have been denied because the loan depended on Judith's income and her six years at Sureco. Harry's year and a half with Arne wasn't long enough.

Judith found a midwife she liked and decided to have the baby at home. When Mom heard about the decision, she warned Harry of the dangers.

"What if there are complications? Judith or the baby might die. Do you want that responsibility? Doctor Thornburg, back in Kansas, said that if he hadn't been there, Jack would have died because he was a breech. I think you should talk to her about it."

Diane tried to convince Judith that natural childbirth would be too painful. "I don't think I could have made it with my four that way," she said. "Not without anaesthetic. The pain is horrible. But then they stick that needle in and the pain just goes away. It's wonderful."

"I want to feel my baby being born," Judith said. "Women had babies for a long time without doctors to help. None of us would be here otherwise."

"It's not civilized," Mom said. "This isn't the reservation."

"But what if there are complications?" Harry asked as they drove back over the mountains.

"Most complications are obvious before the birth," Judith said. "The midwife works with a Birth Center. They can give me any tests that I need. If there is something Bess or I think is dangerous, she has arrangements with an obstetrician. And even if there is some surprise, we are only five minutes from three different hospitals. Don't worry, Harry, I can handle it."

Harry knew that it was Judith's decision.

Just four and a half hours after the first signs of labor, Rebecca was born. Bess remarked on the full head of long, dark hair. Rebecca was healthy and Judith breast fed her. Formula, she said, made babies sick. Bess visited twice more, and recommended a pediatrician. Judith smiled and thanked her, and told Harry later that she would take care of her own baby

She stayed home for almost three months after the birth. She would sit at the loom, Rebecca tied at her breast with a piece of soft cotton she had woven. Harry loved to stand at the door and watch her.

Their new lot allowed Harry to plant a larger garden and he moved most of the fruits and berries he had started at the Ravenna house. The cool, damp climate and the heavy clay soil of the Sammamish Valley limited what he could grow. The people back in Kansas always said the pictures of Washington looked so cool and green. If they only knew how dark and cold it really was. He understood why the first white settlers had attacked the coastal forest as though it were an alien enemy which cast it's dark shadow across the drudgery of their days.

Long Joe once had told him that Native Americans accepted where they were, but everyone else tried to change every place they went into the plains of Africa a million years ago.

"All white men come from Africa," he said. "I read an article about that, when I was at Western. Us, we just come up out of the ground wherever we are."

Harry built a greenhouse and learned many tricks with plastic and insulation to cope with the climate but he would never get used to the hordes of slugs or to having his tomato and cucumber blossoms mildew before they could set. He could grow spinach and cabbage year-round, if he didn't mind sharing with slugs, because the soil never froze for long. But the warm- weather crops he loved, melons and peppers and tomatoes and beans did poorly and were spongy and bland.

The endless storm-driven days depressed him. The long dark of midwinter seemed unreal. He couldn't remember days so short on the east side of the mountains.

The housing business in the entire Puget Sound Basin boomed while inflation raged. Houses bought for twenty thousand dollars a few years before suddenly were worth twice as much and people used their equity to buy larger houses and move into newer subdivisions.

Arne had more work than he could handle and soon Harry had a crew of his own. He thought of starting his own company, but Judith counseled against it. She was afraid that the boom wouldn't last, and besides, how would they ever be able to return to Eastern Washington if they got tied down with a business.

With no warning interest rates started to rise. The housing business reeled. Within six months builders were going bankrupt and payments on new homes were higher than anyone could qualify for.

Arne was conservative, built mostly custom homes, sold before he started them. But his sales started to fall and he consolidated the crews back into one. After three more months with no new sales, he told Harry he had decided to retire.

"By the time this turns around," he said, "I'd be too old anyway. The banks and the big companies are trying to force us little guys out of the business. We've been making too much money." He laughed and gave Harry's shoulder a little shake. "Don't ever make too much money," he said. "They'll just try to steal it from you."

Arne wrote Harry a strong letter of reference and gave him three months' salary as severance pay.

Harry quickly got another job as a Superintendent for a new company called United Homes. The salary wasn't as much as Arne had paid, but there was a bonus plan based on production, several in his position had already earned an extra $5,000 this year. They were impressed that he had been Arne's right hand man and assured him that they knew Arne's reputation well.

The management knew nothing about building. They relied on Harry and the other foremen to get the job done. What they did know was the construction business. They manipulated false loan packages through the banks and faulty plans through city planning departments. They freely lied to both. The pretentious suburban houses he built for United sold for more than Arne ever had dreamed of charging.

He tired of customers' complaints and of the bill collectors from suppliers who had not been paid. There was nothing he could do. If he passed the complaints along to higher management, he was the one blamed for the problem.

Higher management was Lonnie, the General Superintendent, a gray-haired veteran of the business whose own company had failed. He drove around in a tinny little Toyota pickup, visited as many as he could of the dozen jobs that he was expected to oversee. Nearly half his income depended on profits. If he overspent the projected cost, he had to pay half the overruns from his two percent of the job. His bosses squeezed his budget so tight that he often was short. Every hundred dollars of pickup work cost him fifty. He hated pickup work.

Harry was expected to run four jobs, do pickup work when necessary, and "sell" the job to the customers when it was complete. From the time he was given the lot ready for the foundation, he was supposed to complete the house within ninety days. From his two- percent bonus he had to pay a quarter of any overruns on items he controlled, but most of the really risky things like excavation and utilities were on Lonnie's neck.

Lonnie's boss was the company president, Greg Roberts. Greg spent most of his time with prospective customers, squired them around in his Mercedes and flirted with the wives. Harry couldn't prove that Greg ever told anyone the truth. He was sure if he had it was by accident.

Greg hated the uncertainties of the business and would scream at Lonnie when there were overruns. Whenever Greg screamed at Lonnie, Lonnie screamed at Harry and the other Job Superintendents.

On each job there were as many as twenty-five sub contractors, hard-pressed concrete finishers and framers and electricians and plumbers and all the others who hurried in and did their jobs as quickly and cheaply as they could. The subs, squeezed by the large contractors, cut every corner they could when no one was looking. One of their favorite expressions was "quick and dirty." They hated pickup work worse than Lonnie or Greg.

Harry had to do the work himself if he could not get the subs back. Usually, Lonnie and Greg would not authorize enough money to do the extra work. Harry spent more and more of his time and his own money to do the necessary work so that the customer would close the sale. And he learned many ways to hide faults from the customers long enough to get the job sold.

Beyond Lonnie and Greg was the United Homes board of directors and Harry never knew who any of them were. In any case, United Homes was a subsidiary of another corporation, Bartleby Development, which had made a lot of money putting together deals for shopping centers. Bartleby Development had been bought by Associated Tobacco, which was trying to diversify.

One time an Associated Tobacco vice president made a brief appearance at a Superintendents' meeting. His thick Southern accent was so alien that Harry never was sure what he had said. Whatever it was, it was supposed to pump everyone up. Greg and Lonnie and the other General Superintendents laughed and slapped each other on the back when he was through.

One night after Rebecca had gone to bed, Judith told Harry that her boss had become a problem. He would hang around her desk and talk to her while she worked. Whenever she got behind, he would take some of the files she had and assign them to someone else. Several of the other underwriters had complained loudly enough for her to hear.

"I know he's had affairs with at least two other underwriters," she said. "He seems to think because he is the boss, no one can turn him down. And some of the women think he is really good looking."

A few days later she came home with a dozen red roses a florist had delivered with a card from Stan. She showed him the card. "Congratulations to a beautiful lady and great employee of the month," it said. It was signed, "Yours, Stan." Judith explained that along with the roses she had won a hundred-dollar bonus and a dinner with Stan and his boss, the vice president for underwriting.

"I hope you're not going," Harry said. "The bastard is just coming on to you."

I have to go," Judith said. "Otherwise they will say I have a bad attitude. They have been laying-off underwriters."

Stan had selected a Friday evening just a week before Christmas for the dinner. Harry stayed home with Rebecca and helped her wrap some presents for Judith. It was Rebecca's second Christmas and she was excited. She proudly folded and wrapped a batik scarf herself.

Harry built a fire in the fireplace and made her some warm apple cider. She fell asleep in his arms and he carried her to her bed. He found an old bottle of Bacardi, made a hot buttered rum and tried to get into the Christmas spirit himself.

One drink didn't help, so he had another. He stared into the fire and watched the ephemeral flame structures grow and develop and pass. The alcohol soothed his brain but made him slightly nauseous.

Sloppy snow and rain fell among the tall firs left on the north end of their acre. There was no moon, no stars. The dark and the wet closed in around him. He got his old field jacket out of the hall closet and put it on. He sat on the hearth and clung to the fire for comfort.

Judith didn't get home until after midnight. She came in quietly and Harry lifted his head to look at her. She looked upset.

"Hi, honey," she said and took off her shoes.

"Hello," Harry said, "what happened?"

She came towards him and he saw that she was very tired. She kissed him, smelled alcohol. There was a lack of control in her haunted eyes. Harry felt fear but did not know if it was for her or himself.

"What happened?" he asked her again.

She looked away, into the corner. Her head was down.

"Harry, I may lose my job," she said. Her voice was faint and bemused. "He wanted me to go to bed with him and I wouldn't."

"He can't fire you for that." Harry's fog faded. "That son- of-a-bitch. You should make a complaint. Sexual Harassment."

"I can't do that, Harry, I don't have any proof. They would just fire me. We have to have the money"

"How about his boss? I thought there was supposed to be that vice president."

"Don Carlson. Oh, he was there. But he got a call right after they served dinner and had to leave. I think they set it up."

"Those fuckers," Harry said. "Mother-fuckers."

CHAPTER 17

After one particularly bad day at United Homes, when Lonnie had screamed most of the day and Harry hadn't had an excuse to get out into the field, he had several drinks at The Trojan Horse in Kirkland. He watched part of a basketball game. The Supersonics played the Lakers and were beaten badly. At the bar, a large man with a full beard, grumbled that Lenny Wilkens should never have traded away Dennis Johnson the year after the championship. Someone else blamed Fred Brown's cold streak. Everyone blamed someone.

He drove down through Redmond and out into the Valley. When he got home Judith had already cleared the dinner table and she sat at the loom with Rebecca asleep on the floor beside her. Harry asked her if there was anything to eat and she told him to look in the refrigerator. He couldn't find anything he wanted. He went back into the weaving room and told her loudly that he wanted something to eat. Rebecca woke up and looked at him and started to cry. Judith gave her a breast and told Harry to wait a few minutes.

"She's too old to be nursing," he said angrily. "She's damned near two years old. How long are you going to put up with it?"

Judith just looked at him and said nothing, and he went back into the kitchen. She came in after a few minutes and started to fix him something. "Harry," she said, "you need to stop drinking. It's bad for you."

"It's none of your fucking business," he yelled at her. "I'm not some damned Indian that can't handle alcohol."

She burst into tears. "Fine, I'll just go back to my damned Indians and you can do whatever you want."

Harry was sure she meant Nathan. "You aren't going anywhere," he said and stepped towards her.

"Don't threaten me, white man," she said, "I'll go if I please." She moved as though to push by him<. >

He grabbed her by the hair and spun her around and gave her a push and she nearly fell. Her turquoise and silver hair clasp broke open and flew across the room.

Her tears stopped instantly and she said calmly, "Don't ever do that again Harry." The dark fury in her eyes reminded him of the first time he had seen Nathan. She put the food back in the refrigerator and went back to her weaving room. Harry was afraid to follow.

She never did come to bed that night and he had to get up early for a mandatory breakfast meeting at United Homes. He cracked open the door to the weaving room and she was asleep on the floor with Rebecca at her breast, both of them covered with a rainbow blanket Judith had woven.

When he got home late in the evening Judith was gone. She had left a note for him, stick-pinned above the sink.

"Harry, I'm going home for a few days to think about things. Don't try to follow me. I'll talk to you when I'm ready. I love you, Judith."

He sat silently and stared out the window until long after dark.

The next day, at lunchtime, he called for her at Sureco and they told him she had taken an emergency leave of absence. It might be as long as thirty days. "Someone in her family is ill," the lady in personnel told him.

When he got home, he fixed some dinner and watched television for a while then decided he had to get out of the house. He went to the Century Tavern and had several drinks. Then he felt like driving around Seattle, maybe to remember. He drove too fast, slid around corners, but he didn't care. He stopped at a dirty bar in Lake City and had two more drinks and flirted with a skinny waitress in tight designer jeans.

He could try to find someone, as revenge for Nathan. But he wasn't sure he would know how to pick someone up. He wondered if Diane Brown still lived in the same house. He hadn't really thought seriously about a woman other than Judith in several years. His helplessness made him feel sick and he wished for Judith's eyes and herbs.

He awakened with a violent hangover and called in sick. Greg said "Okay, no problem, we'll cover for you, buddy."

Harry went back to sleep until noon, then got up and cleaned the house and felt better. He fixed himself some bacon and eggs and drank a pot of Antigua Guatemala. Twice he started to call Judith's parents in Electric City, but stopped. If she was there, they would know all about it and he didn't want to talk to them. If she wasn't there, they would know something was wrong.

At dinnertime he heated some stew Judith had left and drank another pot of coffee. He was not going out that night. He built a fire and stared into it until his eyes burned and he had to close them.

The torn body of Rebecca floated through his mind, and someone was with her, another child. And the house burned around them. He opened his eyes and the fire flared, dried them, and he blinked to bring the tears. The dark eyes that looked at him, then looked away, held no tears. And he wondered if they mocked him. He pulled the trigger again and again, but the eyes would not go away.

He took a long, hot shower. His brain cleared a little. He drank a cold root beer and it cleared some more. He soaked a towel in cold water and pressed it on his forehead and icy drops ran down his face and splattered on his knees.

He returned to work the next day half an hour early. When Lonnie got there, he called Harry in to give him a bad time for his absence and imply that he could be easily replaced. It was clear that if you were too sick to work, you were too sick to stay at United Homes.

Harry's jobs had all gotten screwed up with just one day away and it took all day to get them back on track. The sub- contractors he could find were silent and sullen. Several did not return his calls.

On Saturday morning, Judith finally called, said she would like to talk to him, but not just yet. She would be back on Wednesday and would like for him to take the day off. He told her he couldn't, that he was already in trouble at work for missing this Thursday and her voice grew distant again and she said okay, she would wait until next Saturday. He couldn't stop her from hanging up.

Harry was determined to quit drinking. He had done it before. Each day he struggled with himself all the way home, but he didn't stop for a drink, and by the end of the week he felt stronger. His love for Judith was more important than anything else. He had to convince her he had solved the problem. And they had to get out of the city. He was tired of pretending that down was up and backwards forwards.

She pulled into their driveway just after ten o'clock Saturday morning, and he knew that she must have left Electric City by six-thirty. He met her at the door and watched her for a sign. She did not kiss him as always before, but she did have a small, strained smile and the irrepressible lights danced in her eyes.

"I'm sorry," he said before she could say anything. "It was my fault and I'm sorry." He was happy that he could say it. "I quit drinking. Completely."

"I hope so, Harry," she said. "I love you, but I hate what alcohol does to you. What it does to anyone, Indian or not."

"I know," he said, wanted desperately to touch her but was afraid. "I didn't mean that. I don't know why I said it, I was just mad. I'll hear it in my head forever."

She handed Rebecca to him and he could see that already he had become a little bit a stranger to her, and it hurt him. He held her carefully, did not want to upset her, and felt tears.

"Look, Daddy," she said and showed him a new rag doll with dark yarn braids. "Gramma made it."

Harry looked at it. "Nice," he said. "Did you have a good time?"

"Yes," she said and hugged the doll. "We missed you. Mommy cried."

He looked at Judith and saw that she had tears in her eyes, too. He put his arm around her and she relaxed against him. He turned her and kissed her gently and she responded. His tears flowed strongly and he laughed and brushed them away.

She smiled at him and asked, "Did you miss me." He couldn't answer, but just held the two of them tightly until Rebecca started to squirm.

"Too tight," she said.

Judith laughed. "You'd better go see how your other toys are doing and introduce Sally."

Rebecca ran off to her bedroom. Judith kissed him again and said, "Harry, we have to get out of here. The city is no good for us. I realized that when I was home. The city is getting sick. Sicker than it ever was. No one cares for anyone else any more. I know you are having a hard time at work. You just can't take it out on Rebecca and me.

"I don't like my job either. I hate Stan. I'm sure he'll fire me. But right now they need me. It's just push, push, push, and people don't matter. Customers are just people we take money from."

"How can we leave?" he asked. "Where can we go? We can't farm. It costs too much to get started."

"We could just get a small place. I don't care if we don't have much money. I hate it here. The Old Man said we could buy their place, on a contract. You know they would love to have us there."

"Their little place wouldn't support us all. And we would have to get a trailer or build a house."

"We could do it if we worked real hard. I could work in town. Anywhere. I'll work in an apple shed."

They spent as much time at home with Rebecca as they could. They stopped seeing friends and turned down party invitations. They often unplugged the telephone. Always there seemed to be someone visiting or calling or watching, someone you could not be sure of.

The Old Man had told him, "Don't worry about men with great power, it's little men with a little power you have to watch out for."

Around them, at work, in the neighborhood, near panic had become chronic. The sudden adrenaline rushes on the freeways ritualized living on the edge. Golden parachutes were not standard issue and everyone negotiated from under the gun.

Almost every weekend they crossed the mountains to visit Judith's family or Harry's grandparents and they looked at small farms for sale, but prices were high. Unless they could sell their house they couldn't even raise a down payment. Each westbound trip back to Seattle was more difficult.

They listed the house with a Realtor who assured them that a house of such quality would be sold in a few weeks. But with interest rates high, hardly anyone came to look at it. The Realtor called and came over and convinced them to lower the price five thousand dollars, but even that did no good.

Harry got a call from Mom on a cold, rain-washed February day. She said that Jack had left the farm to go into the real estate business full-time. Dad would like for him and Judith to come and take the partnership Jack and Diane had given up.

Judith worked overtime that day, came home late. Harry met her at the door with Rebecca in his arms. As he told her about the telephone call, he could see her eyes brighten, the lines of her face soften.

They gave away the equity in their house. They called the Realtor. He called back the same day and said his broker would assume the loan and pay their closing costs. He could use the house for a rental. Harry said, "fine." and they took Rebecca out to dinner to celebrate.

In two weeks when Dad came over in one of the farm trucks to move them they were packed and ready.

Jack wanted them to buy his seventy-foot doublewide, but Harry refused. The payments on the big trailer were high and Judith hated it. They bought a used single-wide and set it up in the rocks along the canal close to his grandparents. Harry ripped out most of the printed woodgrain paneling and replaced it with sheet-rock he textured and painted himself. He built new cabinets and added a ten by twenty greenhouse to the side.

Jack was mad at them, but he set up his doublewide on a small lot in Radfords' trailer park and sold it for a good profit. He was sure he would be a millionaire within a few years.

The season was good, the harvest was good and prices were good. Harry drew a thousand dollars a month from the operating loan and the end of the year would bring a profit share of more than ten thousand dollars, pay off the trailer and leave a little money. Altogether it was less than half what they had made their last year in Seattle, but it did not cost them much to live.

They hardly ever left the farm and Judith spent much of her time with Grandma and learned to grow and preserve much of their food.

One afternoon when Judith and the Old Man worked with Shadow, the Old Man said, "This Filly is yours whether I like it or not." His gentle hand rested on her shoulder. "Not that I don't like it. But she knows her rightful owner."

Judith's eyes and dark smile thanked him.

Judith got pregnant again that summer, and in February gave birth to a son they named Joseph. She had to go home to find a midwife, an old woman from the reservation who had helped in the birth of several of Judith's cousins. It was another short, easy labor.

Not long after Joseph was born, the thaw came and their second year on the farm began. Harry plowed with the old John Deere, gasped in the early Chinook as it awakened the land. He felt that finally all the frayed and tangled threads of his life came together to make a sensible pattern. He began to look forward to a distant time when he could turn the farm over to little Joe.

CHAPTER 18

Harry heard Reject bark. He stood up, kicked the plastic bucket towards the trailer and climbed the canal bank to see what had set off the dog. Several vehicles came up the lane led by a green Continental that he knew belonged to the auctioneer. Another car and a pickup followed. In the rear, a green one-ton truck pulled a long, canopied trailer painted in yellow and green stripes like a circus tent.

Dad met the caravan at the end of the lane and showed them where to park. The auctioneer's two assistants walked around and looked at the equipment. Dad and the auctioneer leaned over the hood of the Continental, read and signed some papers.

The concession trailer stopped at the far end of the lines of equipment, away from the house. Harry watched the auctioneer's wife and a younger woman he guessed was her daughter as they rolled out the awnings, opened the service windows, and then went inside the trailer.

Harry thought it all looked a lot like preparations for a hanging in the old days, a celebration of someone else's misfortune. Hangings were instructive, they said, for children and other potential miscreants.

The breeze strengthened and the little triangular flags that festooned the top of the trailer rippled, popped with a staccato sound like distant gunfire. Harry could hear the hum of the generator and the women appeared to be ready. He decided to go and see if they had coffee yet. Reject stayed close at his heel, alarmed by this invasion of strangers.

The younger woman smiled at Harry, asked him if he would like something.

"Coffee," he answered, "and one of those muffins. Blueberry."

She poured coffee into a Styrofoam cup and gave him a muffin and a yellow and green striped paper napkin.

"Is this your place?" she asked as he started to walk away."

"No," he said, "it belongs to my parents. I just work for them."

"It's a nice place. Where are you moving?"

"I don't know," he said, "I guess I need to figure that out."

She looked at him. "Are you married?"

"Yes," he said. "I mean no. I was."

Her smile brightened and her blue eyes clung to his. She was pretty enough, he thought, and a little younger than he was. Probably divorced. Like most of his generation. So many of them had started their lives late, anyway. Now most of them were trying to start over again.

He called Reject and walked away, towards Dad and the auctioneer. They discussed the reserve prices on the large equipment. If the bids were below a preset level, they did not have to sell. The banker had told Dad what reserve prices to set.

The auctioneer was a little man with a limp who always carried a carved wooden cane. Harry didn't think he really needed it to walk. It was more a badge of office, and when the auctioneer worked he used it dramatically, pointed to the item he was selling or shook it at a prospective bidder, encouraged one more bid. He wore a green vested suit with a Western cut and a white Stetson hat. He could have been a riverboat gambler.

One of his assistants obviously was his son, with the same small, predatory eyes and sharp nose, but he was much taller, and skinny, and carried a short buggy whip. He wore jeans and a plaid shirt, and a fleece-lined denim jacket. His Stetson matched his father's.

The other assistant was an older man with a large belly and soft, round face and his hands showed that he did no real work. He was bundled against the wind in a large brown overcoat and had on the only bowler hat Harry had seen in years. If it weren't for farm auctions, Harry thought, this group would sell Snake Oil.

He listened to Dad and the auctioneer for a while, but he didn't care. It was all just a game. Any way it went the bank got the money. Why should he try to get more for them? If there was a deficiency judgement, he would just disappear. But he wished that Judith hadn't signed the last refinance. And he wished that Shadow and the colt hadn't been on the list of pledged assets.

The day they all had signed that last loan, she kissed him gently in the pickup on the way home and said, "Well, its done, now." Only lately had he realized what she had meant and why her eyes had been too bright. And even knowing, she had stayed and worked and smiled. Until he had driven her away.

He still could not believe how he had treated Judith and the kids. It would be easier not to think about it, but he could not do that. He must think about it. He must never forget.

He had thought the problems were gone, buried with their last year in Seattle. He had made promises to Judith, and to himself, and he had not kept them. He was through with that. If he said it, he would do it, or he would say nothing. To no one. "Useless talk," the Old Man said, "Is the sign of a feeble mind."

He could go out into the coulees, lose himself in that twisted network of dry, ancient flood channels. He could set up camp under one of the rock shelters he and Judith had found and no one would ever find him. They had spent a lot of time in those canyons, hiked and looked for ancient campsites. With all his training in archaeology, he still was not as good as Judith at finding the campsites and lookouts that were scattered through the broken desert.

At first they took turns carrying Rebecca in a backpack and later Harry would carry her and Judith would carry Joseph. They had found numerous chipping grounds where stone points had been made. The ground sparkled with flakes hammered from pieces of flint and agate. There were many broken or flawed arrow heads and lance points thrown away by novices as they practiced their art. When the sun was right, refracted through the scattered fragments, red and blue and green, it looked as if a rainbow had been sprinkled across the earth.

Judith drew power and energy from the old sites. It was as if there she touched a great battery or reservoir, and she would sit silently, and stare into the distance while waves of emotion passed over her face like the cloud shadows that sailed across the desert.

One of their favorite places was a tall chimney rock at the junction of three coulees, a spire too strong to succumb to the great flood. It had taken them three attempts to find a route to the top. Judith noticed several overgrown steps cut by hand into the basalt to bridge the steep last few feet. Without the narrow steps the climb would not have been possible.

There were signs of prehistoric fires and the top of the rock was covered with chips and points left by bored lookouts. There was a view for several miles into all three canyons. They watched the children play at the foot of the tower and speculated about the time when some lookout first saw a white man in the coulees.

They had gone to their Rainbow Tower for a couple of years when one day they climbed the narrow trail to find the top had been dug up in several places and marked out in a grid with orange spray paint. There were several garish yellow signs that said, "KEEP OUT, Archaeological Site, State of Washington Department of Natural Resources." Judith shook her head and said, "The white man discovers America."

They had found several small springs, in notches hidden high in the coulee walls, and he knew that he could survive there. He could grow weed, ditch irrigate it from a spring, and probably make more money that he could ever make on the farm growing legal crops.

Or, he could go to Oregon, south of Ashland, in the Siskiyou Mountains, where Jeff Lasker, his smoking buddy from Viet Nam had gone. Harry had considered Oregon before, about a year after Rebecca was born, at a time when he desperately wanted to farm.

He and Judith had gone down to visit Jeff and his girlfriend, Lisa. Jeff came into Medford to meet them. On the telephone he told Harry with a chuckle that he should not try to get to the place by himself.

Jeff had learned his lessons well from the Viet Cong. A maze of deadly booby traps guarded the ten acres he'd bought on contract. He showed Harry the trip wires that would set off grenades and the false trails that led across cleverly concealed pits full of sharp steel stakes. He had several bear traps, with inch long razor teeth and triggers drenched in hashish oil.

"For the dogs," Jeff said. "They thought they'd get smart, send the dogs in to smell out the fields and then drop in by helicopter and miss the booby traps. The dogs can't resist the hash oil, though. They trained them well." He laughed in the brutal way Harry remembered from Viet Nam.

Jeff had enough firepower in his little hand-made cabin to hold off a battalion. He had handguns and an Ouzi and several high-powered rifles with scopes. He complained that he hadn't yet been able to get an AK-47.

Lisa was a hippie girl who looked about nineteen. She and Jeff had a little boy just older than Rebecca who crawled around in the dirt outside the cabin. Lisa was very happy to see Judith. Her hair was unkempt and it appeared to be impossible to get the cabin or anything in it clean. The orange-red dust clung to everything, and swirled through the air with every hot breeze.

Jeff took Harry up the hill to show him his plantation. He had nearly an acre of marijuana plants, several hundred of them, already over six feet tall and just beginning to flower. Jeff showed Harry the drops of iridescent resin that had begun to ooze from the buds. "That stuff is worth more than gold," he said. I'll make a hundred grand, maybe twice that. Then I'll build a real house."

Harry asked how he got away with it and Jeff asked him how many people he thought would come up the road they'd just traveled. And most of his neighbors, he said, were into the same thing and they protected the area as a whole.

"If you'd tried to drive up here by yourself," Jeff said, "you wouldn't have gotten within five miles. There are a lot of vets up here. Nobody fucks with us. They call us 'Bush Vets' and stay away. Two years ago, one deputy got his foot blown off trying to sneak into a place over the hill. That's the last time we saw anyone from the Sheriff's Department up here."

A neighbor, who lived in an old trailer on ten acres just below Jeff's place was moving to Costa Rica, and Jeff tried hard to convince Harry to move in. "You can just take over the payments. And after one year you can pay it off and not worry about anything."

Jeff drove him down the creek to visit another neighbor, a biker veteran called Reno, who had a small gold dredge. Harry watched the little machine float on the water while Jeff helped Reno use a large, heavy hose to suck up great quantities of silt from the creek bottom which he screened and sluiced and finished in a pan.

After two hours they had accumulated a small pinch of metallic flakes.

"You can make two hundred dollars a day, if you work hard," Jeff said. "You have to duck the Forest Service because they say it tears up the creek. But all these creeks were machine dredged back in the rush."

He showed Harry the huge piles of rocks and gravel the old dredges had spewed out along great stretches of the creek.

"There's still enough in those dredge piles to support you for a long time. Shit, Harry Olson over on Indian Creek found a nugget that weighed over an ounce and sold it to a collector for five thousand dollars."

They offered Harry a turn on the hose, but he declined.

Harry had told Jeff about the memorial to Rod Thornton the town wanted to build and how they made speeches about him at the American Legion on Veterans' Day.

Jeff laughed and said, "If the poor fuckers only knew. Well, I guess he did the right thing to be a hero. It sure would surprise the hell out of him, though. I wish he was here gettin' rich with me instead of turning into a statue covered with pigeon shit."

Jeff and Lisa had come to visit Harry and Judith in Seattle just before Christmas that same year. The crop had been good and they drove up in a brand new four-wheel drive pickup and spent money in a way that Harry had never seen. They took him and Judith to most of the good restaurants in the Seattle area in the two weeks they stayed, and they bought anything that even remotely appealed to them. Jeff seemed to have an endless roll of hundred dollar bills.

They were going to Mexico for the winter, then they would start on their house the next spring. Jeff wanted Harry to come down and oversee the construction for him. Someone else had bought the ten acres below theirs, but he was sure they could find something Harry and Judith would like. He even offered to loan them a down payment at no interest until Harry could get his first crop harvested.

"They're really leavin' us alone," he said. "The bastards know they owe us somethin' for our time in Nam."

Harry had been tempted again, but in the end decided against it. He would not let go of his dream of being a real farmer, growing food. Now, he wasn't so sure. Maybe he had just been a fool not to go.

The coffee from the concession trailer was almost as weak as Mom's. Harry threw the last of it on the ground and gave half the muffin to Reject. He wished again that he had gone into town with Ron.

An old, blue pickup with stock racks came up the lane and parked on the snowy field near the auctioneer's Continental. Two farmers in insulated coveralls got out and started to look at the equipment. Harry retreated to the canal bank and sat on a large rock.

Within a few minutes, two more pickups and a car came up the lane and parked. As he watched the crowd gather, Harry thought again of a hanging, only it was an entire family that was to be executed, while the survivors watched and were happy that this time, at least, they had escaped. He could not blame them, most of them were pressed hard enough as it was, and they had not created the problem. If they could buy equipment cheaper and thereby increase their own chances of survival, he could only wish them well. If the bank lost a little money - well, they had plenty.

It was still half an hour before the auction started, and already a sizable group had gathered. That was good news as far as prices were concerned. A line formed at the concession trailer. The murmur of voices floated with the smell of coffee on the wind. He watched the men in their jeans or coveralls, cowboy hats or baseball caps on their heads, and the women, mostly in jeans and boots. The children ran about madly, climbed on the equipment. These were his people.

"TESTING, TESTING, ONE, TWO, THREE..." the auctioneer checked out his P.A. system. His voice, electronically swollen and distorted, came from a little black box set up in front of the hand tools. He carried a wireless microphone. The antenna trailed from his hand like a skinny black snake. "All right, ladies and gentlemen, we will be starting in about fifteen minutes. There is some very fine stuff to be sold here today, so get your looking done and get ready to bid. There is hot coffee and lots to eat at the yellow and green concession trailer. We will break for lunch between twelve and one, and the big equipment will be sold immediately afterwards. The livestock will be last. Let's have a great auction, folks. I'm sure the Isaacsons will appreciate it." There was a burst of static as he turned off the microphone.

There were at least a hundred people, Harry estimated, and more vehicles came up the lane all the time. He saw Mom walk out on the deck to look at the proceedings then go back inside. Several of the close neighbors were there and many others he recognized. There was no sign of Jack.

Someone had brought a dog, a large German Shepherd, and Reject was gone to investigate before Harry could stop him. There was a flurry of barks and growls before the larger dog backed off in the face of Reject's territorial fury. Harry got up and walked slowly down towards the crowd.

Several people said hello, and he tried to be friendly. He liked them all well enough, he just felt his interest fade as he worked the problem of his own future. If it's done, it's done. Better to turn his back right now, and walk away, get on with his own life. But he had made commitments and wanted to remember this as a day when he, at least, had done what he said he would do.

He heard a horse whinny and looked up towards the corral. A group had collected there to look at the horses. He could see Shadow's head toss as she backed her colt into a safe corner and stood in front of him. Harry went around the back side of the corral and called Shadow over and calmed her. The old Percheron mare stood with head lowered, breathing heavily. He threw them a little more hay and hoped it would help them settle down.

CHAPTER 19

The crowd hushed at the loud pop from the speaker as the microphone was again switched on. "Okay, ladies and gentlemen, this is it. We're going to start here with the hand tools." A small part of the crowd collected around the auctioneer.

He held up a bucket of assorted bolts and nuts. "Now, folks, let's start off easy. Who'll give me a dollar for this?" A farmer in the front nodded his head and the auctioneer handed him the bucket. "Okay. You just give your name to Sally, over there," he gestured towards the blonde woman Harry had talked to earlier. Sally now stood at the edge of the crowd with a thick notebook, ready to record the sales. "And don't forget to pay us, now," the auctioneer reminded the farmer. A ripple of laughter passed through the crowd. Harry knew the auctioneer would first loosen them up, he was a professional.

The two assistants now stood on either side of the auctioneer, watched the crowd with hawk eyes. They would not miss a bid. At least half of those in attendance still roamed around not interested in the small stuff. Many would not even show up until lunchtime.

A few more boxes and buckets of miscellaneous hardware went in the same fashion as the first. A good auctioneer always walked a fine line between the buyers who wanted the lowest possible prices and the sellers, who wanted the highest. If he was successful, both sides would be pleased. His first job was to convince the crowd that things would be given away. Everyone knew the game, but still it worked.

The auctioneer limped over to a stack of shovels, hoes and other tools, and his skinny son carried the amplifier and speaker. "Okay," he said, and kneaded his bad leg briefly, "this fine collection of tools is what everyone needs for a complete farm. Buy them for your son, or daughter, or better yet, for your wife." That drew a general laugh.

"We'll sell these on a per item basis, but you take the whole lot. Who'll give me a dollar apiece?" An Old Man in overalls and a Stetson nodded. "Two dollars?" Someone else nodded. "Three?" Again someone agreed. "Four? Four dollars? Come on, folks, these are first class tools. Well broke-in." Another laugh.

"No? All right, this is your last chance... Sold, three dollars apiece to this gentleman. I hope you know you just stole these, sir."

Next came the table where Harry had put all the Old Man's hand tools, still carefully arranged in wooden and steel toolboxes. The auctioneer opened the lids so the crowd could see, held up a couple of boxes to show those in the back the neat rows of screwdrivers, and chisels and sockets, still polished, bright in the cold sun.

"Now, this is quality," he said and sounded sincere. To Harry, the old tools smelled of time and use. "What do you think?" the auctioneer asked no one in particular, "shall we sell them box at a time, or the whole lot?"

"The whole lot," a man's voice came from the back of the crowd, "let's get movin'. It's cold as hell."

"Okay," the auctioneer assented, "the lot it is. Who'll start it at two hundred dollars? If you went to Sears and bought this it would cost you two thousand. Some of this stuff," he held up a needle-sharp awl, "you can't even find anymore. And this steel. This isn't some cheap Japanese junk; this is real American steel. Two hundred?"

The crowd was silent. A couple of farmers in the front walked away to look at one of the tractors. "I don't believe this," the auctioneer rapped his cane on the table. "I thought we had farmers here. Farmers know tools. Come on, now, two hundred?" His two assistants searched the crowd for a silent bid. Nothing.

"Come on, folks," the skinny son echoed. Still no response.

"One fifty?" Still nothing. The auctioneer shook his head in mock disgust. "The steel alone is worth more. Some of these toolboxes would cost you fifty dollars apiece if they were empty." The crowd was getting restive. "Okay, a hundred dollars."

"I'll give fifty," said an unshaven man in greasy coveralls.

"Fifty dollars?" the auctioneer almost shrieked. "Fifty dollars? Are you folks going to let Jake get away with this?" He nodded towards the man and paused. Three more people walked away, towards the concession trailer. "Fifty dollars it is," he shook his head sadly, then, "Sold to Jake's Scrap Metal."

Next, the auctioneer almost gave away some small equipment items, hydraulic cylinders and hoses and some cultivator tools. Harry knew that he was just trying to get the crowd back, get their appetites up.

Then they started on the Old Man's farm equipment. The auctioneer led them over to the Farmall Model M that the Old Man had hauled out from Kansas, the tractor that had first plowed up the ground where they now stood. Harry went around the side of the tractor, made sure it was out of gear and hit the starter button. The engine exploded into life. Harry revved it a couple of times, then throttled down to a smooth idle.

"This is an old timer," the auctioneer said. He patted the faded red cowling and talked above the sound of the engine, "but obviously well-kept. I happen to know that this belonged to Mr. Isaacson's late father, Henry. Many of you knew Henry, I'm sure, and know how he maintained his equipment. I wouldn't be surprised if this one was running in another twenty years. And it will still out pull any of those Jap machines." He got the laugh he expected.

"Let's start it at five hundred dollars. And I do mean start. We aren't going to let you steal this one." For the first time that day, he broke into the high-pitched familiar chant of the auctioneer. Like a priest's incantation, Harry thought, at a requiem.

"Five hundred, five hundred dollars do I hear five hundred?"

"Yess," his skinny son hissed and sharply cracked the buggy whip, startled a couple of people.

"We have five hundred now five fifty five fifty do I hear five fifty?"

"Yep." This time it was the twangy southern voice of the heavy man in the bowler as he pointed into the crowd.

"Five fifty five fifty now six hundred, Six hundred six hundred now let's have six hundred. Five fifty do I hear six hundred?"

"Yess." Crack.

"Now six fifty six fifty."

"Yep."

"Seven hundred..."

"Yess."

"Seven fifty seven fifty do I hear seven fifty? Seven fifty just seven hundred and fifty dollars." He paused for breath and tipped back his Stetson to wipe his forehead. "This is a good one folks. Do I hear seven fifty?"

"Yep."

"Okay seven fifty do I hear eight? Eight hundred dollars eight hundred eight hundred."

"Yess." Crack.

"Now eight fifty?"

"Yep."

A young longhaired man in patched jeans, with a pretty woman beside him, was bidding against one of the older farmers. Harry wondered if the farmer really wanted the tractor.

He knew most farmers had no use for the hippies who tried to scratch out a living on marginal places. There was something a little too third-worldish about farming by hand with a minimum of power equipment. It made them feel uneasy, as if things were going backwards.

"Nine hundred nine hundred we have eight fifty now nine hundred. We have eight fifty now nine hundred. Nine hundred dollars."

"Yess." Crack.

"Now nine fifty nine fifty we have nine hundred dollars now nine fifty." The auctioneer paused and looked at the older farmer whose turn it was to bid. "Are you going to let him have it, Jim? For nine hundred dollars? That's an awful good buy."

Several people in the crowd agreed.

Harry reached over and hit the ignition switch, killed the engine.

"A thousand dollars," Jim said and looked at the younger man.

"We have a thousand now ten fifty ten fifty."

The younger man nodded his head determinedly.

"Yess."

Jim turned his back, and walked a short distance away, shook his head in disgust.

"Ten fifty ten fifty now eleven. We have ten fifty now eleven."

"Sell it," Harry said in a low voice.

"Okay, sold. To our longhaired friend here. You got a good tractor here, son. I hope you know what to do with it."

Several people laughed, but the young man walked over to the tractor and stroked it. The woman watched him with a smile, and Harry could see tears in her eyes.

Harry introduced himself to them and showed the proud new owner some of the idiosyncrasies of his tractor. His name was Jay Taylor and his wife was Sara.

They had bought a rocky thirty acres between Soap Lake and Stratford. Jay said he drove a hundred miles a day to work in an apple-packing shed near Wenatchee. Sara waited tables at the Basin House in Ephrata. They had managed to save over five thousand dollars in the last year, and Jay intended to buy some more of the Old Man's equipment. Harry told him which pieces he considered the best and talked to Sara while Jay followed the auctioneer.

They wanted to grow organic produce, Sara said, but they had planted only five acres this year, worked the ground with an old rototiller. They had lost a lot to insects, and the soil was more alkaline than they expected, so some crops had turned yellow and never produced. Even so, they had provided a lot of their own food and had sold fifteen hundred dollars worth to a co-op in Seattle.

This year they had made arrangements for a hundred tons of manure from a dairy farmer if they could get a truck to haul it. She was very happy about the tractor.

Harry envied them.

Jay managed to buy the Old Man's offset disc for three hundred and no one bid against him for the cultivator bars and tools, and he got those for his opening bid of a hundred. He also bought a drag harrow and an ancient tumblebug plow.

Jay could do a lot with the old equipment, Harry thought. You couldn't farm a thousand acres with it, but who wanted to. It would handle Jay's thirty acres easily if he took care of it. Besides, it was more equipment than he had, more than the whole family had now. Uncle Paul's eighty out in the rocks was the only Isaacson farm that remained.

Harry wondered where Uncle Paul was. He had said he would be there. It wasn't like Paul to duck it. Paul had more guts than all the rest of them.

The auctioneers moved on. Jay came back to where Harry and Sara stood. "Let's beat the lunch rush," he said, "I want to bid on the trucks afterwards."

Harry said no, he wanted to follow the auction and he watched them walk away, hand in hand. The crowd around the auctioneer was larger now, as they sold some of the newer equipment. The bidding was furious on the field sprayers and fertilizer spreaders. The auctioneer quietly remarked, "This is more like it," and winked at Harry.

Harry had intended to keep a running total, but he had lost track while he talked to Jay and Sara. He saw Sally on the edge of the crowd, notebook in hand, and he maneuvered around behind her, looked over her shoulder. She noticed, smiled up at him. She held the notebook so he could see. The total was barely over fifteen thousand dollars. But they hadn't yet started on the big stuff. The real money would come after lunch.

Sally turned, smiled again. He moved to the other side of the crowd and followed along. As each item sold, he deducted the commission and added the price to the total, applied it against $585,000. There still was a long way to go, even when they sold the land and buildings.

Just before noon another flurry of traffic came up the lane from the highway. For most of them an auction was as much a social occasion as business. Whole families came for lunch. Later there would be a change in the crowd as those interested more in the livestock arrived.

Harry's family had always raised livestock as well as cash crops, but there was a distinction yet between "farmers" and "ranchers." The animosity went back to the late eighteen- hundreds when the large ranches fought against the Homestead Act and bitterly contested the fencing of the plains by homesteaders. Harry was sure Dad would have gotten rid of the livestock long ago, he was a dirt farmer. But the Old Man would never have allowed it.

"The feud," he had once told Harry, "wasn't between farmers and ranchers, it was between outsiders and locals. The big ranches were owned by railroad presidents and English Lords who paid their managers to do whatever kept the profits comin'. If it wasn't for the Homestead Act they would have owned the whole West. They tried hard enough and killed enough people in the process."

Harry knew the story. One of the Old Man's great uncles had been killed in a range war. With three of his brothers, he had filed a homestead on 160 acres along the Arkansas River west of Dodge City in 1872. He happened to pick the favorite fall watering place for one of the British cattle companies.

The ranch boss had tried to buy the land cheap, then to scare the family away. In the end they'd had Uncle Ben shot in the back from cover, bushwhacked. No one had ever been charged with the crime.

The widow hung on with her eight children. The brothers, including the Old Man's grandfather, took turns, guarded the place and helped her work the land until her boys were old enough. In the end they beat the West Arkansas Cattle Co. Harry hoped that there was some of that grit left in him. He had a feeling he would need it.

"Okay, ladies and gentlemen," the auctioneer said, "that's it for this morning. We want to thank you for coming out here on this cold day to help us out. Remember, now, the large equipment will come next, at one o'clock, and the livestock after that. Now have a good lunch and we'll see you at one."

There already was a sizable line at the concession trailer, and Harry saw Sally hurry over to help her mother. He decided to wait until the line was clear before he got something. He could go in the house for lunch, but that would mean talking to Mom again. He wished Jack would show up, after all, so she would have someone to listen to her complain.

"God bless you, Harry." A voice close behind Harry startled him, then he had to check a sarcastic response. He turned slightly and acknowledged Reverend Hale with a distant nod.

"Is your mom in the house?" asked the plump little man. "I came to bring her the love and support of the Lord."

Harry wondered if they taught that sanctimonious voice in Baptist Theological School or if it was a prerequisite.

"Yeah," Harry said, "I guess so."

"We would certainly like to see you in church, Harry." The preacher reached his fat hand towards Harry's.

Harry started to shake it by reflex, but stopped.

"It's at times like this, Harry, that the Lord can help the most." He put his cold-reddened hand back in the pocket of his cheap overcoat. "It is only through prayer that the trials and tribulations of this world make sense." He shivered and turned up his collar. "We must keep our thoughts on His master plan. Remember He has His eye even upon the sparrow."

"It's the bankers HE should keep his eye on," Harry said, "it would do us farmers more good."

"Bitterness does not become you, Harry. Remember, there is a time for every purpose under heaven."

"It's the purpose I can't figure out," Harry said.

"Sometimes, Harry, the only way the Lord can get our attention is to bring us to our knees. Remember what Jesus said about the proud and the stiff-necked."

"That wasn't Jesus," Harry said, "it was Paul. He thought everyone who disagreed with him was proud and stiff-necked. And he didn't even know Jesus, as I recall. He was just a Roman stooge working undercover. They paid him to change sides and rewrite the Gospels."

The preacher nervously clasped his fat belly and rolled his eyes heavenward. "I'll be praying for you, Harry. I'll go see Sister Isaacson, now. She needs me." He waddled towards the house, and Harry could see his head move as though he talked to himself.

Despite the cold wind and the snow on the ground, lunch began to look like a Fourth of July picnic. Children played tag around the machinery. Groups of adults stood here and there or sat on various pieces of equipment. He half-expected someone to come up with a softball and start a game.

The line at the concession trailer was short, so he decided to get some lunch himself. It would be good to talk to some of the neighbors, it might be the last time. He would miss them in a way he never had before.

Harry walked through the crowd, nodded and said hello to a couple of people that he knew, but they were busy talking, didn't notice him. He wished Ron would show up. Ron had said he would be back at lunchtime.

When he found the end of the line, he saw that two of the close neighbors were there, part of the group who met in town every morning for coffee.

"Hello, Ed," Harry said, "Harold."

Both men looked up as if they were surprised to see him. Harold nodded, but didn't make eye contact.

"Oh, hello, Harry," Ed said. "Haven't seen you at coffee in a while."

"No," Harry said, "I don't care much for the new place. Or some of the company." He looked at Harold.

"Oh, the Desert Aire is okay," Ed said, "Kinda out on the edge of town, though, and uppity. I liked it better down at the Owl myself. But, what can you do when you're outvoted?"

"Yeah," Harry said, "I guess."

The two men turned slightly and continued their conversation.

"I don't know, Ed," Harold said, "I know some people are havin' trouble, with interest rates and all."

Harry saw Harold give him a little sideways look. "But I think Reagan has really been good for the country. And for farmers."

"Maybe so," Ed said, "but I don't see it. I think he's too pro-big-business. Things could get out of hand. They want to take everything. Ordinary people need to be protected, too. We need small farmers."

"Farmin's a business, too. Pro-business is pro-farm in my book."

Harry couldn't restrain himself. "The only thing I heard Reagan say about farmers," he said and forced Harold to look him in the eye, "was that they should keep the wheat and export the farmers. Sounds real pro-farm."

"He was talkin' about the lazy farmers," Harold said, "the ones that can't cut it. Like that hippie kid that bought your granddad's tractor. They aren't doin' the country any fuckin' good. I agree with Jim about 'em. Ship 'em to Russia. And it's sure as hell nice to have a president that ain't afraid to stand up to the assholes. I'm sick and tired of this weak-kneed bullshit. Dutch Reagan wouldn't have lost in Viet Nam." Again he looked sideways at Harry.

"I just hope Reagan doesn't start nothin' he can't finish," Ed said. "He's too old. The world has changed. We can't solve our problems by fightin' any more."

"Old, hell. I hope he starts plenty and finishes it, too. We should have kicked the Russians' asses right after World War II. We coulda pushed them all right into fuckin' Siberia where they belong. But Roosevelt always was a pussy when it came to the Russians. His wife was a communist. But Reagan won't never buddy up to those bastards."

"I was there," Ed said, "in Berlin when we hooked up with the Russians. We got along fine. Pretty nice guys, some of them. And I don't think we'd have pushed them anywhere. They were beatin' the Germans bad.

"You sayin' we should be afraid of them bastards?" Harold was belligerent at this.

"No. I'm just sayin' they wouldn't have been a pushover the way you like to think. Besides, they were our allies. They fought hard."

"Allies, hell. That was Roosevelt's fuckin' idea, too. Lend-Lease! We shoulda let Hitler have 'em. Or used the atomic bomb on Moscow. God didn't give America the bomb for nothin'."

"Where were you in the war, Harold? What outfit were you in?" Ed's voice betrayed anger.

"Shit, I wasn't in. You know that. My leg, you know." Harold moved forward a couple of steps with an exaggerated limp. "I got my knee smashed when I was a kid, so I couldn't go. I tried."

"Four F," Ed said. He looked at Harry, but said nothing else.

Harold had told them all, when they still had morning coffee at the Owl, that America had a sacred duty to use nuclear weapons to defeat communism.

"We blew it," Harold said, "in Viet Nam. Disobeyed God, by God. Lost our faith. We shoulda nuked Hanoi. When Jane Fonda was there. Shoulda stuck one right up her pretty little ass."

Everyone but Harry laughed at that.

"I'm not sure you could call it a sacred duty," Reverend Hale said, "but it could all be part of the plan. The Lord does work in mysterious ways."

"I don't think we needed nuclear weapons in Viet Nam," the banker argued. "We just needed the liberal politicians to turn us loose. And some fighting spirit from our soldiers. We needed soldiers who wouldn't be corrupted by drugs and foreign women."

"It was them long-haired bastards," Jim said. They wouldn't shut up. Workin' for the anti-Christ, if you ask me. Every time some gook kid accidentally got shot they put it on the front page. Not a word about our POWs bein' tortured in Hanoi."

"The anti-Christ has many tools," Reverend Hale said, "Many tools." He stretched a fat hand across the table for the sugar, dragged his cuff in his coffee. "There could be one or more of his minions sitting right here in this room." He poured a generous quantity of sugar in his coffee, stirred it and slurped noisily. "I hope you all have sent your letters off to Procter and Gamble. They still use that devil symbol on all their products, that crescent moon with the stars. It's the mark of witchcraft. Same mark the Ayatollah uses, I hear. I have a Xerox of the letter right here that you can copy." He pulled a folded paper out of his pocket and laid it on the table. "How about you, Harry, have you sent a letter yet?"

"No," Harry said, "and I won't. That symbol doesn't mean anything."

"I'm sure you really believe that, Harry, but I was told, and on good authority, that Procter and Gamble made a pact with the devil a long time ago, so they could get the business off the ground. Now their time is comin' to pay him back. We have to battle the anti-Christ wherever he shows himself."

"I saw an article," Harold said, "In the old lady's prophecy magazine. The Chief of Naval Operations said that when the marines got bombed in Beirut last April, it was the work of the anti-Christ. Admiral Watkins, or Watson, or somethin'. Anyways, this preacher or prophet, whatever, writin' in this magazine, says the anti-Christ himself was drivin' that truck and jumped out at the last second. One of the sentries saw him."

"I heard," Jim said, "that the last thing Reagan is gonna do when he leaves office is push the button. The idea, I think it comes from Pat Buchanan or Jerry Falwell or someone. The idea is that if we start World War III, it will force the anti-Christ into Armageddon. The Lord would have to come back, have the Second Comin' right then. He would clean up the environment and everything, heal the land. He says we don't have to worry about all these oil spills and radiation and everything because Jesus will cleanse it all before he starts his thousand-year reign. Make it just like the Garden of Eden."

"Sounds crazy to me," Harry said.

Everyone glared at him but Uncle Paul and Ron Radford. Ron laughed and said, "Right on."

Paul smiled slightly and his eyes met Harry's.

"It's not crazy, Harry," Reverend Hale said. "Where's your faith? I hear the President has people who give him briefings regularly on the Book of Revelations."

"He'd need briefings," Ron said, "or something, to understand all that Gog and Magog nonsense."

"Don't blaspheme, Ron," Reverend Hale said. He took a large bite from a strawberry jelly doughnut, dripped jelly across the table. "We're the last generation. It's up to us to keep the faith until Jesus gets here."

"He better hurry up," Harold said. "These fuckin' Russians worry me. Evil empire the President said. They've got all those space stations and stuff. One of these days they'll just start throwin' bombs out the window when they go over. And we don't have no way to do anything about it."

"Space programs are a waste of time," the preacher said and wiped his mouth with the back of his hand. "Space programs just distract us from preparing for the Second Coming. That Challenger explosion was just a warning from God."

"We don't need to worry about Russia," the banker said. "I heard through my back channel that this Star Wars thing is in the bag. You remember Edward Teller? He's the one that invented the H-bomb and stopped Eisenhower from making peace with the Russians in the fifties. Anyway, Teller has invented an X-ray laser the size of an executive desk that can shoot down a thousand Russian missiles with one shot. They do it with mirrors."

"Bullshit," Harry said. "Every responsible physicist in the country says that Teller is crazy. He's eighty years old, anyway. He's lost touch with reality."

"I don't think you understand these things very well, Harry," the banker said. "My back channel goes right to the White House. I have faith in him."

"Praise the Lord," the preacher said. "If Ronald Reagan believes it, I can believe it. Harold would you pass those doughnuts over here."

CHAPTER 20

"Harry," Ed said. "Harry you're next."

Sally smiled and gave him a slight wink. "What can I do for you?"

"Cheeseburger," Harry said, did not return the smile. "And fries. And coffee."

He carried the plastic-coated cardboard tray over towards one of the trucks. He had seen several of the old United Farms Co-op members there and he decided to eat with them. But apparently they were finished, and left as he approached. He sat on the bed of the truck anyway.

The cheeseburger was dried out from the microwave, the fries still frozen in the middle. He threw the cheeseburger to Reject, tossed the fries under the truck. With all the other litter scattered around the place today, it wouldn't make any difference."

He jumped off the truck and headed for his trailer. He needed to get away. He couldn't make any decisions out here, pissed off.

He avoided the crowd. There was no point in more close encounters of the weird kind. Halfway to the trailer, he saw Ron's Mitsubishi coming up the lane. He cut across, intercepted Ron before he had a chance to park. He got in. "Get the fuck out of here, he said."

"What's wrong with you?" Ron asked as he turned the little car around. "You look like you just saw the devil."

"No," Harry said, "But that son-of-a-bitch was out here this mornin' too, in his Mercedes."

Ron laughed. "He really has gotten to be an asshole, hasn't he? The last time I saw him he was on my case about drugs. Said he'd heard I was a cocaine addict. He was tryin' to give me the idea that my dad couldn't get any more loans if I didn't straighten out. I don't do that much coke, and I didn't ask him for any fuckin' loan. Or advice."

"Yeah," Harry said, "he's a regular asshole."

"Want a hit?" Ron asked and held out a little bronze colored bottle, a tiny silver spoon. "It'll do you good. Make you forget that asshole and the rest of them."

"No," Harry said. "I need to keep my head straight. I need to figure out what the fuck I'm goin' to do. There isn't much that sounds good."

"I told you, you could work for us, any time. Dad would hire you. Be a fuckin' executive. It beats the hell out of farmin'."

"No, I'm not goin' back to the coast."

"Judith's there," Ron said and Harry winced. "She'd like to see you. You know she would."

"No thanks. I screwed that up enough."

"So what's got you so pissed off?"

"Oh, just Ed and Harold arguin' again. Made me think of havin' coffee at the Owl and that really pissed me off."

"You know Harold," Ron said. "He's always blowin' his mouth about somethin' he doesn't know nothin' about. Remember how he used to carry on about Gog and Magog and the anti-Christ hidin' behind every sagebrush?"

"Yeah, I know, but nobody used to listen to him, everyone knew he was just a jerk. Now they either agree with him, or you can tell they're afraid to argue, even though they know it's all bullshit."

Ron laughed. "Like 'Supply Side Economics?' Have you heard him explain that one?

"Hey," Harry said, "there are a lot of people who believe it. Think Reagan has come up with a miracle."

"He's a miracle all right," Ron said. "Like Herbert Hoover returned from the dead, that's what your Uncle Paul told me. He said trickle-down economics means we get what trickles down their legs."

"The thing that worries me," Harry said, "is Reagan tryin' to start a war, like Ed says. He tries every time there's a chance."

"Just like Harold, for sure," Ron said. "Never been in a war, except the movies, so it sounds like great fun. Someone else gets to fight, while he talks macho."

"And passes out medals, like the one they gave Rod," Harry said.

"You should tell 'em all, Harry. About Rod. Maybe it would wake some of 'em up."

"I don't think so. Besides, it wasn't his fault. He was just like the rest of us. If they want to think he was a hero, let 'em. He was, in a way. Someone has to be."

They had come to the interchange with I-90. "What do you want to do, Harry?"

"I don't care."

Ron took the entrance to the freeway, and headed West towards Vantage. He maneuvered around a semi and a camper, then accelerated. The little car leapt forward; the turbo's scream fell behind. Harry watched the speedometer climb over a hundred and level off at a hundred and twenty. He lay back in the seat and closed his eyes. If he was lucky, maybe Ron would lose control, cross the median and take a truck head-on. Or go over the cliffs into the Columbia. He understood Rod more all the time.

Rod had been too sick to do it himself. They watched the sick ones, sometimes took away their ammunition. And it wasn't the sort of thing you could ask someone in your platoon to do. But there was a way. He could still carry a rifle, he could volunteer to walk the point once more. If they thought he had his shit back together, they'd let him do it. He was a good point.

It fit, he told Harry, he had walked point many times, cheated death. He owed it. For the balance. His hand shook violently as he gripped Harry's arm. And he wanted to do it straight, not wasted. In three more days he could control the shaking. They weren't due out until the day after.

Rod's reddened eyes glistened. "Who knows?" he said, "I might get a medal. Purple heart, at least." He had pulled his field-jacket tight around him.

It would be easier, Harry thought, to crash through the guardrail and tumble, slowly, irrevocably, down into the strangled river. Even if you missed the water, were dashed to death against the rocks it would be better, sudden, no other human to blame. Death always mocks the killer.

Shadows flickered across Harry's eyes, and he opened them, still alive, saw through the open sunroof the green arches of the Columbia River bridge. "Let's get a cup of coffee," he said, "I'm not ready to go back yet."

"Okay," Ron said. "I've got nothin' to do. As usual. I hate that, you know. Sometimes I wish to God we were still farmin'. It wasn't that bad, I mean the work. And at the end of harvest there was always this feelin' like you had done somethin' real. And important. I hate nursin' homes. People are just brought there to die, and the quicker they get it done, the cheaper it'll be for their family. They just throw the old folks away. I told Dad once that 'Radford Retirement Environments' should be 'Radford Human Refuse Disposal.' It really pissed him off."

Harry laughed. "I can't imagine the Old Man in a nursing home. He would have raised bloody hell."

"For sure," Ron said as he parked in front of the Riverside Cafe. "Old Henry sure did say what he thought."

"You know," Harry said, "I think they send the old people away because they don't want to hear what they have to say. Mom was always on Dad's back to make the Old Man retire so they could do whatever they wanted with the place. It only took them five years after he died to run it into the ground. And it was the Old Man's place, really, his money. I think they would have sold out long ago and gone south, but by the time the Old Man died they were in too deep."

"The old people are dangerous," Ron said. "Lock 'em up and say they're senile."

"That generation wants to throw everything old away, includin' their parents," Harry said. "I guess when their time comes we'll just throw them away, too."

"It'll serve 'em right."

They ordered coffee and it was good, for restaurant coffee. Harry drank his greedily. "God, I need my stimulants," he said.

"I've got a better one," Ron winked. "A guaranteed wake- up."

"No," Harry answered. "No thanks."

"Well, I'm goin' to," Ron headed for the restroom. He was back in a few minutes, rubbed his nose with a smile. "Better already," he said.

Harry finished his coffee. Ron was restless. His face was flushed and there was a fine film of sweat in the hollows beside his nose.

"Let's go," Harry said. "I may as well get back and face it."

They drove for a while, did not talk. Harry listened to the high whine of the engine and the tumult of the air as they passed through it.

Then Ron said, "You know, Harry, it's still too bad the United Farms Co-op didn't work out. Everyone thought you had a great idea. But they were afraid they would lose control. As if they had any control."

"Your family, your dad has control all right," Harry said.

"No, not really. It just seems that way, but it's an illusion. You just do what they tell you to do and it looks like you have control. All you really get is money."

"But that first nursing home move, that was a good move, timed just right."

"Sure it was. By accident. The bank ordered it. Not ordered, I guess. Let's say strongly suggested. The banker had a friend on the coast, a developer, builds nursin' homes. He needed to sell one, bad, and we had the money. No, actually, we had the credit. The banker set it all up. My dad didn't know a nursin' home from a hardware store. "

"Is that why he fought the co-op, too? The banker?"

"Yeah. More or less. The banker kept tellin' him, tellin' everyone that you were just tryin' to compete with legitimate institutions and that everyone involved would live to regret it. That's why all the neighbors gave in, on the takeover. That and the couple of thousand they made sellin' their stock to his buddies from the coast. I think the banker was scared to death. The farmers wouldn't have needed him, if the co-op worked."

"That son-of-a-bitch," Harry said, "sometimes I can just see his rodent face in my rifle sights."

Ron grinned.

At Adams road, Ron nudged Harry's arm. "Hey, man. You ready to go back?"

"No," Harry said. "Not yet."

"Let's go into town," Ron said, "Have a cup of coffee at The Owl. I want to show you somethin'. At the Extension Office."

"What?" A new secretary?"

"A satellite picture."

"A satellite picture?"

"Yeah, of the Black Sands."

"I don't care," Harry said. "I could use another cup of coffee."

Ron parked on the side street and they walked around to the front of the building, followed the sign, "Grant County Agricultural Extension Office."

"You gotta see this," Ron said.

The satellite photo was on the wall across from the counter. It was a beautiful enlargement, about three by six feet, a view of a part of the Earth from space.

"Now, get oriented," Ron said. "Here's I-90 cuttin' across and makin' the turn to Vantage. This is the old Morrison Road crossin' the White Trail. Now, straight across, see all these circles, like somebody shot it with buckshot? That's the Black Sands. See that one, and that one?" He showed Harry two of the dark, round spots, which stood out from the patchwork of the photograph. "And these two over here. Those are ours. This was taken in spring, last year. I was workin' over there all

Spring. I'll bet with a good magnifyin' glass you could see me sittin' in a Bearcat cab, plowin' away."

Harry laughed. "How deep did you go for water?" "Almost eighteen-hundred feet on one. Bet a bundle on that one. But if it works, it's like winnin' the lottery. Free money."

Roulette, Harry thought, on a grand scale. You could see the wheels from space. Plainer than the Russian missiles they showed during the Cuban Missile crisis.

Harry stood back a little and noticed a dark shadow, which ran from the northeast corner, down across the photograph, from the head of the Grand Coulee to the barren scab-rock of the Potholes country. It was the mark of the Great Spokane Flood and the multitude of small lakes pockmarking the shadow lay in crevices and basins whose soil the flood had boiled away.

"Let's go over to the Owl," Ron said. Have a cup, and see if Jeanette is there."

"I'll skip Jeanette," Harry said, "and take the coffee."

"You used to like her pretty good, in High School. She's divorced, now, and horny as ever."

"No, thanks," Harry said, "more important things on my mind."

"Since when is there somethin' more important than pussy?"

"Since I grew up," Harry said. "About a month ago."

They crossed the street, walked to the south end of the block. "Owl Cafe" the sign said in pale red and green neon. The professorial owl flashed his wide electrical wink. The sun streamed through the side-window blinds and bounced off the Kelly green naugahyde booths. The tabletop still was the same green marblette Harry had stared into so many times. The absence of wind inside annoyed him. It was too quiet; someone might hear his thoughts.

They sat down in a booth near the back.

"Hi, Doris," Ron said to the waitress who brought water and menus.

"Hi, Ron," Doris said and smiled a tired smile. "Harry! I haven't seen you in here in ages." She looked in his eyes. "Where ya been?"

"Just on the farm," Harry said.

"Yeah," Doris said, "I heard. I'm really sorry. It was so excitin' when you were havin' those co-op meetin's in here. It sounded like a real good idea. What do you boys want? Need a minute?"

"No," Ron said, "Just coffee, I guess. Want somethin' to eat, Harry."

"No, I'm not hungry. Just coffee."

"This place sure stirs up some ghosts for me," Ron said, when she left. "This used to be the center of the world."

"No shit," Harry said. "Couples used to come here for dinner on prom night. Now, they all have to go out to the Desert- Aire, be seen with the right crowd."

"And Sundays," Ron said, "we used to come here after church on Sundays. There would be a dozen farm families in here. And there's been a lot of business done in this old place."

"Business worked better when everyone did it here," Harry said. "I can remember

Matt Johnson takin' loan applications right here on Sunday afternoons. Then he'd come out and poke your sows in the belly and know how many pigs they were gonna have."

"Shit," Ron said, "This new banker wouldn't know a pig from a combine."

"No," Harry said, "But he sure knows how to talk you into puttin' it all on his asset lists. He'd like to have your grandmother on his asset list. Foreclose on her ass."

"Assets are all just shit," Ron said, "You can get shit again. It don't matter."

"No, some things aren't just shit," Harry said. "They're sellin' Shadow. And the colt."

"Judith's mare? So that's what's eatin' you."

"Yeah," Harry said, "That's the worst. And the Old Man's mare. They'll butcher her for dog food."

"Why don't you buy 'em?"

"I haven't got that much money. At least not enough for Shadow. Besides, if we fall short and there's a deficiency judgment, the bank could seize them by court order and sell them again."

"Why'd you put Shadow on the list? She was Judith's, she could have kept her off."

"She did," Harry said. "But I put her on, later, to get the banker off my back, and didn't tell her."

"Oh, shit," Ron said. "Is that why she left?"

"That was one reason. That, and me yellin' all the time. I wasn't a pretty sight. I was drunk for about two weeks straight after we found out the loans were called. I would have left, too."

"Why'd the banker want a horse on the list? They usually don't mess with that kind of stuff."

"Just didn't like me, I think," Harry said. "He was always tellin' me it looked like I was tryin' to hold out on 'em. Said the board needed to know I was really committed. And Judith. So I signed an amendment."

"But, if Judith didn't sign it..."

"No," Harry said, "I signed her name, too. At the time it seemed like there wasn't any choice. He held up last year's operatin' loan until I did it."

"How about your folks?"

"Oh, they knew. They both signed it, too. And Mom reminded 'em to add the Old Man's mare. Said we had to show good faith."

CHAPTER 21

"We'd better go," Harry said, "It's almost one thirty."

"No problem," Ron said, "We'll be there in less than ten minutes."

"That's okay," Harry said, "I want to be alive when I get there."

They had to park way out along the lane and walk through a sizable crowd. There were more rancher's hats and boots among the baseball caps.

"There they are," Ron said, and pointed out two new Ford pickups sitting side by side. The door of one had a sign that said SUNNY DALE FARMS, INC. The other, Harry knew, without looking at the sign, was from United Farms Corporation.

The auctioneer had almost finished the trucks. Harry thought for a moment that he saw Nathan up by the corral, but that was impossible. He had Judith on his mind too much.

Jay was bidding on one of the older trucks, a one-ton with a grain box that the Old Man had liked. Both Harold and Jim bid against him.

"Eleven fifty now twelve hundred twelve hundred. Eleven fifty now twelve hundred."

"Yess." As usual, Skinny punctuated the bid acknowledgement with his buggy whip.

"I have twelve now twelve fifty. Twelve fifty do I hear twelve fifty twelve fifty."

"Yep."

"And now thirteen."

"Yess." Crack.

"Thirteen fifty." The auctioneer paused and took a drink of water from a Styrofoam cup. He tipped back his hat, mopped the sweat from his forehead and then again attacked the microphone. "Do I hear thirteen fifty? Thirteen now thirteen fifty just thirteen hundred and fifty dollars."

Jay had bid thirteen. The auctioneer and his fat assistant both looked at Harold, who faintly shook his head, then they looked at Jim.

"Well, Jim, thirteen fifty?"

"Buy it, Jim," Harold shouted, "I'll go up to a thousand on halvers." Several people laughed.

"Fifteen hundred," Jim said and smiled.

"Fifteen now fifteen fifty."

Jay nodded.

"Yess," Skinny screamed.

"Fifteen fifty now sixteen, sixteen do I hear sixteen?"

"Two thousand," Jim said.

The auctioneer looked at him intently, then said with a grin, "Okay, Jim. I have two thousand now twenty fifty."

Jay turned away, his shoulders slumped a little, and he shook his head.

"Sold to Jim Thompson," the auctioneer said to Sally. Jim smiled triumphantly and went over to talk to Harold. Harry went over to look at Sally's notebook again. The total was now over fifty thousand.

"Harry," someone said close behind him, and for a moment Harry thought it was the Old Man. He turned and the hat, too, could have been the Old Man's. But not the eyes, one of them winked through the scar.

"Hi, Paul, "he said. "I wondered where you were."

"Had a little problem," Paul said and indicated with his head that he wanted to talk, away from Sally. Harry followed him to the edge of the crowd.

"That fuckin' banker was hangin' around out at my place this mornin'. Looked to me like he was takin' pictures of your Dad's trailer. Before I could get up there, he was gone, but I know it was his Mercedes. It looked like there was someone else with him, but I wasn't close enough to see good. Anyway, it bothered me, so I decided I better move the trailer."

"That bastard," Harry said. "I wonder who told him about the trailer. It's in your name, anyway. He can't do shit about it."

"He could, if they could prove your Dad bought it from farm proceeds. They could claim an illegal transfer."

"Fuck," Harry said. "Where did you put it?"

"Up at Ben's, you know, my neighbor with all the windmills. We stuck it in the barn and covered it with tarps. Ben don't like the banker nohow. Said he'd shoot the son-of-a-bitch if he came pokin' around there."

"Good," Harry said. "Someone ought to do it."

Paul looked at him hard, put his hand on his shoulder. "Don't be doin' anythin' stupid, Harry. It won't help nothin', now."

"Yeah," Harry said, "I suppose not, but it sure would feel good."

"Where you stayin' tonight?"

"Shit, I don't know. Sleep in my pickup, I suppose. I've slept in worse places."

"Come over to my place," Paul said, "I've got an extra bed. Then we can get your folks off in the mornin'"

"Okay," Harry said. "Where you goin'?"

"Back home. I can't do no good here. Besides, if that asshole comes around askin' questions, I might get mad and do somethin' stupid myself. Stay away from him, Harry. He'd love to have one of us in jail." Paul walked away, towards the lane.

In the relative quiet as the auctioneer led the crowd to the next truck, Harry heard someone call his name and involuntarily he turned, saw Mom on the deck. She called to him and waved. He threaded his way through the crowd, walked across the yard to stand beneath the deck.

"Have you seen your Dad," she asked him. "I haven't seen him for a while. The banker called and it sounded important."

"Not likely," Harry said. "No, I haven't seen him."

"Would you look for him, Harry. He needs to talk to the banker. He said he was coming right out. He asked me if you were here, too."

Harry got a sudden jolt of adrenaline in his stomach. "Yeah. I'll see if I can find him."

He worked his way back through the crowd, made no real effort to find Dad. He turned to look and saw that Mom had gone back inside, so he cut across to the canal bank and walked towards his pickup.

He saw Dad and three of his friends coming down the far canal bank, from the direction of the old place. One of them put a flask back in an inside jacket pocket.

Harry jumped across and walked to meet them. Dad looked up at him with a guilty smile.

"Hi, Harry," Chuck Henry, the one with the flask, said. "Wanta drink?"

"No," Harry said. "Dad, the banker wants to talk to you. He called Mom and said he would be right out."

"Shit," Dad said, and Harry could tell he had drunk quite a lot.

"Fuck 'im," Chuck said, and elbowed Dad in the ribs, "tell 'im to go to hell."

Dad laughed, swayed a little. Then his eyes cleared and he said, "No, I better go talk to him."

"I haven't seen him yet," Harry said, "but he told Mom he was coming."

"Okay," Dad said.

The other three men split off from them, walked towards the concession trailer. Dad and Harry headed for the heart of the crowd.

"There he is," Harry said and pointed to the near end of the lane where the Mercedes was parked, blocking in several other cars.

Dad turned to walk that direction, looked back at Harry. "Comin' with me?"

"No," Harry said, "I'd just get mad. That wouldn't do anyone any good."

He watched Dad walk, shuffle along, really. He looked so old, older than the Old Man when he died. The banker got out of his car and Harry saw that there was someone else with him, a tall man with sunglasses and a dark overcoat. Looks like a goddamned hit man, Harry thought, or a stockbroker. Probably one of the new board members Washington First appointed. They must be afraid of losing a bundle on this one.

Harry watched them sell the other trucks. They were all newer, and Jay didn't bid on any of them. He saw Ron and went over to stand beside him. "The banker's here," he said, "talkin' to Dad."

"Why don't you shoot him and get it over with."

Harry didn't laugh. Ron looked at him. "Hey, man, any time you want to get out of here, just let me know."

"Okay," Harry said.

Dad and the banker and the other man came towards them, and Harry felt that they talked about him. He turned his back to them, watched the bidding.

The auctioneer finished with the trucks and went on to the heavier stuff. The big potato digger went at a good price. Potato prices had been up last season, so there was a demand. Harry was sorry to see the big John Deere combine sell. He had spent many hours in the combine cab, listened to music on the tape deck while he watched the flow of wheat or corn or beans the augers whirled into the machine's four-foot throat. He would miss harvest.

With the disastrous conditions in the cattle market, they had expected the hay equipment to go cheap and it did. A wiry old rancher with a weathered face and a battered hat bought the self-propelled swather for $2,200. He told Sally he was from Chesaw, in the Okanogan Highlands, and Harry thought the Old Man would have liked the rancher. Perhaps the Old Man's spirit was somewhere still, hidden away, watching, waiting.

The two smaller tractors, a Massey-Ferguson and the John Deere Harry liked the best, were next. The Massey drew a lot of bids and sold for forty-five hundred. Then they started on the John Deere.

"Stay here," Ron said, "and watch this." He moved about thirty feet away, took off his dark glasses, and put on his serious face.

The bid started at twenty-five hundred and three farmers quickly bid it up to thirty-two. At that point Ron made a slight gesture caught by the fat assistant auctioneer. He focused on Ron who nodded.

"Yep," the fat man called and the auctioneer upped the bid a hundred. With four bidders the price climbed quickly. Harry kept his face serious and watched.

At four thousand, one of the farmers dropped out, but the other two stayed with Ron. At forty-five hundred another dropped out and Harry heard him say, "He's a ringer."

The remaining farmer had gotten into the competition. Harry watched him and Ron closely. All talk in the immediate area stopped. Ron looked at no one but the fat man and each time as soon as the auctioneer's skinny son hissed his "Yess." and cracked the whip, Ron nodded and the bid was thrown back immediately on the farmer.

At fifty-one, the farmer hesitated and Harry wondered if Ron would lose the game. But the "yess" came and this time Ron waited a few seconds as if he were at his limit. Then he nodded.

"Yep," said the fat man and this time the farmer did not hesitate to bid. Harry saw the corner of Ron's lip twitch, almost smile. Ron slowly nodded again, appeared on the point of defeat.

Immediately the farmer bid. Ron pulled out his checkbook and looked inside, pondered, then nodded.

"And now fifty-six," the auctioneer turned towards the farmer who said "Yes."

Ron spun on his heel and moved back to Harry's side, smiled. "That dumb bastard," he said, "There's a John Deere just like that one sittin' in at Donohoe's for forty-two with a guarantee and everything. Well it'll help a little."

"Thanks," Harry said.

He moved over to look at Sally's notebook. A quick estimate told him they were over seventy-five thousand. If the two big Bearcats brought the forty thousand they were worth, they would be within spitting distance of $585,000 once the land and the livestock sold.

Harry could see Dad and the banker and the other man just behind Ron, so he stayed where he was.

Sally smiled at him and winked. "How we doin'?"

"Fine," Harry said. The bid stopped at twelve five on the first Bearcat, just five hundred over the reserve price. No one else bid and the auctioneer said, "Sold, Sunny Dale Farms, twelve- five," and Sally wrote it down.

They started the second Bearcat at five thousand and worked it up slowly to seventy-five hundred. A farmer Harry didn't know bid against Matt Swenson, the manager from United Farms. Harry wondered where the manager from Sunny Dale had gone. If the other Bearcat was worth twelve-five to him, why didn't he bid on this one, too.

Then he realized that the Sunny Dale manager had made a deal with Swenson. They had come to the auction with an agreement not to bid against each other on the Bearcats. That way they each could steal one.

Harry saw that the banker and his friend had moved away and Dad's three drinking buddies were back, stood in a little circle around him.

"I have seventy-five now eight do I hear eight," the auctioneer chanted while his assistants searched the crowd. "Folks," he said, "you know this tractor is worth twice this, three times. Surely someone can use a fine machine like this." There was no response and a lot of the crowd was already on the way up to the corral, to get in position for the livestock. The auctioneer switched off the microphone, talked to Matt Swenson. Then he switched it back on. "We'll find out," his voice faded in, "I see the principal standing right over there. Mr. Isaacson." Harry looked at Dad and saw the flush, the dull eyes.

"Mr. Isaacson." Dad focused on the auctioneer. "The bid is seventy-five hundred. That's below your reserve price. Do we sell it or not?"

No, Harry thought, no fucking way. I'll burn the son-of-a- bitch for the insurance.

Dad swayed a little; Chuck talked to him. He shook his head and Chuck said something else.

"Oh, what the hell," Dad said loudly and waved his arm in a grand drunken gesture, "Let it go. I'm retired." Chuck smiled. Several people in the crowd laughed.

Harry turned and almost ran over the banker. The banker said, "Hello, Harry," and held out his hand. Harry pretended not to see it. "Harry, this is a friend of mine, Jerry Maxwell. He has something very interesting to talk to you about. When you have time."

"Not now," Harry said and ignored Jerry's hand also. "I need to get up to the barn. I have to help with the livestock."

"We'll wait," the banker said, gave Harry a level look, insisted.

Harry turned and walked towards the barn.

Dad and Chuck and the other two headed in the direction of the old place. Harry caught up with them, pushed in between Dad and Chuck. Dad looked up at him a little startled. "I had to do it," he said. There wasn't no point in fightin' it."

"I don't care," Harry said, "it's just a tractor. Come on up to the barn with me. See how we do on the stock."

Chuck looked at Dad, then glared at Harry.

"No, Dad said, "me'n the boys was just goin' to, uh, we're just goin' for a walk."

"I know," Harry said, "Mom's worried about you."

"About me, about what?" Dad's eyes were clearer, more focused and his voice was stronger.

"I don't know," Harry said, and squeezed Dad's shoulder, hard, tried to get through to him. "She just wants to see you, I guess."

"Well, tell that woman," Dad said and stopped, swayed a little as he tried to look at Harry. Chuck laughed his nasty little laugh.

"Tell her," Dad repeated, "we got business out here. We ain't got time for no prayin'. If prayin' was gonna help we wouldn't be havin' no auction. I saw the preacher comin' in his fuckin' Cadillac. She can do her prayin' with him. Or whatever."

Chuck started to laugh again, but Harry stopped it with a hard look.

"Okay," Harry said. "I'm goin' up to the barn." He watched them walk away. They laughed, bumped into each other like a group of high school kids.

CHAPTER 22

When Harry got to the corral, they were selling the yearling calves in lots of ten. He worked his way to the front and leaned on the top rail to watch. The late sun cast a golden shadow across their red and white hides and twin blasts of steam pulsed from their nostrils as they circled the cracking whip. Each group sold with two or three bids. Most went to the buyer from United Beef's feedlot operation. Most of the two-year-old breeding heifers also sold at feedlot prices.

The brood cows, each with a winter born calf, came next. It wasn't often that a quality breeding herd was broken up, and the prices were good. The rancher from Chesaw bought several of the best cows. Harry was happy that the buyer from United Beef showed no interest.

When the first of the bulls was let into the main corral Skinny scrambled up the fence which drew a laugh from the crowd. He sat on the top rail across from Harry, bravely cracked his whip and hissed his bid acknowledgements. Harry's favorite young bull would go to the Okanogan Highlands.

The auctioneer paused for a cup of water and said, "That's all the cattle, folks. We have the horses coming and that's it." About half the remaining crowd began to leave at that.

Harry's first impulse was to leave also. He really didn't want to watch. But he held his place and looked at the ground as the Old Man's Percheron mare was led in. Even when the whip cracked near her, then burned across her back, she stood stolidly in the center of the corral with her head down. Harry glanced at her, saw that her frightened eyes were on him. She tossed her head and pawed the ground in her confusion. Skinny jerked her head down with the halter and again put the whip across her back. She trembled and gasped through flared nostrils as the auctioneer's chant ordained her fate. When she was led away, she did not struggle, but stumbled woodenly, and her eyes showed Harry no recognition.

She went for two hundred dollars to a dirty, unshaven man Harry had seen leaning against a decrepit and stinking Chevy truck. He was a scavenger, a kind of carrion bird who roamed the farm country, hauled away dead animals to sell to the rendering plants and bought old or unwanted animals for the pet food companies. Skinny laid the whip across her once more, and closed the gate behind her.

Tears, how he hated tears. Long Joe had once told him that tears were the manifestation of the spirit, to be given as an offering to the dead. But it seemed to him now that everything made him cry, required an offering.

The wind gusted, drove dust into his eyes, and he was grateful for it. There had been no dust that day on the hill above Gook Town, and no rain, no excuse to give Jeff for the water that rolled down his face.

"It's kids, Harry," Jeff had said as they watched the procession. "They must've killed some kids. Look at that, four of 'em. Those crazy bastards. It's a good thing they're goin' back out. There's gonna be some trouble. There ain't no V.C in Gook Town."

Harry saw the woman he knew was their mother walk with another woman close behind the men who carried the cloth-wrapped bundles. He had known anyway, before he saw her, he had been sure. The heat weighed on his chest. The slight breeze that stirred carried the smell of human excrement.

"Hey, Harry. That's her. That's their mother, isn't it? I thought that was the hooch that was burnin'. Why the hell did they do that? Just celebratin' the Fourth?"

"I don't know," Harry had said.

"I heard some of 'em talkin', sayin' they didn't have no respect for Americans in Gook Town. Said they were gonna teach 'em a little lesson, show those whores how to act proper. But I never thought they'd just shoot up the place. It don't make no sense killin' kids."

"No," Harry said, "It doesn't make any sense."

"Ain't that the outfit your friend is in, that Rod, the junky?"

"Yes," Harry said.

"Well, shit, buddy, I guess them kids ain't gonna follow you around no more, with those big brown eyes, callin' you Daddy."

"No," Harry had said, "I guess not," and he had struggled against the tears. It was as if from that day forward his own pale blue eyes had looked out through those round dark eyes, and the world was different. He had tried to believe again, to have faith. But it wasn't all right. And he had sometimes wished that he had been with Rod four days later when he walked the point for the last time, gallantly led his platoon into an obvious V.C. ambush. For the balance.

There was a commotion in one of the holding pens and Harry saw the auctioneer's two helpers trying to separate Shadow from her colt. The mare whirled around to block the gate, reared and sliced her front hooves close to the fat one's face, knocked the Derby off his bald head. He staggered back and she struck at Skinny with a rear hoof. The colt shivered behind her and she pressed him against the fence. Her neck arched, her eyes glowed. Flecks of foam lathered her chest.

"Sell them together," someone called from the crowd. "That colt won't bring much anyway."

"Okay, boys, let's sell them together," the auctioneer boomed.

Skinny opened the gate and a tremor passed through the small crowd as Shadow danced into the main corral. The colt rubbed against her for comfort. Skinny cracked his whip once and Harry caught his eye and he did not do it again. The auctioneer quickly got a bid of five hundred dollars from a rancher Harry did not recognize.

Immediately the Okanogan Highlander jumped in, then Skinny hissed a bid from someone further into the crowd that Harry couldn't see.

Shadow reared again as she turned in the corner and the ripple of late shadows across her Appaloosa markings made the scene seem to pulse in negative/positive flashes. The taut colt clung to her and Harry could see the sweat slick his coat.

All three bidders were still in, although at fifteen hundred they responded a little more slowly. At two thousand the rancher Harry didn't know dropped out, but the Highland rancher and the unseen bidder continued. Finally at twenty-eight hundred the Highlander gave the horses a long, fond look then shook his head.

"Sold." The auctioneer switched off the microphone for the last time. "Who was it, son?"

"Who are you?" Skinny called into the crowd. There was a response Harry couldn't hear. Then, "Joe..." Skinny said, turned again to listen. "Joseph Longeaux, from Nespelem."

Harry braced himself against the corral and looked quickly down, shook away the unwanted tears. He felt intense relief. He was sure that Shadow and the colt would go to the freedom of Cache Creek. Then he realized that it must have been Nathan he had seen earlier, that Nathan had brought Long Joe to save Judith's most prized possession, her link with her mother's people. He was sure of Nathan's motives.

He wanted to see Long Joe. If anyone could give him a better perspective it would be that little man with the deep eyes. Harry ducked into the corral and helped Skinny move the horses into a holding pen near the loading chute. Then he slipped between the rails on the far side and pushed into the dispersing crowd to look for Long Joe.

He saw them from the back, first Nathan's tall, strong frame and square-cut hair, and beside him Long Joe's single shining braid. Harry put his hand on Long Joe's shoulder, and he turned, already smiled.

"Hello, Harry."

Nathan also turned and his eyes burned into Harry, probed him. He nodded silently and Harry returned it.

"Thanks," Harry said and felt foolish.

"No thanks," Long Joe said, "We have the horses. We should thank you."

"Judith will appreciate it," Harry said. "She loves that mare."

"Someone has to take care of her," Nathan said. "If not her own people, then who."

"Her other people," Long Joe said, "She has the blessing of two peoples."

"Some blessing," Nathan said, "My grandfather was white. It's certainly been a great blessing."

Long Joe chuckled. "Sometimes we don't recognize our blessings until it's too late."

"How did you know?" Harry asked, "about the auction?"

"A spirit came to me," Long Joe said and exchanged grins with Nathan. "In the city. It told me to get out of there, I'd had enough time in the big psychiatric ward. I was needed to help my friends Judith and Harry."

"Are you taking her to Cache Creek?" Harry asked, remembered the herd he and Judith had watched there.

"Yes," Long Joe said, "She deserves some freedom. And Nathan wants to ride her in the parade at the Stampede in Omak next summer. If it's okay?"

"She's your horse," Harry said.

"No," Nathan said, "She belongs to Judith. By gift. Horses should not be sold, only given. And Judith is with you."

"Judith isn't with me any more," Harry said and felt the fear rise in him.

"I know that," Nathan said, "But she loves you. I know that, too. Women, like horses, are not to be bought and sold. It is not your choice. And there are children. Your children." His look made Harry feel guilty.

"What are you going to do, Harry?" Long Joe asked softly. "I don't know," Harry answered. "I wish I did. I wish the Old Man was here.

"The old ones are always talking in our heads, if we just listen." Long Joe had turned those unfathomable eyes on him. "What do you want in your deepest dreams?"

Harry gritted his teeth against tears. "I just want to have my wife and family. And to grow things, produce food. To feel what I do matters."

"So do it," Long Joe said.

"But how? Land costs too much, and operating costs, you have to borrow money. I can't do that, now."

"Do you want to farm? Or play monopoly?" Long Joe asked.

Nathan laughed.

"There is always land," Long Joe continued. "And if you can't buy a tractor, get a horse. They're cheap. Except for flashy saddle horses like we just bought." He grinned. "But she wouldn't pull a plow anyway. Too uppity. I thought she'd kill one of those auctioneers."

"She should have," Nathan said.

"Where is there land?" Harry asked. "The only cheap land is no good." He thought of Jay and Sara struggling in the rocks over by Soap Lake.

"We have land," Long Joe said. "Good farmland even. Nathan's family has an allotment on the San Poil, just below Cache Creek, that his grandfather used to farm. A long time ago, with horses, too. I'll bet they would work something out." He grinned at Nathan. "For enough money."

"Maybe," Nathan said, and he looked at Harry through narrowed eyes. "My aunt has a hundred and sixty there. Did Judith show you? It's mostly rocks and timber, but there's about forty along the river, good bottomland. We run horses there sometimes, in the fall. She has a water right on the San Poil."

"I'd need a place to live. And I couldn't pay much. It doesn't seem possible."

"Probably not," Long Joe said. "It would be too much work. And it's not like playing with the big boys."

"I don't mind the work," Harry said. "I love the work. And I'm sick of this game. There's no way to win in it. They just use us."

"The big game," Long Joe said. "They want you to feel big and important, for a while. If you do as they say, you can play. If not, they will destroy you. White people all came here as slaves, and you have not yet learned to be free. You thought you were escaping, when you came from Europe, but you brought the slave system with you. Your churches, your governments, your businesses, all depend on slaves. Soul slaves, war slaves, work slaves. That's why they killed most of us, we didn't make good slaves. They said we were lazy and useless, because we would not do their work."

"How is it good to have televisions and cars and big houses, if you have no control over your life? If your children grow up as slaves? And in the end, you are taken away to die in 'Rest Homes,' alone and confused, like cattle waiting for slaughter? How is that freedom? My people have more freedom in a hut in the woods. We decide, we depend on ourselves. We die in the arms of our families. That is freedom. Freedom isn't things. When you were in the war, you didn't fight for freedom; you fought for things, things for other people. And wild ideas, slave ideas. What you call communism or capitalism is the same. Slaves working for bosses."

Harry saw Long Joe's eyes focus on something just behind him, and Nathan's followed.

CHAPTER 23

"Harry," the banker said, didn't acknowledge Long Joe and Nathan, "You need to talk to Jerry. We may have a way for you to take care of this - problem." His gesture vaguely included all of Harry's life. "I think you know we're a long way from where we need to be. Probably a hundred thousand or so." He talked as if Long Joe and Nathan weren't listening. Long Joe turned, and his finger tips lightly brushed Harry's hand. He led Nathan towards the corral.

"I guess I'll have to solve my own - problem," Harry said and started as if to follow Long Joe and Nathan. The banker put out his arm to restrain Harry, and Harry knocked it down. Several people in the departing crowd had noticed and turned to watch.

"Harry," the banker said, "I'm trying to help you. And your family. I know about the trailer over at your Uncle Paul's. I haven't told the board yet. And, like I told your Dad, I don't want to."

"That's his business," Harry said. "I don't have shit."

"But you might be able to help them. Don't you owe them that? I know your Christian spirit can't be completely dead."

Harry started to hit him, but he felt the trace of Long Joe's touch on his hand, and he had the strength not to do it.

"We want to help you, Harry, but a hundred thousand dollars is a lot of money. Much more than the trailer is worth. Is Judith still employed?"

"No," Harry said. "She lost her job. Nothing you can steal, there." He felt a momentary satisfaction in that. If you had anything, they would take it. If you had nothing, they forgot you, you ceased to exist. Instead of minus $585,000, you were nothing.

"We aren't the ones who steal, Harry. It is the failures in life who steal from all of us, the whole country. But sometimes we just have to take what we can get and be satisfied."

Harry knew then that he had to get out of the situation any way possible or he might kill the bastard. He remembered Jerry, behind the banker, probably armed. "You got what you're goin' to get, here."

"Well, you have no reason to be mad at Jerry," the banker said, "At least listen to what he has to say. I think it might appeal to you."

Harry felt them look at his tightly clenched fists and he forced his hands to open, to relax. Then he shrugged.

Again Jerry put out his hand, and again Harry ignored it. Instead, he walked towards the canal bank, indicated with a sideways nod that Jerry could follow. He moved into the long oblique shadow below the bank, turned and looked at Jerry. Even in the near dark Jerry retained the sunglasses, but Harry's eyes adjusted to the shadows, he could partly see through them. The eyes weren't deadly, but uncertain. Harry waited, enjoyed Jerry's discomfiture.

"We need your help, Harry," Jerry began, and his voice was higher than Harry expected.

"Who needs my help?" Harry asked, "The bank?"

"Not the bank. The country. I represent a group of people, patriotic, Christian people, who are very concerned about what's happening down in Central America. They are afraid the Communists will take over completely, including Mexico. It would be like sharing a border with the Soviet Union. We can't allow that."

"CIA," Harry said. Just like Viet Nam.

"No, this is a private group. But I can assure you the government shares our goals and objectives. At the highest levels. But their hands are tied by Congressional misunderstanding. Many of us feel liberal congressmen are part of a conspiracy to weaken the country, turn it over to the communists."

"I served my country once. In Viet Nam."

"We know that, Harry. We chose you because of your distinguished record."

"Not that distinguished," Harry said, "no more than many others."

"I've seen the records, Harry. You should be proud."

"How have you seen them? I thought this was a private group."

"It is. But I was in the military until recently. I retired to serve the group I work for now."

Retired, Harry thought. He can't be even forty. CIA.

"I know what you're thinking, Harry. But it's legitimate. We work from friendly foreign countries in the area. They are glad to have us, have faith in our program. You'd be a hero. To the people there, and to Americans, once they come to their senses."

A hero to the bankers there, Harry thought, and here. And the corporations. But not the people.

"What is it," he asked, "that you think I would be so capable of doing?"

"Like in Viet Nam. Supply. Logistics. There are plenty of freedom fighters there, in-country nationals. We just have to get the materiel to them. No combat. Just loading planes and keeping things straight, in a friendly country. A vacation, really, most of the time. One week off out of four. You can R&R in Belize or Cancun. They're almost as good as Saigon in the old days."

"I never cared for Saigon," Harry said. "They always acted like I was a foreigner."

Jerry ignored it. "We really need your help. And it could help your family a lot."

"It must pay pretty well, if it will help that much." He thought, if it's enough I could go for a while, save the money, take Judith and the kids somewhere, start over, sure as hell not give it to the bank."

"It doesn't pay that well. About two thousand a month. Of course you could draw some living expenses. And R&R transportation is free."

"How will that help? You heard him say a hundred thousand dollars." Harry started to walk away. "I'm not goin' down there for five years."

"No, wait," Jerry said and started to restrain him. He thought better of it, dropped his arm and stepped back. "We can't pay a lot, because the money is so limited. At least for right now. We're dependent on private donations. Not like the CIA. But we have friends, so we can pay in other ways."

"What other ways. The banker wants money."

"It would take care of that. Your friend," he gestured towards the banker, "helps us all he can. He believes that he can convince his board of directors to drop the deficiency judgment, write off the balance - if he can tell them that you're helping us, helping the country. He's only thinking of you. And your family."

Harry noticed that Long Joe and Nathan watched from the shadows beyond the corral, and he wondered what they would do if a fight started. Probably just watch the white men destroy each other. As Long Joe had always said they would. And wait.

"No thanks," Harry said. "Like they say, I've spent my time in hell."

"I'm sorry you feel that way," Jerry said. His voice dropped, artificially flattened, "I hope nothing bad happens to you. Or your family. This administration cares about our brave veterans."

"I can see you do," Harry said, and wondered if Jerry had the capacity to perceive irony. "If I change my mind, I'm sure 'my friend' can find you."

"He sure can," Jerry said and seemed to be relieved that the interview was over. "Think about it, Harry. Your country needs you."

Harry turned and walked towards where he'd last seen Long Joe and Nathan. I need some human company, he thought.

The north wind grew as the sun set, its icy teeth tore at Harry's wrists, burned his eyes. He rolled his stocking cap down over his ears and the wind throbbed through the strands of wool, a rhythmic hum he felt rather than heard, like distant helicopters. Obstructed by the homestead, the wind shrieked among the ragged fence-posts and wailed around the corner of the Old Man's horse barn. A litter of paper plates and foam cups swirled in the lee eddies of the buildings, birds of ill omen, come to seek shelter. Harry could almost believe he heard a gunshot flee, like a whisper, down the wind.

The sun, cut in half by the keen desert horizon, bled across the fields, clotted blackly in the long shadows among the cornstalks. Reject shivered into place beside Harry's knee and nipped at him. Harry pulled away in surprise. The dog barked and sat and would not move. Harry shrugged and continued on.

Close to the corral, he could see Shadow and the colt faced into the wind, reading it with flared nostrils. Even the old mare ignored her fate, arched her massive neck. Her swayed back straightened as she tasted the future on the wild northern air. Her one visible eye burned red against the blackness and Harry felt that she looked through and beyond him. Reject rejoined him, whimpered and circled. Harry could not see Long Joe and Nathan, but he knew they would return for Shadow. They had probably gone to get a truck.

He would go get his pickup and come back to wait for them. He wanted to say goodbye, finish it right. He turned and let his feet feel the way up the rocky canal bank. Reject jumped across the ice to go to the old place but Harry whistled and the dog turned reluctantly, followed him.

Harry felt a flash of vertigo as the last rays from the dying sun threw his shadow upward, hurled it into space, and the darkness came without twilight.

The pickup seat was chilled and stiff and the cold-blooded engine started reluctantly. He slid the heat control to Hi and resisted the urge to turn on the fan. The truck shuddered slightly in the wind but it was tight and the lack of motion of the air inside was like a vacuum, unnatural. After a minute or two he eased off the choke and the truck settled into a slow idle. His breath already had fogged the windows and he felt isolated, wiped a patch in front of him. But in the darkness he could see only the reflection of his own eyes.

He tried the heater fan, and the air from it seemed warmer than the air in the cab, so he left it on. He eased the clutch in and wiped a new spot to see through. Just as the truck started to roll, someone knocked on the passenger side window. He stopped, wiped the fog from the window and saw Mom, opened the door for her. The wind forced the door closed behind her and she was breathing hard. She had no coat over her suit and her hair was blown apart.

"Harry," she said, "I need to talk to you."

"I know," Harry said, "you're worried about Dad." He mocked her, but he was worried, too, a kind of diffuse anxiety that ebbed and flowed with the wind. He saw the hurt in her eyes.

"I'm sorry," he said, "It's been a long day."

"I really am worried, Harry. He hasn't come back to the house at all. Not since lunch."

"He was drinking with Chuck the last I saw him."

"Where?"

"They were going up towards the old place. He was pretty drunk."

"Find him. We have to find him."

"He's okay," Harry said and she shook her head. "Maybe they went to town for a drink. Sounded like they were giving him a retirement party."

The mascara had run onto her cheeks and she looked to him like a little girl. "You know he doesn't go to bars," she said, "he's a good Christian man."

"He was tying on a good Christian drunk when I saw him," Harry said.

Mom glared at him, started to be angry, then looked down and slowly shook her head.

"I'm sorry," Harry said again. He put his hand on her shoulder, and realized how long it had been since he had touched her, so long since he had touched anyone in the family. She leaned towards the touch, he felt her hunger.

"You should have helped him, Harry. Made him come in the house. That Chuck is no good for him. Whenever they get together, it's like they're back in the war or something." Harry drew back his hand.

"I think I've helped all I can."

He put the pickup in gear. "We'll go up to the old place, see if he's there." Without lights, he crept up the incline they had built for access to the canal bank. The wheels slipped slightly, and Mom gripped the armrest hard. She stared into the darkness ahead, but Harry didn't think she could see anything. Her lips moved silently in fear or prayer.

He switched on the headlights and Mom started as the familiar road leapt into reality. She looked over at Harry and started to reach out to him, then stopped.

"I'm going to be so glad to get away from here, Harry. I used to love it so much; it was going to always be my home. Now I don't see how I could have felt that way. It's so cold here, and dark, and the wind never stops. I can't wait to get to Arizona or California."

"It's warmer there, for sure," Harry said.

"And the people," Mom said, "I'm sure the people there haven't changed the way they have here. Remember when we were there, Harry, in Monterey, you and me and Dad and Jack and Meg? The time you found the nautilus shell and Jack broke it? The people were so friendly and the sun was shining every day."

"That was more than twenty-five years ago. It's probably changed some," Harry said.

"I hope not, Harry. We were all so happy, then."

Across from the old place Harry stopped the pickup. He took his flashlight from the glove compartment, checked it. He opened the door and looked to see if she was coming, but she stared out the window. He saw tears roll down the windshield reflection of her face.

Reject had followed the pickup, was beside Harry as he touched the ground. They jumped across the ice and the dog anxiously led the way to the old house.

"Dad," Harry called. "Are you here? Mom's looking for you." The shadows from the flashlight jumped and swayed in front of him. Reject ran ahead, out of range, and Harry followed him. He heard rustling in the sagebrush to his left, flashed the light there, and a jackrabbit darted away. There were many tracks in the snow along the path to the old house, obliterating his own tracks from the morning. The light caught something to the side and he steadied it, saw several beer cans and the yellow stain where someone had urinated beside the path.

Reject barked uncertainly, then again, near the porch of the old house. Harry could see that the front door was slightly open and he remembered closing it when he left. Maybe they had gone inside to drink. He stamped the snow from his boots and pushed the door open.

"Dad," he called again. No answer. They must have gone into town.

He started to turn back, but Reject growled, pulled at something on the floor between the table and the cookstove. Harry flashed the light down and saw boots, Dad's boots and legs. The hair on the back of his neck bristled as a chill passed through him.

"Dad," he said. He must have passed out, from the drinking.

He moved the light up towards Dad's head and saw blood, lots of blood. Who would have hurt him? Not Chuck or his other buddies. He was face down. He must have fallen, hit his head on the stove. There was too much blood. He was badly hurt.

"Dad," he said, "Dad, can you hear me?"

Reject licked the blood near Dad's head, whined and looked up at Harry. In the light Harry could see a great black wound where the back of his father's head should be. And near his hand, half covered with blood, was the soft shine of the souvenir Beretta Dad had brought home from the war.

Harry's anger boiled and raged through him. His body shook and tightened, his chest and biceps ached from the tension. It must have been a minute before he realized he had stopped breathing. He gasped for breath and it was a sob that seemed to tear him open. Something spattered onto his hand, wet the light, and he welcomed tears that seemed to ease the tightness. Even as he looked at the body, the numbers ran through his mind. There was over a hundred thousand dollars in an old life insurance policy Dad had bought right after the war, and the loan on the new house had been covered with credit life, would pay off automatically. He couldn't remember a suicide clause. The banker would move to attach the life insurance, you could be sure of that. But even so, when the house was sold there would be money left.

But not for him. The banker could have it, and Mom. And Jack would be there with his hand out. For his birthright. He would think Harry was a fool to refuse it, but so much the better for him.

Harry would be happy with zero. It was more of a legacy than he had expected. All that his father had bought him with his life and his death. Nothing.

He thought of the Old Man who had died in almost that same spot, how much he had left them all. He wondered if in those final moments Dad had chosen to die there in an attempt to follow the Old Man.

Harry would follow the Old Man. Long Joe had told him, "When you choose your life, you choose your death," and he knew which death he wanted.

Reject whined again and licked blood from Dad's hand, tried to rouse him. "Come," Harry said, bent down and patted Reject on the head, "we can't do him any good, now." The dog licked tears from Harry's cheek and Harry could smell his father's blood.

"Come on, now," he said and buried his face in the dog's soft hair for a moment. "We have to take care of the living."

CHAPTER 24

Harry walked slowly back to the pickup. Mom would be devastated. She still stared out the far window when he got in. He could see from the reflection that her tears had stopped and she watched him, thought he could not see her.

"He... he's there," Harry stammered, "but he's hurt. He shot himself... I think. He's dead."

Mom turned to look at him, her eyes were dry now. "I thought so," she said. "When I couldn't find him, I looked for his gun. It wasn't there." She took a deep breath. "I knew he would find a way. He always found a way. He saved us, Harry. Don't you see. He sacrificed himself for us. I knew he was a good Christian man. Everything will be fine, now."

Harry stared at her. "He's dead."

"But now we can pay the bank. The family will be fine. He always wanted the best for his family. He did it for us. It was a noble sacrifice"

"It was a coward's way out," Harry said, jammed the pickup into gear.

"Don't say that, Harry. He was a hero. He was always a hero. He tried so hard. And in the end he found a way. Don't tell me he wasn't a hero. He did his best for us."

"Most people don't see suicide as heroic," Harry said. He turned the pickup around, nearly drove into the canal.

"It wasn't suicide," Mom said, "it was sacrifice. Like in war, so those who remain can live and be free. Suicide is for nothing. God will forgive him."

"I suppose so," Harry said, "your God seems to forgive anything *you* want him to."

"He isn't my God, Harry. He's everyone's God. He is good and kind. He sacrificed his own son, remember?"

"Yeah," Harry said. "How could I forget? He seems to like sacrifice a lot."

"We better call the sheriff," Harry said when they got in the house. "They'll have to make a report. And the funeral home."

"I'll call," Mom said. "Would you make some coffee? I need a cup of coffee. And a cigarette." She got out a cigarette and lit it. Harry noticed that her hand seemed steadier than it had been in a while.

He put coffee in the percolator basket, filled the pot with water and plugged it in. It started to hiss and bubble. Mom dialed the sheriff, got a busy signal and dialed again.

"Call 911," Harry said. "They would consider this an emergency."

"Yes," Mom said, "I guess they would." She dialed, got an answer. "I need to report a death, a shooting." She waited a moment. "It's my husband," she said. "He's dead, he's been shot. Oh, he shot himself. I'm Mrs. Isaacson, out in block eighty-eight. No, county road number five. I don't know, I didn't actually see him. Here, you better talk to someone else." She handed the telephone to Harry.

"Hello," he said. "This is Harry Isaacson. It's my father."

"Are you sure he's... deceased?" the dispatcher asked. "Should we send an ambulance?"

"No," Harry said, "I don't think so. The whole back of his head is blown off." Mom winced, walked into the living room where she couldn't hear.

"Where is he now?"

"Over at the old house. My grandparents place. Across the canal from us."

"I have a deputy in your area, I'll send him over."

"Should I call the coroner?" Harry asked.

"No, I'll do that when I hear from the deputy. You might want to call the funeral home, though, get them prepared."

"Okay," Harry said, "I will." He heard the dial tone as the dispatcher disconnected.

"I don't understand it," Mom said. "They told us, just one telephone call, day or night, and they would handle the rest. Now all I get is a recording that says no one will be in until tomorrow morning at nine, please leave a message. This is supposed to be easy. That's why they call it Easy-After."

"So, call them in the morning," Harry said. "The coroner will keep him until then."

"Well, I've never done this before. How am I supposed to know?" She lit another cigarette and glared at him. "This isn't easy for me, you know."

"You better call Jack. And Meg."

"I don't feel like doing that, Harry. Would you call them? He was your father. You can help."

"Give me the telephone," Harry said.

He dialed Jack's number.

Diane answered, "Hello, Isaacson residence."

"Diane, this is Harry. Is Jack there?"

"No he isn't. Would you kids shut up, I can barely hear? He's at the office. He has a very important closing this evening."

"Okay, I'll call him there."

"I wouldn't do that, Harry. This is a very important deal. A six thousand dollar commission to us. He doesn't want to be disturbed. Can I take a message."

"No," Harry said, "This is very important too."

"Harry..." she warned him as he cut her off.

He dialed Jack's office. A woman answered. "Town and Country Realty, may I help you?"

"Is Jack Isaacson there?"

"Jack is in conference. May I help you?"

"No. This is his brother. This is very important, I need to speak to Jack."

"I'm sorry, Jack asked not to be disturbed. I'll be happy to give him a message."

"Tell him his father is dead," Harry said.

"I'll get him right away." She put the line on hold, Glen Campbell sang Wichita Lineman.

After about two minutes Jack came on. "I hope you have a good reason to interrupt this Harry. It means a lot of money to me."

"It's Dad. He's dead. He shot himself."

"Harry, are you drunk. I don't have time for some bullshit."

"I'm serious," Harry said, "He shot himself after the auction. Up at the old place."

There was a silence.

"Why the hell weren't you with him? Someone should have been with him."

"Why the hell weren't you with him?" Harry asked.

"I wasn't there. I was busy. You were there. You shouldn't have left him alone. This is really going to fuck up my closing. Do you need me for anything?"

"No, Jack, we don't need you for anything." Harry hung up the telephone. It rang almost immediately. "Hello," he said.

"This is Jack. Let me talk to Mom. Someone has to take care of her."

Harry handed the telephone to her.

"Hello," she said. "Oh, hi, Jack. No, I'm fine. No, it's okay, you finish your meeting, dear. I know you're busy." She hung up. "What did you say to him, Harry? He's really mad at you."

"You heard what I said. You were sitting right here." "Well, you have no reason to take it out on Jack. He tries real hard."

Meg wasn't home, so he left a message on her machine to call as soon as she could. Then he called Uncle Paul.

"Hello."

"Paul, this is Harry. It's Dad. He killed himself. Up at the old place."

"I was afraid somethin' would happen," Paul said. "He's been actin' kind of weird. Talkin' to me about when we were kids and how much better he liked Kansas. I didn't know this was what he was up to, though. How's your Mom?"

"She's okay," Harry said.

"Are you still comin' over tonight? You should get some rest. There ain't much you can do."

"Yes, I'll be over later. I'll have to talk to the sheriff, first, though. I found the body, so they'll have to have a statement."

"Okay. But come over as soon as you're finished. You should take your Mom into Jack and Diane's. Don't leave her alone."

"Okay Paul. I'll see you later."

"What do you mean telling him I'm fine?" Mom asked as he hung up. "This isn't easy for me."

"He thinks you should go spend the night with Jack and Diane, not stay out here alone."

"I don't need to do that. I'm fine."

A light flashed across the window and Harry looked out, saw headlights up by the corral. It might be Long Joe and Nathan. "I better go up there," he said. "It's probably the deputy, got himself lost." He put on his hat and coat, got his gloves. "I'll be back in a little while."

When he got near the corral, he saw that it was the scavenger's truck backed into the loading chute, not Long Joe and Nathan. He swung the headlights around so that they shone on the chute, left them on.

As he got out, he saw the scavenger try to drag the old mare up the chute onto his truck. She lowered her head and braced her front feet against the bottom boards.

"Howdy," the scavenger said, flashed Harry a gap-toothed grin. "Ya wanna gimme a han' with this ol' piece o' meat? She's stubborner'n hell. Damn near wore me out a'ready." He slapped the mare across her face and she swung her head, tried to hit him. "Dammit," he said, "If they din't pay more for 'em alive I'd cut 'er goddamn throat right now. An' enjoy it some, too." He wiped sweat from his face with a greasy hand.

"Get your hands off her," Harry said and stepped towards him. "Now."

"Hey, man, I bought this goddamn horse. I do whatever I fuckin' wanna wit' 'er." He slapped her again and she jerked her head into the chute, blood trickled down the side of her face.

"Get your hands off that horse or I'll cut your throat," Harry said. He started to climb over the fence.

The scavenger backed up a step and the mare hit him in the back with her head, knocked him against the side of the chute.

"Son-om-a-bitch." He gingerly touched his head, left a mark of blood. "I go call the sherf right now. I got me a fuckin' bill o' sale right 'ere in m' truck." He dropped the rope, climbed the side of the chute.

"You paid two hundred dollars for her, right? I'll give you the two hundred and you can sign her over to me."

"No fuckin' way. I gotta make me a livin'. The cann'ry 'd pay near four hunnert dollar, much as she weighs. I ain't losin' m' profit."

"You're goin' to lose more than your profit if you touch her again. I'll give you two fifty and you get the fuck out of here."

"Three hunnert."

"Two fifty," Harry said and jumped down beside him. "I think I'd enjoy kickin' your ass." He raised a fist and stepped towards him. "I may kick it anyway."

"Okay, two fifty, but if'n you touch me, I call the sherf, sure."

"Get the bill of sale," Harry said, "I'll get the money."

While they were making the exchange in the light of the headlights, the deputy drove up, flashed his spotlight on them.

"You guys got a problem?" he asked.

"Nope," Harry answered. "Just talkin' to a man about a horse." He looked hard at the scavenger.

"No, sir, no problem here. No, sir."

"Is one of you Harry Isaacson?"

"I am," Harry said.

"Your mother said I'd find you up here. You want to show me where the body is?"

"Sure," Harry said. "Just a minute. Soon as I finish with this guy."

The scavenger's hands began to shake. He hurriedly endorsed the bill of sale.

"Okay," Harry said to the deputy. "It's across the canal." The scavenger got in his truck and spun the tires in the snow as he bounced away.

"That guy looked like he'd just seen a ghost," the deputy said as Harry led him across the canal.

"I don't know," Harry said, "maybe so. I was just buyin' a horse from him and givin' him a profit, too."

"This an old homestead?" the deputy asked as they approached the old house.

"Not that old," Harry said, "Just about thirty years. Belonged to my grandfather."

"I didn't know they still built like this thirty years ago. Looks a lot older than that."

"Yeah," Harry said, "he was an old timer. Didn't care for modern ways."

Inside they both shone their flashlights on Dad's body.

The deputy whistled softly. "No offense," he said, "but he sure did a good job of it. It was quick." He moved his light to the Beretta. "Whose gun?"

"His," Harry said. "A World War II souvenir. I've never even seen him shoot it."

"It's a nice one," the deputy said. "Nickel steel. Cost you a pretty penny now." He picked it up carefully by the barrel with his thumb and forefinger. He took a plastic bag out of his jacket pocket, put the gun in, smeared blood on the plastic. "We'll have to take this in, just for a day or two. Then you can pick it up. I'd hang on to this. It's a collector's item for sure."

"I don't want it," Harry said. "My brother might."

"Whatever," the deputy said. "This how you found the body? You didn't move it?"

"No," Harry said. "I didn't touch it."

"Let's go back over to the car," the deputy said. "I'll write my report and radio in for the dispatcher to call the coroner. They want a coroner's report on suicides."

"Okay," Harry said.

The report was short and simple. Suicide by gunshot. Probable cause, despondency over financial problems.

"That should be all we need," the deputy said. "I don't think they'll need to talk to you any more. Sorry about this. Is everyone else okay? Your mother need any help?"

"No," Harry said, "She's fine."

After the deputy left, Harry moved the old mare back into the main corral with Shadow and the colt, found some grain and fresh hay for them. Shadow nuzzled against him and he put his arms around her neck, buried his face in her mane. The old mare nibbled at his shoulder. He turned and put an arm around her neck also.

He didn't know what to do with the old mare. Maybe he could get Long Joe and Nathan to take her to Cache Creek. She would have to be fed, though; she was too old to survive on her own.

Too bad there weren't any horse farmers any more. With the right care she could still pull light equipment for several years, maybe even have a foal or two, continue the line. But draft horses were just toys now, for rich people and beer companies, and the old mare wouldn't make a very fancy toy.

The wind had subsided, the breeze that remained passed for stillness on the desert. The clouds had fled eastward on the jetstream. From the magnified night sky the stars pressed down on him, forced him to look up. The sliver of moon far in the west reminded him of Judith's Navajo earrings, and he wondered if she watched it, too. The sky was so dim in the city. The moon there was not silver, but muddy orange, and the stars receded, turned their backs on the Earth.

He had to get Judith and the children out of the city. It no longer mattered to him if she loved someone else, had lost faith in him. If Nathan was her choice, then he would help her. He could understand. She was not to be owned, or bought and sold. She had loved him and he was happy for that. If she loved him again, he would take it as the gift that it was.

He had thought with the loss of the farm that he would have no legacy for Rebecca and little Joe. But he could see the difference between heritage and inheritance. He did have a birthright for his children, something beyond the animals and land and equipment that had been the farm, something beyond even the memories of the Old Man. He would learn with his children how to live here, not as a stranger, a foreigner, but as a part of the Earth itself. "You've got to play the hand that's dealt you," that's what the Old Man always said.

The old mare raised her head to chew the hay, and he felt the strength of her great neck. There was still some of the Old Man's harness, hung on the wall in the barn. If he could not find horse-drawn implements, he could adapt some of the older mechanized equipment. The Old Man's forge was still in his shop, and the anvil, they had thought no one would want it. He had the cookstove. He could build a cabin.

"So, Harry, I see you have a plowhorse." Long Joe stepped out of the darkness at the back of the corral. Nathan followed him. They were almost indistinguishable from the shadows except for their eyes, which seemed to reflect the starlight.

Harry wondered how long they had been there. No one had driven in since the deputy left.

"Yes," he said, "I bought her back."

Long Joe chuckled, Nathan echoed it. So they had been watching.

"I am sorry about your father," Long Joe said, "but he chose his own path."

"Yes," Harry said, "I know that."

"We each choose our own lives and our own deaths."

"Yes, I know that, too. I remember. I choose life."

"Does that mean you want the San Poil place?" Nathan asked.

"My grandfather would like that. That place is very lonely without him."

"Yes," Harry said. "If we can work something out. I don't have any money."

"We don't need money," Nathan said. "Money is poison. But there is something you can do for me."

"What?" Harry asked. "I will do anything I can."

"I have a second cousin," Nathan said. "Someone I care about very much. I need someone to care for her and her children. And her horses. She is trapped, in the city, and we must get her out of there."

Harry stared at Nathan, could see the white flash of his grin.

CHAPTER 25

The tires sang on the frozen pavement as the International danced northward up the coulee. Harry pushed the old rig, loaded as it was. He wanted to be on the Manila Creek summit by daybreak. The headlights reflected from the coulee walls, refracted through the streams of ice from frozen springs. Snow swirled away from his wheels at the edge of the highway, glittered briefly as he passed.

Even in the faint starlight, the dark mass of Steamboat Rock was visible to the west. The broken north end of the rock made a black shadow on the ice of the frozen lake, but the bright reflections of the stars shone through it. Two ravens started up on the side of the road; their dark wings seemed to brush the windshield as they flew over him.

Electric City was still asleep. He passed through without seeing anyone. The other little towns were quiet also, and even Grand Coulee Dam seemed deserted, marked only by the red lights flashing along the buoy line and on the tops of the powerhouses. He wondered if some day the dam would break apart, as the great ice dam once had, and free the river, let the salmon pass upstream to their ancient spawning grounds on the Kettle and the San Poil.

The night had passed quickly. He had helped Long Joe and Nathan load the horses, and talked for a while before they began the long drive to Cache Creek. Then he had gone back to the old place, loaded the forge and a few tools that had been overlooked.

When he went back for the cookstove, he noticed that the old man's black wool coat still hung on its hook. He shook the worst of the dust off it and put it on. It fit him about right. He tossed the field-jacket in the pickup. Then he searched the barn for harness and found more than he expected.

He unloaded his guns and packed them in the back. It didn't seem like he would need them right away.

When he got to Uncle Paul's it was past midnight. He had called Judith, awakened her, but she didn't seem to mind. He felt the relief and excitement in her voice when he told her of his plan. He wanted her to spend the summer with Hattie, as she had long wanted to do, learn how to heal in the old ways. He would take care of the children. She had said that she loved him.

He had fallen asleep immediately. Dark eyes greeted him, but they did not threaten. He thought they even smiled a little.

He wanted to get the cabin built as soon as he could. Nathan had said he would help and they could buy rough-sawn lumber cheap from the little mills in the mountains.

He needed a barn, too, for the horses. And he wanted to be ready to plow as soon as the ground thawed.

He had asked Long Joe if he would teach him some of the ways of his people, help him learn how to live with the Earth. Long Joe had smiled at him and gripped his arm and said, "When you're ready, Harry."

The Manila Creek road was icy and treacherous and he picked his way carefully up the switchbacks below the summit. When he pulled off onto the turnout it was still dark although he could feel the imminence of the dawn. He turned off the engine and got out. The dry snow crunched beneath his boots.

The air stirred with the dawn wind and cooled his face. He took off his hat and his gloves to feel the cold. Ice froze on his beard from the steam of his breath. He started with the west, faced each of the four directions and thought of the path ahead of him, the path he must choose. When he turned at last to the south, he could just make out the faint shadow line of the cliffs on the far side of the river. Above the cliffs, the sky lightened, the stars faded, a new day began.

Printed in the United States
1275400005B/355-372